THE TRANSFERENCE

The Transference
Copyright © 2022
Jeff S. Bray

ISBN: ISBN: 978-1-957344-12-6

Cover concept & design by Mike Parker

Published by WordCrafts Press
Cody, Wyoming 82414
www.wordcrafts.net

The Transference

a novel of suspense

JEFF S. BRAY

WordCrafts Press

To our law enforcement officers and their families.
Thank you for your dedicated service.

Chapter One

Saturday, February 1, 22:05

Do we have a name yet?" Lt. Daniel Masters asked the officer on-scene.

"No, he wasn't carrying identification, but with prison tatts, it shouldn't be too hard," the officer said, lowering the sheet over the body with four bullet holes to the center of his chest. "What do you suppose he was thinking? I mean, suicide by cop? I don't understand."

"Sometimes these perps don't like it on the outside. They lose it. Or…" he trailed off as the ambulance wailed and drove off with the survivor, "he just picked the wrong time to commit the crime."

"At least they were able to save Mr. Nelson," the officer said, nodding toward the window as the flashing lights faded into the distance.

"What do we know?" Masters looked over the scene, playing out the scenario in his mind. Something was missing. He scratched his salt-and-peppered chin and paced the room.

"I'm no forensic, but I'd say some sort of torture for information?" the officer said. "Sorry, where are my manners. The name's Lawson," he stood and extended his hand.

"Lt. Daniel Masters," Master said, receiving the welcome, "Possible. My only question is, Lawson, with the perp now on a slab, where's the weapon?"

Lawson had a perplexed look on his face. He didn't have an answer.

"Well, Lawson, go find me that weapon."

Lawson disappeared to confer with the first officers on the scene.

Masters pulled his phone out of his pocket and dialed a number.

"Sergeant Atwood," the raspy voice answered.

"Hey there, sweet lady," Masters cooed.

"Lieutenant, I know you are not using official channels to perpetuate sexual harassment," the desk sergeant snapped.

Sergeant Laureen Atwood had been on the force nearly as long as he had. They had a long-standing professional relationship with a share of back-and-forth ribbing attuned with a big sister-little brother relationship.

"My apologies, *Atwood*," he cleared his throat and chuckled. "I'm over here in the Delmont district at the KBC incident and—"

"Masters…" Atwood interrupted, "You have a partner for this. Why are you calling a desk sergeant for help when all I can do is sit here, stamp paperwork, and make your life a living hell?"

"Gradiosa?" Masters said. He was reluctant to have a new partner this late in the game. He had been without one since his last partner resigned after a case went sour two years ago—which he partway blamed on himself. Since then, Atwood was determined to make him a mentor to some rookie who would wretch his guts over the sight of a little blood or seemed more determined to make an impression than to listen to orders. Why would this Gradiosa be any different?

"Yes, Gradiosa. And he goes by Grady." Atwood corrected. "This one you better treat right. He is a long-time detective. He came down from Rampart District. His wife got a transfer with her job, and they moved into the area. So play nice. He is well-seasoned and not like the others. Got it?"

"Yeah, yeah," Masters said. He was impressed Gradiosa was from Rampart. They were known for not letting their ranks get muddled with the need to promote—you had to earn your stripes. To become a detective in Rampart meant something. "What's his number?"

"It's already on your cell. I took the liberty of programming it for you the last time you were here. I figured you were gonna need it."

"Alright, I'll call him," he said and hung up.

Once again, big sister was intruding on little brother's privacy by touching his belongings. Masters scrolled through his phone. Sure enough, Grady's number was there. He hit *dial*, and three rings later, it went to voice mail. "Not a good start, *Grady*," Masters mumbled. He swiped his phone and put it in his pocket.

The coroner nodded at the bag with the tattooed, deceased body, and it was loaded onto a gurney. They wheeled it into the van for transport. Soon they would have his ID and hopefully some answers.

"Lizzy," James "Grady" Gradiosa called out from the bathroom where he was shaving. "Where's my phone? I can hear it buzzing."

"Probably where you put it last," she snapped from her home office. He pictured her rolling her blue eyes, with her head under a stack of paperwork, unnerved at the disturbance. He knew she was about to close on a home for a client, and when she was at the end, she had tunnel vision.

Elizabeth was a real estate agent and a good one. Her Atlanta office was expanding and setting up shop in an unexplored area of Georgia, and she had earned the merit of heading the team to open the new offices. This meant Grady would follow *her* aspirations, give up his Atlanta badge, and relocate to Savannah. Now he was partnered with a brute veteran who did not like slackers and had been rumored to make more than one rookie cry. And now he just may have ignored one of his phone calls.

Grady mumbled under his breath something he had to ask forgiveness for. He wiped his half-shaved face and went in search of his phone. As his wife had surmised, it was on the coffee table, right where he left it. It wasn't blinking with a voicemail message, but the missed call number was unfamiliar. He hit redial and waited for the scolding he knew he was about to receive.

"Was this the first or the last?" the answering voice said.

Taking the hint, Grady said, "The last."

"Great. With that out of the way, how quick can you get down to Center and Twentieth Street?"

Grady was still getting used to the area and not entirely sure where that would be in relation to where he lived. Hoping for the best, "Twenty minutes."

"You better hustle, the scene is still fresh, and I need your young expert eyes to show me you're not just hot air from up north," his lieutenant said and hung up.

"Liz?" he cringed, "Sorry, do you know where Center and Twentieth is?" He was praying for *across the street*, or another miracle but would receive no such comfort.

"The other side of town. Near Forsythe Park," she said without a beat.

"Like that helps," he said, grabbing his jeans and boots.

"If you're going to *protect and serve*, you really need to get to know your city, Grade," his wife jested.

"Yes, babe." *Tell me something I don't know*, he added to himself. Right now, he was more interested in not getting shot by his new partner. He finished with a coat, a kiss to the back of his wife's head, and was out the door.

Chapter Two

Saturday, February 1, 22:50

Thirty-two minutes, two wrong turns, and a coffee stop for good measure, Grady made his way through Forsythe Park. Luckily, he had caught his forgotten face in the rearview mirror and grabbed an emergency Bic he stored in the glove box. Now clean-shaven, and with only a couple of nicks for his trouble, he was ready for anything.

Only two sets of lights were now flashing. They belonged to the officers first on-scene. He found his lieutenant fast enough. He was the towering figure in the dark trench coat with steam coming from his ears leaning on his staple Caprice. He half-jogged over, not wanting to drop the coffee.

"Whatcha do, walk?" Masters said, seeing him come out of the park.

"Not entirely. I passed up the street, and it's one way. Didn't want to make the turnaround. So I parked and backtracked. Easier," Grady said out of breath, extending the coffee peace offering. "It's black. I have creamer and sugar in a bag in my coat pocket."

"Don't take it," Masters said, removing the lid and taking a sip.

That's a good gesture, Grady told himself. "Sorry, I didn't realize I lived so far from here."

Masters sipped his coffee again without answering. He sat up and walked toward the building. "Follow me."

Grady took a quick drag of his coffee and did as he was told. The air was cold with the deep chill of winter. A front had blown in the day before, and the winds had just settled that afternoon. He hoped the coffee would show his new partner he was thinking of these things. Masters hadn't yelled, that was a good thing, but the night was still young.

They approached an apartment building where an officer stood at attention like he was guarding Buckingham Palace. Masters noticed as well. "At ease, soldier," he said, "no one is going to bite. Lawson still inside?"

"Yes, sir. Finishing up his report with the two who shot the perpetrator," he said.

"Thank you, officer," he said, giving him a firm pat on the arm, "as you were."

Guess he does have a sense of humor, Grady thought, following close behind.

"I'm with him," Grady pointed with a slight chuckle, but got no response.

The entryway was dark. The fluorescent bulb was out—poor maintenance by the super. The hall was better lit, but not by much. Grady could just make out gold-plated mailboxes on each side. After the mailboxes, a narrow hallway followed. It ended with two doors, set like a mirror image—apartments 1A and 1B—then a stairway to the right, just past the door to 1B. Masters proceeded up the flight to the next level. The stairs creaked under his large figure, which filled the entire frame. Grady followed, but several steps behind.

Nearing the top, Grady could hear a heated conversation, but it wasn't between officers—not unless one of them was an older woman. From his guess, the landlord was unhappy that her place was now the location of a homicide. Or more likely that she was no longer going to be collecting rent.

Masters stopped short of the door and turned to Grady with an eye roll, the first real acknowledgment of his presence. He rapped on the door but didn't wait for a response before entering, "Lawson, where are we at?"

Lawson was speaking with an older woman in a purple

muumuu with shoulder-length black hair. She was standing on her tippy toes and pointing into his face. The other two officers were near the window in the corner, both with grins, trying not to laugh.

"Lt. Masters. This is Eunice Keppler," Lawson explained calmly, but his face was red and his fists were clenched tight. "She is the building owner and would like this apartment vacated as soon as possible."

"Who was the tenant, Mrs. Keppler?" Masters began with the landlord.

Keppler blushed, and her voice softening at the sight of the strapping newcomer. "First of all, it's Ms. I'm not married, Lieutenant ..."

"Oh, brother," Lawson muttered, flapping his arms at his side.

Ms. Keppler continued, walking toward Masters, "... and Mr. Nelson *was* my tenant. Now that he is diseased, I need to vacate this place so I can rent it out."

"Yes, of course, *Ms.* Keppler. But Mr. Nelson is *not* diseased, nor is he *deceased*. EMTs were able to save his life. He's on his way to the hospital now. And when he is up and ready to come back, he will want a place to come back to. So can you take care of this place for him until then?"

Ms. Keppler's old nose crinkled. She faced an internal debate. Was it worth missing a month or two of rent for the chance at this hunk of a man to give her a call? She looked him up and down, and that crinkle gave way to a mouth full of teeth, much more than he expected. "I s'pose I can hold it for a bit. But I need to eat too. Can't pay my bills when my tenants ain't around to pay theirs."

"I completely understand," Masters said.

"What if I need to reach ya?"

Masters grinned at Grady. "My partner is going to give you his card. If you have any questions, you can give him a call."

"What 'bout you?" Ms. Keppler asked, never giving Grady a glance.

"I'm fresh out of them," Masters lied.

"All I have are my Atlanta cards. I haven't had the chance to transfer them yet," Grady said, pulling one from his coat.

"Just give her the main line to Atwood," Masters suggested.

"Right," Grady said with enough delayed tone that Master again rolled his eyes, grabbed the card, and wrote the number himself. He handed the card to Ms. Keppler.

"Now, if you will excuse us, we have official business to finish up here, Ms. Keppler," Masters said, escorting her to the door and locking it behind her.

"Holy Guacamole, I thought we'd never be able to get rid of her," one of the officers said from the window.

"You okay, Lawson?" the other asked.

Lawson was back to a gentle shade of pink, but he didn't reply. He picked up his notebook and continued with his questions. Both Grady and Masters listened as the two officers recounted what occurred up to and after they came upstairs while their superior officer secured the perimeter downstairs.

Clarke and Ryan arrived at 21:30, on the heels of Lawson. He exited the building after speaking to the man who had called in the disturbance. His downstairs neighbor, Mr. Nelson, was heard arguing with a visitor just before a series of violent yells, then nothing. The man reported that after the second piercing scream, he was frightened enough to dial 9-1-1.

By the time Lawson arrived, the man who didn't want to be named said the screaming had stopped for approximately five minutes. The man also reported hearing a loud truck pulling up to the rear of the complex. He pointed out there was a rear entrance that only residents had access to with a key. He learned that much information from the witness when Clarke and Ryan arrived. He sent them inside while he went around back to check out the truck.

Clarke ran point, and the two headed up the stairs minding

the creaks each step made, but it made no difference, the noise above drowned out every sound they made. It was a terrible verbal chanting. Neither officer could make out what was said. Lawson underlined this twice in his notes, not even a guess or a vernacular representation; it was complete gibberish to the two.

There was little doubt which door it was coming from—straight left from the head of the stairs. Their gut told them there was someone seriously hurt, possibly with fatal injuries. Once both officers reached the landing, the chanting stopped, leaving them in silence. They needed to act.

Clarke wanted to burst in—surprise was the best element they had. Catch him off guard. If they went in softly, it may allow the perp to get his weapon or be in a position to attack. Ryan felt the softer approach of talking him down would be best if there was a hostage. It turned out they would need neither approach—a voice called to them from behind the closed door.

"If you want him to live, you will get the hell in here right now," the voice bellowed.

"He called to you?" Masters interrupted.

"Yes, sir," Clarke said. "It was the darndest thing. Never had that happen before."

"Go on," Lawson said, flipping the page of his notepad. "What happened next?"

Both men just stared at each other, almost daring the other to reach for the knob. The voice shouted a few obscenities appealing to their manhood. They both shook their heads and laughed it off.

Clarke took a step toward the door and turned the knob as the nervousness returned to his stomach. His eyes met Ryan's, and they revealed that he wasn't the only one anxious about their situation. In silence, they both agreed which way each would go and how they would face this criminal together; it was what they were trained for.

Clarke opened the door and went high right; Ryan low straight ahead, both weapons drawn, fixed on their target. The tattooed criminal sat on a chair with a cigarette in his mouth. Mr. Nelson was lying on a coffee table next to him, unconscious, bleeding from lacerations to both arms and legs; he was half-naked, wearing only his boxers and a blood-soaked t-shirt.

The tattooed man blew a series of circles into the air, smiled through his handlebar mustache, and said, *"He's got about twelve minutes, so I hope you have EMS on their way. I don't have much time."*

"Not much time for what?" Masters asked.

"I don't know," Clarke replied, "he didn't say."

"Masters, can you please save your questions for later? Let me get their statements while they are fresh in their minds. We can comb through follow-up questions later."

"Fine." Masters said.

"Go on," Lawson said, again flipping the page of his notepad, "please continue."

The blood was pooling under the table. Ryan couldn't believe that Mr. Nelson was still alive. He was certainly dead by now. Ryan took his eyes off the victim; he couldn't bear it. The tattooed man was just staring at them. It was a stalemate. Clarke was first to speak, asking the man his name. He wouldn't reply. Then Ryan tried to Mirandize the man. But the tattooed man wouldn't have it. He just laughed and continued to puff on his cigarette, telling them they were wasting time. Clarke called for EMS—that seemed to appease the tattooed man. He didn't speak again, just switching his attention between the two of them and his watch.

Once the sirens were within ear range, he rechecked his watch, then grinned ear to ear and nodded. He closed his eyes and began to mumble under his breath. It was the familiar cadence they heard coming up the stairs. Both officers looked at each other, guns still drawn, knowing something was about to happen. They spoke to him, trying to get him to stop. They tried again to read him his Miranda, but his chanting only grew louder.

He stood. They gave warning. He walked over to Mr. Nelson—another warning. The tattooed man folded his hands like he was praying. He then raised them over his head and screamed. The officers gave a final warning, and before the tattooed man could thrust whatever he may have had in his hands down into the man's chest, the officers fired, two shots each, center mass, just as they had been trained, ending the life of the unknown man.

Chapter Three

Sunday, February 2, 01:05

The coroner's van that drove the unknown tattooed man's body to the morgue took a haphazard route through the chilly night. It had been a long day, and although it would be their last drop-off, neither man was in a hurry. They had no clue that a sandy-haired lieutenant was sitting at his desk across town, waiting for a phone call with an identification. They were unaware that his new partner was sitting across from that desk just as eager, but for different reasons. The coroner was similarly ignorant. He signed the chain of custody paperwork, assigned the first slot he found, and called it an evening. By the time Masters had enough waiting and called the coroner's office, all he heard was a ringing phone. Not even the courtesy of an answering service or machine.

Masters slammed the phone down and swore, which made Grady jump. Grady looked up at the clock on the wall. It was a little after one in the morning. The coroner would be well gone by now, but he dared not say anything. He watched as his partner read over the statements of the two officers.

Masters flipped back over the pages like he remembered something. "O77 prison tatts," he said. "Pretty hardcore. Known for multiple homicides outside and inside the State Prison system."

"Yeah, they did some damage up in Atlanta. They can touch anyone, anywhere. You think this was a hit?" Grady asked.

"Not sure yet," Masters flipped the pages back to where he was.

The notebook looked familiar to Grady. Then it dawned on him. "How did you get Lawson's notebook?"

Masters didn't look up. "I asked nicely."

Masters flipped to the section on Nelson. He spent some time looking through his information, shaking his head. Nothing there either, Grady assumed. Masters tossed the notebook to him. "Take a look."

Grady flipped pages. Nelson seemed clean. From the books in his room, he could have been a college student; he was an Uber driver, from the decals noted. He appeared to live alone. If anything, this was a shakedown from a loan shark, if that's who Mr. Tattoos was. A student loan repayment plan went bad; who knows. "Student loan gone sideways? Uber drivers have been known to be a good cover for drug runners and help fund a college education. Too bad we don't have bank records."

"Impressive thinking," Masters said, nodding without a smile, "but yeah, too soon to get that type of info. Carmen will be in at seven. She can pull bank, medical, school, military records. Hell, she could tell you if he had a pet turtle when he was five if you wanted to know."

Grady looked up at the clock again.

Masters must've read his mind. "Not much else we can do tonight. Go home and get some rest. Be back here at seven. We'll hit it again when Carmen gets those records, and the coroner gives us an ID," Masters said. "Make it eight—give her time to do her magic and you time to get settled in."

Grady didn't acknowledge or complain. He didn't want to be sentenced to an all-nighter of speculating the unknown. He set down the notebook, said good night, and headed back to his sleeping wife.

Sunday, February 2, 07:05

Carmen Albanese was as good as Masters made her out to be, maybe better. When Grady buzzed his way upstairs onto the detective's floor, she was dancing between two desks on either side of her, glancing between four monitors. Two printers were spitting out copies of what her hard work had discovered.

"You must be Gradiosa," she said without looking up from one of the screens. Her large-framed glasses reflected the monitor's glow, and a lock of dark brown hair tangled with the arm of her frames and hung to the desk where she leaned.

"Yeah. People call me Grady," he said.

"Don't like your name?" Carmen said, still with her eyes locked on her screen.

"It's not that. Just easier to say. Too many people flub it up."

"10-4. I hear ya. Can't tell how many times I hear Alban-ess-ee, or Alban-ess." she said.

"Is the lieutenant in?" Grady asked as he took a couple of slow steps toward her electronic cave.

"This early?" Carmen said with a hearty laugh.

"I'll take that as a no."

"He'll be here in about an hour," she said, looking up at the clock. Then to Grady for the first time. "Well, given a case like this, maybe sooner."

"Speaking of, anything new?"

"I'm not here to just pretty up the place. I have everything on your Uber driver." Carmen went back to her screen and made a few clicks of her mouse. She waved Grady to join her at the computer. "He's clean. Nothing out of the ordinary. His bank records are about what you would expect for a college student. Parents send him money now and then, student loans come in and then are gone to pay tuitions, an occasional deposit here and there, maybe his job. But nothing substantial."

"But that doesn't mean anything, really."

"Right. If you are dealing drugs, you aren't going to write *drug money* on your deposit slip."

"Any credit cards, insurance purchases, protection plans?"

"Auto insurance. But other than that, nada," she said. Carmen reached around Grady, grabbed a thin file folder from the desk, and handed it to him.

"This is it?" Grady asked, giving it a quick thumb through.

"Yep, not even a parking ticket."

"Could it be cleaned? Deliberate?"

"Hmm. I doubt it. There would be signs of a professional cleaner. Plus, Nelson's too young. He just doesn't have a record."

"Mr. Tattoo must have had—"

"Who?"

"Sorry, we don't have an ID on the—"

"Stephen Allan Tanner," Carmen said, reaching again and handing him a much thicker file. "That's your corpse."

Grady sat at a desk next to Carmen's and opened the file. A hardened face, scarred from his forehead to his chin, and O77 tattooed just below his breastbone, stared at him. His vacant eyes were the eyes of a man bent on doing harm. Somehow it set him at ease that this man was no longer walking among the living. Grady looked over to his Bio: Stephen Allan Tanner, 37, 5'10", 275 lbs, Aggravated Assault with Deadly weapon 2009, Burglary 2009, Grand Theft Auto 2010, Georgia State Penitentiary 2010-2015, Assault Deadly Weapon 2015, Attempted Murder 2017.

"This guy didn't know when to quit. Five years in GSP? I wonder how he got out and why the other later charges didn't send him back?"

"That's the penal system for ya," Carmen said, typing on her terminal.

"Then he went quiet for the last few years—dropped off the radar."

"Maybe the O77s told him to straighten up?" Carmen suggested.

"Or gave him a job to do?" Grady said.

"Like find college boys and rough them up?" suggested Carmen.

"What makes you say that? Are their similar cases to Mr. Nelson?"

"I researched cases that included injuries similar to Mr. Nelson's. Doctors report he had cuts to both femoral veins as well as his brachial veins. They were deep enough to cause bleeding but not in the right place to cause him to bleed out. He would have to lacerate an artery to do that. Tanner knew what he was doing. That made me wonder. Why would he not complete the job and check out the way he did? So, I expanded my search to include any open cases regarding femoral and brachial injuries where the victim died."

"And?"

Carmen plopped down three files on the desk in front of Grady. "Three cases?"

"All open and unsolved. No forensics linking anything or anyone to any of them," Carmen explained.

"Until today," said Grady.

"Until today."

"Does Masters know?"

"Hey, I'm just finding all of this out myself," she said. "I haven't had the time to call him. He should be here any minute anyhow."

Grady picked up the three files and looked through each one. Two male, one female. Sure enough, each victim's arm and leg cuts were identical to the cuts inflicted upon Mr. Nelson. Each victim was placed flat on a coffee table and was dressed in nothing but undergarments. The photos did reveal one difference, the amount of blood. There seemed to be an excessive amount in the photos—much more than the Nelson crime scene.

"Where were these other murders?"

"One in South Carolina, one in Florida, the last in Alabama," Carmen said with a bit of hesitance. "All in just the last month."

"Are you serious?" Grady asked.

"That's as far as I set my parameters," she said.

"So, there could be more?"

"Possibly," she said.

"We need to call Masters," Grady said.

"Call me for what?" A gruff voice called from the stairwell just as the entry buzzer sounded.

For the next half hour, Carmen filled Masters in. Masters went through two cups of coffee, taking it all in without interruption, allowing Carmen to give her point of view, her speculations, and even interject Grady's name here and there.

Grady learned that Masters was not as hard as he seemed to be. He was reasonable. At least when he respected you. And Grady could tell that Carmen's opinion was held high. He hoped that he would earn that level of respect. He also understood that Carmen had earned it.

"So, what do you think we should do next, Grady?" Masters asked, half looking at Carmen.

Was this a test? Grady looked at the notebook. He figured that Tanner, himself, would be a dead end. Their real lead would be the connection Tanner had to Nelson. And his first hunch was a possible drug-running tie through his position as an Uber driver.

"Search Nelson's car," Grady said. "If he were running drugs, there would be evidence of it. We need to do it before he has a chance to dispose of it. While we're at it, we should search his place top to bottom. If we have a forensics team there, we may as well sweep it for anything suspicious. Then we'd know for sure."

Masters nodded. "Do it."

Carmen smiled at him in recognition. He must have made an impression.

"You may still need a warrant for the car," Carmen said. "You're clear on the apartment. It's a crime scene. I'll make a call. I know a clerk or two who can get hold of a judge on a Sunday," she added with a wink. "I'll have your warrant by lunch."

Masters stood and nodded toward the entrance gate, "The rest of the team will be up soon. I'll have you coordinate with them. You'll run one team to search the car. Send the other to the apartment. We need quick answers before Mr. Nelson is released from the hospital. If he is involved, we need to know."

"Understood."

Masters went into his office and picked up his phone to make a call. He walked back to the door and shut it.

Carmen turned to Grady. "I think he likes you."

"Let's hope so. I didn't make too good of an impression last night."

"He's like that with everyone at first. Sarge downstairs has put him with so many newbies the last couple of months I'm surprised he hasn't gone mental."

"What did he do? Sounds like punishment."

"No. His partner cut out a few months ago. The case went bad. I can't really discuss it. It's not my place. But Chief wants him with a partner and put Atwood is in charge of doing that. So, in a way, newbie detectives can be a punishment to a seasoned veteran. But Atwood and Lieu go way back. I think she is just toying with him to loosen him up, but now she's done. She gave him you. It surprised him. He expected just another wet-behind-the-ears rookie. But you have common sense and have shown him you can think. Don't let it go to your head, and don't screw this one up. You still need to prove yourself out there."

Grady smiled, somewhat relieved. "Where's Nelson's vehicle?"

"All his personal property is at his residence. We didn't take anything. No reason to. He was the victim," said Carmen.

A group of voices grew louder through the stairwell—the team. They were coming up from the morning debriefing with the chief. The buzzer sounded, and the gate creaked. Four officers, all in street clothes, walked in. If they weren't in the station, you probably couldn't label them as detectives, and that was the point. Other than identical holsters, each bore their own style. Three men and one female. They took him in just as he was checking each of them out.

Grady stood to introduce himself.

"LaCrosse," the first detective said in a voice that was as gruff as his look. "You must be Gradiosa. Glad to have you part of the team."

LaCrosse stood a bit taller than he did. His firm handshake bore the callouses of a hardworking man. He wasn't always an officer, Grady concluded. His slightly graying brown hair and mustache that extended below his lips showed that he was the group's eldest member and probably the senior officer.

"Thank you. I go by Grady. Good to meet you. I look forward to serving with you."

"Damn, boy. You don't need to sound so formal. We're all on the same level here."

The whole team laughed. Grady shied back a bit, unsure how to react, but faked a laugh to keep from feeling more uncomfortable than he already was.

"Sorry, yes. First day jitters, I guess."

The next two in line approached him. "Hey, Grady. I'm Detective Mesa."

"And I'm Nettles. Great to have you part of the team."

Mesa and Nettles were practically twins, although opposite sex. Same height, dirty blonde hair color, and they carried themselves in the same manner. The only difference was one was left-handed. Grady could tell from their shoulder holsters straps. Nettles was the righty, her grip near as firm as LaCrosse, save the callouses. Mesa, the southpaw, extended his fist and gave a bump, and a head nod completed his welcome.

"That's Branson," Mesa said. "He's fairly distant when it comes to newbies. Give it time. When I came aboard, it took him two weeks before he would even speak to me."

Branson was meeting with Carmen. Grady figured he would need to begin addressing her as Albanese, which he would need to check. *Just don't screw this one up.* He joined them and introduced himself. Branson's narrow jaw and tight lips stabbed at him without a touch. He just grunted when Carmen, or Albanese, told him that Grady would be running point on the Nelson search.

Grady got it wrong. LaCrosse was not the senior detective; Branson was. He also couldn't help but notice that Branson was older than he was. *This should be interesting. Just don't screw this one up, Grady.*

Chapter Four

Sunday, February 2, 08:15

The twins headed out with Branson to give Nelson's apartment a once over. Grady had his money on the car. He wanted to be in on that because Tanner had been inside the apartment. If this was a drug or a money issue, he would've had evidence on him. But, the suicide by cop was the one wild card that threw off the whole drug premise. Neither cop's statement referred to Tanner talking about money, drugs, or trying to talk his way out of that room. The room was a dead end. If there *was* anything to find, it would be in the car.

Grady sat on a chair outside Masters' office. Masters was inside with LaCrosse, who had asked for a moment of his time. Carmen, as she preferred to be called, was out to lunch. She had been in since five and needed the break.

LaCrosse exited Masters' office and looked down at Grady, "Let's go. We have an appointment with a Prius."

"What about Masters?"

"He's busy," LaCrosse said, already heading toward the stairs.

"But—"

"But nothing. Let's go, kid."

Grady followed without another word. *Kid?*

They headed downstairs, past Desk Sergeant Atwood, who shook her head at LaCrosse, and into the motor pool. They got into what looked like Masters' Caprice but smelled of cigar smoke, so it definitely wasn't his. "You remember how to get there?" LaCrosse asked.

"It was dark. Not really. All I remember was Forsythe Park. It was across the street."

"That's good enough," he said, peeling out, and they headed toward Nelson's apartment.

LaCrosse didn't say much on the drive. After a couple of small talk questions with one-word answers, Grady quit pressing. When the surroundings became familiar, Grady pointed over to where he saw Nelson's entrance. There were no signs of a Prius on the street. "The notes said there is additional parking behind the building. The vehicle may be back there."

LaCrosse followed the side alley and found the tenant parking next to a two-story parking structure. They drove through the two-aisle parking lot, and on the corner of the closest aisle was an aqua blue Prius.

"Let's hope Branson has the keys that go with it," LaCrosse said. He called Branson, who confirmed they had them. "Mesa's on his way down."

Grady nodded, and the car again filled with silence.

"So, how long were you up in Atlanta?" LaCrosse asked, breaking the silence.

"Five years. Three as an officer, two as a detective," Grady said as if it was no big deal.

"Is that right?" LaCrosse said, sounding more impressed than he expected to hear.

"Thought I was a rookie too?"

"I knew you had experience, just not that much."

"Yeah," Grady said, shaking his head, "I've seen a thing or two."

"And this?"

"Not the worst, but it's not something you want to see every day."

"I don't think there is much we would want to see every day," LaCrosse said, stroking his stubble, which also showed the subtle shades of gray his hair revealed.

"But Tanner? The guy we took out was bad news. We're looking at a possible three homicide connection—same MO, but Nelson lived. Tanner had every chance to inflict the same lethal wounds and disappear; the question is, why didn't he?

"Perhaps he's just a copycat who flubbed it up. Maybe that's why he pulled his SBC stunt. Afraid to go back to solitary up at State. Too many questions right now," Grady reasoned.

"And they didn't find the weapon after they shot him?" LaCrosse asked.

"Nope. Part of the reason Branson is up there now. That's the strangest part. The weapon just disappeared. Did he use one of Nelson's knives, then clean up and put it back in the drawer? That's too deliberate and meticulous, not the sign of someone in a crazed mental state who was mumbling gibberish and gave the officers no choice but to shoot him."

"Mumbling?"

"The officers who shot him say that he was mumbling while he was standing over Nelson. Crazy stuff, they couldn't make any of it out," Grady explained. "Then he raised his hands over his head, and he appeared to have something in his hands. They thought it was the knife. But afterward, they found his hands empty. There was no sign of a weapon anywhere."

There was a rap on the window that made LaCrosse jump. He turned, and Mesa was there with a fob in his hand. Both men exited the car, and LaCrosse took the key.

"I hope this is it," Mesa said.

LaCrosse pushed the button. A musical *chirp* came from the car, and the lights danced, showing it was safe to proceed.

"Anything upstairs?" Grady asked.

Mesa looked up at the apartment, almost like he was nervous about revealing a secret. "Nothing really. Still a bit messy up there. Residual blood, scratch marks from what appears to be a knife, but no knife."

LaCrosse looked at Grady, then back at Mesa, "Bag and tag every piece of cutlery in the kitchen similar to our suspected weapon. We may have a courteous felon here. Hotshot over here thinks he may have cleaned up after himself."

Mesa lifted a finger to say something but thought otherwise. He turned and headed back into the building. LaCrosse's shoulders danced as he walked away.

"Well, thanks for that. Branson has it in for me as it is. I haven't been here a day, and even I can tell that."

"You'll be fine. He'll get over it. He just doesn't like it when the new guy gets to call the shots on his first day."

"How long has he been with the force?"

"Couple of years as a cop. Almost a year as a detective."

"Well, that makes me feel a little bit better. At least I carry some sense of seniority."

LaCrosse chuckled, opening the passenger side door. "Let's see what secrets this oversized battery is holding."

An hour later, they discovered two things about Stuart Taylor Nelson. One, he had a serious gum fetish. The front seats were littered with scrunched gum wrappers. Orbit seemed to be his preference. And two, he was not a drug runner. The car was entirely too clean, and there were no places to hide drugs. Most drug vehicles had hollowed-out compartments to hide as much product as possible. Door panels, under seating, under the hood, and the obvious trunk compartments. Nothing. No drugs, no money.

"So now what?" asked LaCrosse.

"Lock it back up and see what Branson found," said Grady, trying not to let the defeat reflect in his voice.

The hall didn't seem as small this time around; he was in the lead and not behind the massive Masters. Once he reached the top, he was reminded of the voracious Ms. Keppler, but to his relief, she was nowhere to be seen or heard. He thought of warning LaCrosse but didn't want to spend more time in the open than needed. He hurried both of them into Nelson's apartment and would explain later.

The apartment wasn't much different than it was 12 hours earlier. Other than the missing bodies, it was undisturbed. Branson and Nettles were in the back room discovering what he and

LaCrosse found in the car: Nelson had no interest in drugs, had no hidden stashes of cash, and there was no bloody knife to be found. Mesa, as the bearer of the bad news, pulled kitchen duty. A flashbulb could be seen every so often from his cataloging Nelson's collection of steak and butter knives.

Grady went to make peace, "Sorry, didn't mean for you to have to go through all of this."

"Don't be. We have to cover every angle. It was good insight. Masters would've been set off if we had missed it. Good job," Mesa said.

"Need help?" Grady offered.

"Nope. Last one now." Mesa said, taking the last photograph. He wrote length, handle color, and general type of knife on the bag and sealed the evidence bag. Then dropped it into a box on the counter.

Grady picked up the box while Mesa collected his kit. "Thanks. And don't worry about Branson. He'll be fine. He's always anxious around new badges, especially ones with experience."

"So, I've heard."

"I think we're done in here, but I don't think any of these blades caused those wounds. There are a couple of chopping knives, but they are as dull as Nettles' jokes," Mesa jested.

"I heard that!" called a voice from the hall.

Mesa laughed. Grady echoed.

"Forensics will still look at them, though. No stone unturned. We're that thorough."

When they entered the living room, both Branson and Nettles were there with LaCrosse. Nettles had a box under her arm too. "A couple of hunting knives. Short blades tucked in a closet. That and a straight razor for shaving. Both doubtful, but no stone unturned."

Grady looked around, then fixed his eyes under the coffee table. He could see the condition of Mr. Nelson when he entered the room. His mind flashed to the three other scenes. From what little he remembered, they seemed identical. What was he missing? That piece was here, staring him in the face. He looked at the chair where Tanner was sitting right before he chose to end his life. To the left and just behind the victim.

"What are you thinking, Grady?" LaCrosse asked.

"He's thinking he sent us on a damn wild goose chase with this drug angle," Branson said. "Complete waste of time."

"Branson, shut up," Nettles said. "What is this team's motto? We never leave a stone unturned. So, take your ego and shove it. If Grady is part of our team now, his ideas are going to be explored."

Grady wasn't listening to the exchange. He stood at the chair and took the steps Tanner had taken to get into the position of his demise. Four steps. Four good steps, just about six feet. He looked at the chair again, then at his feet. Nettles joined him, not entirely sure what Grady was looking at but studying all the same.

"I have to get back to the station," Grady said, his eyes darting around the crime scene.

"Why, what's wrong?" Mesa questioned, exchanging glances with the chair and Grady.

"I need to see the older case files photos. Something is missing here."

Chapter Five

Sunday, February 2, 17:30

Carmen had retrieved the files Grady requested by the time he returned to the station. He found an empty room with a large enough table to spread the out files and went to work examining each case, confirming his suspicions. Three hours later, when he was comfortable enough with his theory, he called in LaCrosse and Nettles.

"Where's Masters?" Grady asked. "He should be here for this."

"He's on his way," Nettles said, entering the floor with four cups of coffee.

Grady led them back to the empty room, which was now lined with photos, statements, and file notes, all painting a picture of what Grady saw, or rather what he didn't see, in Nelson's apartment.

Grady had combed through each of the three files from the past crime scenes. Each had detailed descriptions of gruesome murders that had taken place over the last month. Two male, one female, twenties to mid-forties. All were ritualistic, committed on top of coffee tables where the victim was in their undergarments with incisions that severed their femoral and brachial arteries, leaving the victim to bleed to death. The only apparent difference with Nelson was that he survived.

Grady also noted the lack of defensive wounds on the victims. Nor did the scenes show any sign of struggle, but a witness account reported screaming at the Nelson scene. So, he was incapacitated enough not to struggle but aware enough to experience pain. He talked Nettles and LaCrosse through his findings. He was glad to get their perspective before bringing it to Masters. *Just don't screw this one up.*

"So, what do you guys think?"

"Forensics and medical records are still out on Nelson. They're slow, it being Sunday and all," Carmen said. She looked at her watch, which was reversed like a nurse, "He's probably in recovery by now. I should have something by the end of day tomorrow."

"I think you have a point, kid," said LaCrosse. "I wasn't there, but if you see something connecting these cases, it's worth looking into."

Carmen loaded the photos taken at the Nelson scene onto the monitor in the corner of the room. "Could they get any further from the body?" She stood and walked closer to the 32" plasma monitor, continuing to click through the two dozen photos. "At least they took multiple angles."

"And why weren't we called on this one? It's our jurisdiction," Nettles asked.

"It was called in as a domestic dispute," Masters said. His voice and the buzzer from the gate announcing his entry onto the floor.

Nettles spun from the doorway where she stood, "Sorry, sir. Meant no disrespect."

"By the time it looked different, it was wrapped up in a body bag. I had Grady on the way, and their team was on-scene, so I decided to let you guys get your beauty sleep. I didn't realize it would get this complicated. Had I known, I would've done things different. Whatcha got Grady?" Masters dropped his jacket and holster on a desk and joined Nettles at the doorway. "Can I join the party?"

"Somethings not right about this case when we consider the other three cases. I won't know for sure until forensics comes back on Nelson, but I believe they're all connected."

"How so?" Masters asked, his eyebrows raised and arms folded against his chest.

Grady walked over to and pointed to the screen. "These aren't the best, but you and I were there, so our memories may better serve us. You saw the cuts—they were straight line, and placement was along the arm and leg. You may also remember that they were superficial, deep enough to cause bleeding but not deep enough to cause Mr. Nelson to bleed out. Tanner knew what he was doing."

"Okay, and how does this relate to the other cases?" His arms were still tight, but his face relaxed, showing a bit more concern. Grady was reaching him.

He walked over to the displayed folders and pushed up two photos from each case file. Each showed a full-length photo of the victim on the coffee table, each frozen in their death pose, covered in blood. Next was the photo of them lying on the coroner's table cleaned up, with their four cuts visible. Four clean, straight-line cuts along the femoral and brachial arteries, identical to the photos on the monitor.

"My theory is that Tanner did these," Grady said, pointing to the table. "I believe he may be the murderer in these unsolved cases. Why he didn't murder Nelson, I don't know. Why he chose to commit suicide by cop, I have no clue. Why there isn't a murder weapon is the biggest mystery, and I have no answer. But those are my current thoughts on the case right now. I will have more once the results on the cut patterns on Nelson are in."

Masters locked eyes with Grady for a long moment, studying him. Grady felt a grating sensation, like he was being peeled back layer by layer. Masters walked to the table that held the spread of documents and file information. He picked up the victim's photo previous to Mr. Nelson, a 41-year-old male, office clerk. He went missing a week ago, found by a concerned neighbor when his mail began to pile up.

"What do you think, Carmen?"

"Grady's case has teeth," she said. "It makes sense. It does have some loose ends, but in 12 hours, many of them will be tied up. Either Tanner is an exceptional copycat, or he's your killer. Why he chose to do what he did is beyond all of us, but it's one less scumbag off the streets and less paperwork for me to have to deal with."

Masters picked up another photo—33-year-old male, banker. Same scars, same clothing and positioning, same blood poured over the scene. The final photo was the oldest, the first of the collection. The female was just a bit different than the rest, maybe she was the first—a bit of first-kill jitters, but still masterful.

"You see it?" Grady asked, his head peeking around Masters. "The difference? What's missing?"

Masters looked down at each picture, then up to the screen. He looked at the wide-angle photo and saw it. "The chair. It's the only thing in the Nelson photo that's not in the others. Otherwise, the scenes are identical."

"Right, and none of the files say anything about a chair either," Grady said.

"But that doesn't mean anything," Masters said. "He could have moved it back to where he got it.

"Or it was never there in the first place," LaCrosse said. "Sorry kid, just covering every base."

"No, I completely agree. I know we need to keep an open mind. I have done my fair share of chasing wild geese. Whether Tanner has a connection with these cases remains to be seen. I just have a gut feeling that I need to pursue," Grady admitted.

"So, the two key elements *here* are the chair and the missing weapon," Masters said, pointing to the screen. "We know the chair was there because, *if* Tanner is our killer, he never got the chance to move it. But that doesn't explain the missing weapon."

"We combed that place high and low," Mesa said. "There was no weapon to find. The knives we did find we bagged and tagged and sent to Evidence, but none of them could have caused straight-lined cuts like what we see in the photographs, they were too dull."

"So, Tanner would've had to dispose of the actual weapon before the officers entered the room," Masters said.

"Boss, again, we turned that place inside out. There was no

weapon. He would've had to toss it out a window... or something," Nettles said.

"Did you check out that possibility?"

Nettles was silent for a moment. "Well, no."

"Then we need to head back and check the windows. All stones, Nettles. All stones. Anything else?"

"Not until tomorrow," said Grady.

"Well, it's getting late, and we need the forensic report on Nelson anyway. We'll know if his wounds are consistent with these other cases then," Carmen said.

"Okay, everyone. Let's call it a day. Meet back here at ten. We should have something by then," instructed Masters. "Nettles, get with Mesa and check those windows on your way in."

"10-4, boss."

Grady began to gather up the case files and organize them according to the timeline. Everyone filed out except Masters. Grady could feel his gaze—he was waiting for the room to empty before he spoke. "Night, boss," LaCrosse said as he shut the gate and headed downstairs.

"You're doing a fine job, Grady," Masters said. "I may have come off rough, but I'm not used to having experience at my side. Atwood has been giving me nothing but first years for the last six months. I had expected nothing more when she handed you off to me. When she told me you were from up north, things changed. I've worked with a couple of guys from Rampart. I know what they put you through, which carries weight. But with that respect comes expectations. So far, you have performed well. Just don't screw that up."

"I understand. I don't plan to. Atwood has advised me the same," Grady admitted with a grin. He considered Carmen's warning but didn't want to mention it and put her in the doghouse.

"Smart woman," Masters chuckled, his eyes thinned, the first time he had shown an emotion other than the grumpy old man.

Grady looked at his stack, then back to Masters with an exhale, "There's something here. I can feel it."

Masters just nodded. "Go. Go home and see your wife while

it's still early. We'll see if that hunch pans out when we get Nelson's medical records."

"What about Tanner?"

"Tanner? Four shots center mass by a cop, and he was an ex-con— no need for autopsy to reveal cause of death. It's obvious. Suicide." Masters said.

"We may still need the report. Could give reason to his state of mind when he did it. Medical reason, perhaps?"

"Carmen didn't find medical records on him. And the Pen is pretty strict on keeping those records up to date and accessible."

"Is that how Carmen got his name so quickly?" Grady asked.

Masters nodded. "Yeah, I took a drive up to Georgia State Prison last night after I left you. I have a pigeon up there. He helps me out when I need information, so I assist with his accommodations. He knows the biker circle fairly well, especially the O77s, so I paid him a visit. Tanner was up there on a five to ten stretch—got out after serving six of those years."

"Interesting. Does your bird know where Tanner went after he was released?"

"He laughed when I asked. But it makes sense. Why would a lifer keep tabs on a parolee's steps, even if he could?"

"If he were to be given a job, that task could have been given from the inside?"

"From whom?" Masters asked.

"Your pigeon," Grady said. "It's not uncommon for an informant to play both sides. To give you just enough to keep you happy and to keep enough info from you to stay alive and under the radar of the group he's informing on."

Masters rubbed his stubble. Something he may not have considered possible. He looked at Grady through squinted eyes. Grady again felt studied. "Garrison would be in deep if he were to be playing me, and he knows it."

"The question becomes, *if* this was a list of jobs, then what connection do all these victims have, and the bigger question, why was Nelson spared?"

"A question we can begin exploring tomorrow. Now go home and see your wife."

Chapter Six

Tuesday, February 18

The headlines returned to normal within a week. A dead ex-con was a comfort to most people, especially at the hands of local authorities. It showed their tax dollars put to good use. Stuart Nelson had been released from the hospital but hadn't been near his freshly cleaned apartment. He had informed Ms. Kepler of his intention to move out; although the apartment showed no sign of the attack, he couldn't live in the place where he almost died. The word was he had been staying with a friend on the other end of town, closer to the college. But with no forwarding address, there wasn't any clue about his whereabouts. And with the knowledge of what happened in the apartment, Ms. Keppler was doubtful she could rent the place even at a cheaper rate.

Masters read Nettles' report on Nelson's place. She and Mesa had searched the window sills, fire escape, and the alleyway. They came up with an array of items varying from a dozen plasticware knives, two nail files, four 9mm casings, and a saw blade, none of which were the murder weapon. But the 9mms were an interesting find and handed over to Forensics. The weapon had just vanished. The coroner's report didn't reveal much more. It didn't list any items on Tanner's body. Just him and his clothing. The only metal on him was in his teeth—and the four slugs they pulled from his chest.

While events around the precinct had returned to normal, the case still didn't sit right with Grady. He knew there was more to it but wasn't ready to admit it out loud. He was still struggling with being the new kid on the block. And the gut of the new guy is a bit farfetched to base further reaction on for his taste.

The most significant setback was that Tanner was now looking more like a botched copycat. While his cuts were practically identical, he didn't sever Nelson's arteries. He cut his veins. So, instead of producing assured death, the injury caused a slow bleed that gave Nelson a chance of survival. The going theory was when Nelson didn't die, Tanner panicked and chose suicide by cop rather than going back to jail on another attempted murder charge. At least that's what the now-closed file said.

Grady wasn't happy about it. *But what can you do when all the evidence points to one conclusion,* he mused.

There was a knock at Masters door. "Come in."

"You called for me?" Grady peered in.

"Yes, Carmen needs the after-action report on the Isaacs' robbery from Wednesday. She says you haven't sent it to her yet."

"Finishing it up now," Grady said with diverted eyes.

"Grady, have a seat," Masters said, pointing to a chair.

Grady closed the door behind him and sat. His shoulders were close to his chin, and his attention was everywhere but on his boss.

"What do you expect me to do, Grady?"

"I don't know what you mean." Grady tried to keep a straight face.

"This isn't the man who walked into this precinct a month ago ready to prove himself to me and everyone in this station house. What would Branson say?"

"I blew it. That's what *he* would say. Even though both you and I know that's bull. The file is wrong. But we have been around long enough to know there's not much you can do with a closed file until something can unclose it. I don't know why it being closed is making me so uneasy. If Tanner is responsible for those other cases, a murderer is dead and justice has been served. It's just that—there is something not right about this whole thing. I can't put my finger on it. Maybe it's the whole missing weapon thing."

"For all we know the paramedics took it," Masters said. "A souvenir. Who's going to miss it? The victim survived, the perp is dead—no harm done. And they won't fess up now. A simple, 'Nope, never saw it,' will suffice."

Grady sighed. "Maybe your right."

"So, stop with the distractions, and get your current work completed. Staring at cold cases will not solve them. It just keeps current cases from being solved. And puts your current job in jeopardy."

Grady looked up from the ground, finally meeting Masters' eyes.

"Ah, that got your attention," Masters said.

"Won't happen again, boss."

"I'm sure it will. But I would expect nothing less from a dedicated detective."

"Yes, sir." Grady stood and headed for the door.

"When you go back out there, make sure you tell them I ripped you a new one. I have to maintain my image of a hardass."

"Consider my ass chewed."

"We'll figure this out, Grady. Just not now. But in all seriousness, don't do anything foolish. I have your back, but go against me out there," Masters nodded toward the door, "and I won't hesitate to knock you off your high horse, even in front of Branson."

"Understood."

Grady left, shoulders back to normal position, head a little higher. Masters opened his top drawer and pulled out the Tanner file. *Where is that damned weapon?*

"How many times do we have to say it, man. We didn't take nothin'," the paramedic said.

"We picked up the body, transported it to the morgue, and went to eat," his partner recounted.

It was the same story in the report, the same story that he had heard two weeks ago, the same story Grady was triple checking now. "I'm just making sure. If you did, just come clean—no harm done, no foul. We just need to know, so we can clear this case."

"We have told you everything we know. You keep asking the same questions. I don't know what more you want," said the partner.

"This is borderin' harassment, bro," the first added, his jaw tensing.

"I'm not trying to harass anyone," said Grady.

"Could'a fooled me," said the first.

"Can we go now? We have a John Doe to pick up," said the second.

Grady looked them both in the eye. The first had a fiery glare. Grady knew that look; he didn't do anything. The second was innocent as well. Only he wasn't burning a hole through him.

"Yes. You can go. Sorry, gentlemen."

The paramedic mumbled under his breath as he jumped into their rig. The second remained silent, simply rolling his eyes, and circled to the passenger side. The ambulance peeled out, leaving Grady with a bit of regret for shaking the tree again. But he had to be sure, and now he was. A couple of enemies made, but two names scratched off the list of where the weapon could have gone.

Grady was determined. Despite Masters' stern warning to let it go, the case wouldn't leave his mind. It kept him awake—even Elizabeth gave him grief over it. He wasn't sure if it was over Masters' warning or that there was something more to the case.

"James, just come to bed," Elizabeth said for the third time.

"In a minute, babe," Grady reassured.

"You said that an hour ago."

He looked up at her. She had her hand on her hip, the way she always did when she meant business.

Grady smiled. "On my way." He closed the file in front of him and placed it on the stack he had accumulated during the last week. He had background checks on the two paramedics, schematics of the apartment building, details of the owner, and records into the whereabouts of Stuart Nelson. Something was staring him in the face, but he couldn't see it. He was convinced of that.

After reorganizing, he followed Elizabeth back to their room. He had been staying up far too late for both of their tastes and neglecting their time together as well as church time, which was something he had promised he wouldn't do. He could tell it weighed on her, but neither of them had spoken of it yet.

"What's so important about those files, James?" Elizabeth asked, sitting on the edge of their bed.

"I need to find something out."

"I thought you said the case was closed."

"It is," he answered as they both slipped under the covers of their king-sized bed.

"Then why are you still working on it?"

"Something isn't right," Grady said, leaning up onto his elbow.

"What's not right?"

Grady shook his head. "If I could answer that, then I wouldn't be so confused." Grady rolled over and turned out the lamp.

"Have you prayed about it?" Elizabeth said in the darkness of the room.

Grady stayed silent a moment. He hadn't thought about it that way. "Not as much as I should, I suppose. Stuff like this seems strange to pray about."

"Well, you know that God hears, no matter how simple or complicated the issue."

"I know." Grady loved that about his wife. She could see spiritual things more clearly than he could. He tended to get lost in what he was doing and was glad to have her to set him straight and remind him what matters.

Elizabeth turned to him and put her head on his chest. "Speaking of God, I'd really like to find a church. We haven't been since we moved down here. I miss going."

"Me too. I'll ask around the station. Maybe one of the guys knows of a place. I haven't heard anyone talk about church, much less God, but I can ask."

Once again, she had him. When they were in Atlanta, they attended regularly. It was tough leaving their church family. Maybe being away from the church was the reason for his disconnected feeling. He had been so busy trying to adjust that he had neglected his relationship with God. He couldn't remember the last time he picked up a Bible, and that had once been a daily habit.

Elizabeth reached up, kissed him, and rolled over. He watched her for a moment, and like every other night, she was asleep in seconds. A talent he envied. His mind, though, never stopped. It was the analytical mind of a cop, always recalculating a current situation, trying to piece it together and solve the case. He remembered Elizabeth's words and closed his eyes.

"Lord, sorry we haven't spoken in a while. I didn't mean to push you aside. I could use your help. I'm struggling to understand this case. I know that it's closed, but I don't feel right about it. Is this uneasiness from you? If it is, please direct me on how I should go forward. Please show me the answer that everyone else is missing. If it isn't, please give me peace and the strength to move on. Amen."

Grady opened his eyes, feeling a little better. His wife was gently snoring, another thing he loved about her. He didn't know what tomorrow would hold, but he now knew that he wouldn't have to carry the weight he had been slothing around. The answer was out there. He just needed to be patient and vigilant. Minutes later, he too was asleep, dueling sleep sounds with his spouse.

Chapter Seven

Thursday, February 20, 20:20

Are you sure?" Masters questioned his cell phone. "That's not possible."

More silence.

"Exactly the same?" Masters gave Grady a look of disbelief he was trying to deliver to the person on the other end of the line. "We're on our way."

"That doesn't sound promising," Grady said.

"For you, it might," Masters said. "It's regarding the Tanner case."

"The Tanner case? You're kidding," Grady's eyebrows furrowed.

"Well, maybe not directly. There has been a murder down on the Southside. It's consistent with the Tanner case. Similar to Nelson, but more like the victims murdered before him."

"How consistent?"

"According to officers on-scene, identical. That's why they called us."

"I don't understand."

"Neither do I. We need to head over there for answers. We may have a copycat on our hands."

"Did they say anything about who did this? Was it another killed-by-cop standoff?"

"They didn't say." Masters opened a file cabinet and grabbed his gun and credentials. "Let's go."

The car ride to the scene was spent in silence, other than the police band radio squawking. They managed to avoid a pileup on the Truman Parkway, just before the Vernon River. Taking the side streets across Highway 204 added to their trip, but not as much time as waiting out the accident. They still managed to beat the coroner, who must've been caught in the mess.

Masters turned off the highway onto a side street. It was a neighborhood of single-family homes. There was still daylight left, but the flashing lights from the crime scene could be seen from down the block. At the end of the first street, an officer in a heavy coat signaled them to stop with his flashlight. "Can I help you?"

"Lieutenant Daniel Masters and Detective James Gradiosa. Officer Odem called us."

"One second, Lieutenant." The officer stepped back and grabbed the walkie at his waist. After a brief discussion with someone up ahead, he waved them through.

For a single murder, there was far more commotion than Grady expected. The street was blocked off by the officer they just met, and four squad cars were parked in front of a two-story house. As Masters pulled up, Grady could see a half dozen officers standing on a wraparound porch, and an ambulance was parked behind another detective's vehicle.

"LaCrosse," Masters said, nodding to the car up the block. He guided his sedan and parked in front of him."

Masters was the first out of the car after putting it into park. He didn't say anything as he headed to the home. Nor did he acknowledge the officers standing there. Grady understood. He had to know for sure. While Masters felt this case was sealed up in a body bag long ago, not finding the murder weapon had haunted him as much as it did Grady. The biggest question was, was this a copycat?

When Grady entered the house, another set of officers added to the group on the porch. The smell of cannabis perfumed the air. Other than the odor, the home was immaculate. Not what you would expect from a druggie. The décor was that of a grandmother. There were knick-knacks and porcelain figures on shelves along the wall. A hutch displayed plates with handprints and children's smiling faces. For a moment, Grady was lost in his surroundings. Then a familiar voice grabbed him.

"Masters. Grady. Back here," LaCrosse called.

Grady looked to the back of the room. LaCrosse was in sweats and a Doors T-shirt.

"Nice of you to dress up for the occasion," Masters said.

"My tux is at the cleaners," LaCrosse ribbed. "Body's back here. It's not pretty."

"Is it him?" Grady asked.

"Can't tell yet. Too much—well, you'll see."

"The team?" Masters asked.

"I phoned Mesa and Nettles just before you pulled up. They're fifteen out. I told them to hold the perimeter, get the officers' statements, and talk with possible witnesses," LaCrosse explained.

"What about Branson?" Masters asked, wondering why his team lead wasn't called first.

"Couldn't reach him."

"Understood," Masters said. He had other things to be concerned with than a team member not answering his phone. "Where are we going?"

"This way," LaCrosse led Masters and Grady through a hallway into a large room that looked like a study. It was much different than the living area. This room had wall-to-wall paneling. There was a large desk at the back of the room and bookcases along the walls, overloaded with books. In the middle of the room was a couch and a coffee table. On that table was a middle-aged man soaked with his blood.

"Sure looks like Tanner's handiwork," Masters said. "But I don't understand it. That bastard is dead. I saw the body."

"I don't know. Look at the blood here. It's looking more like Tanner was a copycat, and that's why Nelson didn't die," LaCrosse said.

"Not possible," Grady said, shaking his head. "There are too many similarities to the originals. Tanner's MO was identical."

"*Except* Nelson didn't die," LaCrosse stressed. "There's a difference."

"Why is that then?" Masters asked. "Why the difference? What caused this guy here to bleed out, and Nelson didn't?"

"You just got there in time?" LaCrosse offered.

Masters sighed and walked up to the body. "Do we have a time of death?"

LaCrosse thumbed through his notes, "9-1-1 call came in two hours ago. First officer was on-scene five minutes later. The medical examiner arrived about a half-hour ago. She determined death was roughly an hour before the initial 9-1-1 came in."

"You see," Masters began. "Nelson lasted twice that long and survived. Why is it different this time?"

"So, you think we're looking at the wrong guy?" Grady asked.

"We have to consider the evidence in front of us, Grady. First, Tanner's victim didn't die like the first three victims. Second, the murder weapon is still missing. And third, well, it's on a coffee table in front of us."

"You're thinking, either Tanner has a partner, or Tanner was a copycat," Grady said.

"Either way, *if* Tanner is our man, he had help," said Masters. "That's the only way to explain the missing murder weapon. Since we have no physical evidence of another perpetrator, either it grew legs and walked out on its own, or Nelson was in on his attempted murder, and he snuck the weapon out himself."

"What if he *was* in on it?" LaCrosse thought aloud.

"Nelson?" Grady asked. "I looked at that angle. He coded three times during surgery. He almost died. You think he would risk that? What would he gain?"

No one could answer.

"The other option is we got it wrong. Tanner isn't our guy. And the real suspect is still out there killing again." LaCrosse said, pointing an open hand toward the body.

"That still brings us back to the missing knife," Grady said.

The room again went silent. None of the men could respond.

The silence was broken by the EMTs entering with a gurney. To Grady's relief, it was not the same men who took Tanner's body.

"Excuse us, gentlemen." Two men in medical coveralls and gloves, driving a gurney, eased past them.

"Well, this is going to be messy," one said to the other.

"We want everything that your examiner finds. And I mean everything," Masters ordered, handing him one of his cards.

"We will pass it on," one of the coverall clad examiners said. Then he and his partner loaded the deceased into the body bag and headed out of the room.

Two officers with coffee cups entered the study, debating the difference between an armoire and a hutch.

"Do you have an ID on the victim? Did he live here?" Masters asked.

They both looked at each other, then at Masters, "And you are?"

"Where's Odem?" Masters asked.

"He's up front talking to the reporter from KNWS. That doesn't answer my question."

"Lieutenant Daniel Masters. North Savannah District. Odem called me about this victim. He's part of a possible string of murders that have occurred across the state. Same MO. Now, do you have a name or not?"

"William Dale, 45, attorney at law. No, he didn't live here, but he did know the resident. However, she wasn't home at the time of the murder. She's in Florida visiting a relative," the officer on the left said—*Simmons*, his badge read.

"If the homeowner was out of town, why was he here?"

"Your guess is as good as mine, Lieutenant," Simmons answered.

"And the pot smell? Have you been able to determine where it came from?"

"Again, we would only be guessing at this point."

Masters shook his head with a sigh. "Has your forensics team at least gone over this room?"

"Just around the body. No weapon or prints: finger or shoe. Whoever it was did a good job of hiding that much. We'll still comb the room. But doubt we'll find anything," the second, Jacobs, explained.

"Why's that?" Grady asked.

"If he went through the trouble of cleaning up around the body, do you think he'd be careless enough to leave prints around the room, Detective?"

Masters knew Jacobs was right. If this were their guy, they'd find nothing—not today and not tomorrow. Searching would be useless. But they would still join the search. It was the team's motto: No stone unturned. Police work was always built on the hope of the payoff of the criminal making that one mistake that would lead to their capture.

Masters gave Simmons one of his cards and explained he expected a full report of all their findings. Then he added, "By the way, in the dining room? It's a hutch. The difference is that an armoire is a full-length piece and usually has doors. A hutch is a two-part piece for either storing china or displaying knick-knacks, like the lady of the house has here."

Grady exited the front door and followed the porch toward the driveway. Nettles was there with her notepad in hand, scribbling like it meant something. "What you got?" he asked.

"There's no car," she said.

"She's out of town. Probably took it with her," Grady explained.

"Not her. Her name is Perkins, by the way. Evangeline Perkins. She and her husband have lived here for nearly 60 years. He passed about five years ago. But that is beside the point. Yes, she is in Florida with her sister. William Dale rents the room in the back for his law firm. He's out of Atlanta and is a family friend. He relocated after the husband passed but retained clientele down here. She offered the room to him so he could save money on office space."

"And the smell?" Grady said, waving his hand in front of his nose.

"Medical marijuana," Nettles laughed.

"Ahh, okay," Grady nodded. "And you figured all of this out in less than an hour?"

"Well, no, not me. That was Carmen. She called with the information. I'm finalizing her notes," Nettles explained.

"I should've known."

"William Dale had a late model silver Mercedes. If he's here, it should be here. Our killer may have taken off with it. Carmen's issued a BOLO on it."

"Good work, Nettles. Have you told Masters?"

"Not yet. You're the first one I've seen since I received the update."

"Okay. We should let him know. Where's Mesa?" Grady asked.

"Talking to the neighbor. He may have seen something. He was telling us he saw the Mercedes pull up earlier today, but I had to take the call from Carmen, so I left Mesa to take his statement."

"Did Carmen say anything else?" Grady asked, half expecting her to say something about the resemblance to the previous cases.

"Other than she thinks that Masters is going to have a field day with this, she didn't say much else."

"Yeah, I bet. Did you see the scene?"

"No, I've had perimeter duty. But I've heard the officer's talk. A couple of them even made use of the bushes over there," Nettles nodded to Mrs. Perkins' rose bushes that lined the driveway.

"It looks a lot like what we saw with Nelson," Grady said. "Only more blood. Sure looks like Tanner's work."

"But he was killed by those two officers," Nettles said.

"Master's thinks there may have been more than one, that we're missing something."

"How does that make sense?" Nettles flapped her arms at her side. "There wasn't evidence of two people in Nelson's apartment or at any of the other scenes. Hell, there was barely evidence of one perp."

"That's the going theory."

"You don't agree," Nettles said, seeing through his frustration.

"Who am I to argue with the boss? But no, I disagree with Masters that there is more than one. I stand by my belief that Tanner acted alone."

"Then how do you explain the missing weapon?"

"I can't. At least not yet," Grady said, then looked at the ground.

"But?" Nettles asked.

"The scene in there." Grady looked back to the house. "If the same weapon made those incisions, what does that mean?"

"It means that you're that much closer to finding your answers."

"True, but it also means it's in the hands of another murderer. Obviously, with the same skills as Tanner. And that takes us back to Masters' premise of second a perpetrator."

Nettles was silent. Grady could feel her eyes boring holes through him.

"I'm missing something. I just know it. And it's staring me in the face," Grady said.

"Let's go talk to Mesa. Maybe he has some answers."

Chapter Eight

Friday, February 21, 09:30

The information that Mesa had only confirmed what they already knew. William Dale drove his silver 2010 Mercedes E350 to the residence around 13:00 that afternoon. The neighbor who gave the statement said that he was alone and brought in a bag that appeared to be from a local eatery. He went in through the back entrance, which was normal—there was a door to the office he kept back there.

Later, around 17:00, she thought she heard squealing tires. She was certain of the time because it was during her favorite television show, *Cooks of Savannah*. It was also why she didn't get up to see where the noise came from, but she said it was close and in the direction of Dale's office. When she went to her kitchen at 18:00 to start cooking dinner, she looked out her window, and the Mercedes was gone.

Officers found a McClary's Deli take-out bag in the trash basket and skid marks on the street that confirmed the witness' statement. And the timeline matched the 9-1-1 call, the tire screeching, and her television show. The lunch contents showed a meal for one, so Mr. Dale was not expecting his executioner for lunch. Nor did his appointment ledger reveal anything of worth. It seemed he had a clear schedule for the day. His next appointment on his log was not until 09:00 the following day.

"This guy sure kept himself busy," Grady asked, flipping through the ledger for the third time. "Have we found Mr. Howard?"

"LaCrosse is on his way to speak to him now," Masters said from his side of the desk, sipping his second cup of coffee. "Then he's heading up to Atlanta to Dale's main office. He'll be back on Monday."

"Mesa and Nettles have a list of names they are meeting with today as well."

"I'm a little concerned with ours. I have kept it to myself because I didn't want to mention it until I was sure. And I wanted it to be you to make this visit."

"Okay, Grady, cut the theatrics. Whose name is on the list?" Masters said, circling his hand.

"Dale's first appointment yesterday morning was with Branson. I don't know if it's why he was MIA last night, and I don't know if he was a client or just meeting with him."

Masters never broke eye contact with his partner while receiving the news. He then looked up to the small window that cast a bit of natural light into the room. You couldn't see out the window, but Masters seemed like he was looking at something. He remained silent for a long moment, then said, "No, Branson wasn't MIA. He called me around lunchtime. He asked for a PTO day—said he had to go out of town on a personal matter, and he would be back this afternoon."

"Did he say what this personal matter was?"

"No, and I didn't pry," Masters said firmly. "I've worked with Branson for 10 years, and I shouldn't have to ask details. I did ask if everything was alright. He confirmed everything was kosher, and I left it at that."

"Gotcha," Grady said. But something inside him wasn't so sure. The coincidence seemed too coincidental. "So, do we take him off the list?"

Masters turned and tilted his head. With squinted eyes, he looked to the ground, "No, I suppose not. We need to do this right. No stone unturned."

Grady still wasn't sure about Branson. He'd had more than one run-in with him. He knew he was the team lead, but he didn't seem to act like it. From what he had seen thus far, LaCrosse had more of a lead style about him. Maybe the relationship with Masters had something to do with it. He just didn't see Masters as showing favoritism.

"Do you know any of these other names?"

Masters looked down the eight other names. His eyebrows raised a few times. "Some yes, others no. Mainly collars officers' downstairs have made. Petty offenses, nothing major. We may have seen one or two."

"Where do we begin?"

Masters looked over the list and handed it back to Grady. "Ariella Matthews, then Nancy Blevins."

"Why them?"

"They're the only two women on the list, they live close to each other, and they live near the strip. We can catch lunch. I'm hungry."

"Gotcha, boss." Grady grabbed his coat and the case file.

Neither woman knew anything about Dale's murder. Both had met with him early in the week and had their cases settled out of court. Matthews was on bounced checks; Blevins was in a domestic dispute with a neighbor that the other party instigated. While officers were called out in Blevins' case, no criminal charges were officially filed, and the other party realized they were at fault and dropped their accusations even before Dale could file a motion to settle the case.

They wrapped those two with such ease they had plenty of time to scan their list and find that one of their next interviewees was Joshua McClary, owner of McClary's Deli. "Interview and lunch. Two birds with one stone?" Grady offered.

Masters spun the car around and headed up the highway. Grady could see his lieutenant was in thought. He was still learning when to speak and when to keep silent but had grown comfortable enough to ask, "What's up, boss?"

"Maybe Dale didn't tip well?" Masters jested.

"Could be, but if it is McClary, you would think he would take the food bag with him after the crime, not leave it for us to find," Grady volleyed back.

"Or cleaning it up would show more guilt because he'd know we'd be looking for it, so he'd leave it."

"All over a tip?" Grady chuckled.

"Hey, I've seen people lose it because you didn't say 'thank you' the correct way."

"What a shame," Grady said. "McClary better have a rock-solid alibi."

Fifteen minutes later, they were sitting at a booth in the back corner of McClary's Deli. The place was rather sophisticated for a hole-in-the-wall. McClary must be doing something right, or wrong. The dining area was darker than expected, and the walls were lined with rustic wallpaper depicting Irish headlands overlooking the North Atlantic. The tables had fabric tablecloths. The place had more of an Irish pub feel than a delicatessen. Not long after they sat, they had complimentary pretzel bites with cheese delivered to their table. Maybe they were made when they arrived. Cops tend to stand out in some neighborhoods. The waitress returned to take their order. Masters asked for a pastrami on rye; Grady had the Rueben.

"So, detective, what do you make of this?" Masters questioned, nodding toward the room.

Grady looked around in a daze. A bit overwhelmed but still focused. "It's all new. Two, maybe three months. Fresh money for sure."

"And how do you draw that conclusion?"

"No frays," Grady replied.

"Frays?"

"On the tablecloths. Either they change them out frequently, then my timing would be off, or they are still new and haven't had time to age and fray. Even the best cloth will fray on some level. The wallpaper would show signs of age as well, especially near the ceiling where the cleaning staff cannot, or will not, reach up to clean."

The sandwiches arrived, and Grady bowed his head in prayer. He took little notice that his partner didn't and dove into his meal. They both must have been hungry because neither said a word as they consumed the first half of their meal.

Masters was the first to break the silence. "How do you know so much about cloth wear?"

"My wife is a realtor. Part of her job is showing homes. She has a team stage the home for viewings. She ensures all materials are top quality and changes them out frequently. I guess I pay attention."

Masters nodded in what appeared to be approval, another notch of endorsement from his partner, easing Grady's tension. It always seemed he was taking one step forward, then two steps back with his boss. Any advancement was good. Now, if he could only keep the momentum.

Feeling another lull coming and wanting to keep the conversation going, Grady took another risk. "So, is there a Mrs. Masters?"

Masters' eyes glazed over like he had left the room and sailed to another time and place. The smile left his stubbly chin, and he looked to the table and shook his head. "No, I've never married," he said and left it at that.

Grady understood there was more to the story, but he didn't press. He just nodded in acceptance of his answer.

"I guess you can say I'm married to the job," Masters said as he looked up to Grady again, smiling, but the glassy look remained in his eyes.

"10-4, boss," Grady replied. Elizabeth had accused him more than once of having an affair with his badge. He understood the late nights, the missed dinners, the canceled plans, and the tears that followed. In a way, he was envious. It wasn't that he regretted being married. Grady wouldn't change his life for the world, he loved Elizabeth, but he hated putting her through the choices he was forced to make.

The server came back to clear their empty trays, and Masters asked if McCleary was in. She said he was in his office and was expecting them.

Grady raised his eyebrows at Masters, who shrugged. They both stood, and Emily, their server, led them down a hallway past the restrooms and through a set of swinging doors. The kitchen was ahead of them, and two twenty-something prep cooks were cutting vegetables. One was chopping lettuce, and the other focused on slicing tomatoes.

Emily stopped at a closed door and tapped on the door. A stern voice beckoned them in, and Emily entered the room. A man in his forties sat with an opened file on his desk. "Officers," the man said.

"Detectives," Masters corrected.

"My apologies, detectives, please have a seat," the man said, gesturing to two chairs in front of his desk.

As they sat, Grady noticed that they seemed out of place for the tiny office area. "Are you Joshua McClary?"

"I am not," the man said. He immediately went back to the file he had in his hands, thumbed a couple of pages, and exhaled deeply. "I'm Eric McClary. Joshua is my son. What sort of trouble has he fallen into this time?"

"This time?" Grady asked, exchanging glances with his partner.

"Yes, if it's not one thing, it's another. Petty theft as a teen, stolen checks out of high school, identity theft a few months ago. He was talking with an attorney because he is facing his third misdemeanor—"

"—which would be considered a felony," Masters finished the sentence.

"Right. So, his attorney was trying to get his third pleaded down."

"Who was his attorney?" Grady asked as straight-faced as he could, as if the answer would be a surprise.

Mr. McClary took turns looking at each of them. Grady could

tell he already knew what had happened. His eyes showed the pain of a father who was sure of his son's innocence but not entirely sure of his confidence behind it. "Look. I know why you are here. Yes, William Dale was my son's attorney. Yes, Mr. Dale was in here yesterday around 11:30. He ordered a Philly cheesesteak to go. No, my son didn't see him yesterday. I know that because he's in Atlanta visiting his cousin. I spoke to him last night. He did have an appointment with Mr. Dale the day before yesterday to go over some paperwork for his hearing next week."

"You seem to have all the answers, Mr. McClary," Masters said.

"With a son like mine, you need to, Detective," Mr. McClary said matter-of-factly.

Masters nodded. Grady watched the interaction. It was his first time to witness his partner question a person of interest. He was taking the back seat and letting him run with this one.

"How did that appointment go? What did Joshua tell you on your phone call?"

"Nothing much. Josh said he had to sign papers for the court appearance next week. He didn't get into details," Mr. McClary said, breaking eye contact with Masters for the first time. Grady caught the tell. Would Masters?

"You sure?" Masters asked. "You know with just a phone call, we can find out everything."

McClary paused for a moment, then took a breath. "Josh wasn't happy. His attorney thought he might have to face jail time. The D.A. wanted five years. Mr. Dale was trying to get him probation and time served. He had already spent three months before being released on bail. But during his last meeting, he had discussed that judges are far less lenient with the third offenses. 'Laws are on the books for a reason,' he explained."

"Was he angry enough to harm Mr. Dale?"

"Hell, no," McClary said, raising his voice. "Sorry. Joshua wouldn't harm a fly. Yeah, he used to be a criminal, but most of his stuff was white collar. He isn't violent. That's why he's fighting so hard not to go to prison. He's afraid to go."

"So, he wouldn't get his hands dirty, then," Masters suggested.

"Don't go putting words in my mouth. He doesn't hang around people like that."

"But it wouldn't be far-fetched to say that he could have gotten mixed up accidentally with the wrong crowd? Stolen the wrong ID, perhaps?"

Mr. McClary was at a loss for words. He didn't have an answer to Masters' question. It was obvious that sort of scenario had not occurred to him. "No, I guess it wouldn't. It's plausible, but I don't think it happened that way. He would've said something."

"You never know, Mr. McClary. Kids nowadays. You said yourself he was scared to go to prison. That in itself can make a normal person do the unspeakable." Masters paused for effect, then continued, "We will need the number and address of where Joshua is staying. We need to speak to him directly. Until we speak to him, he is still a person of interest."

"Of course," Mr. McClary pulled a blank sheet of paper from the copy machine and gave the requested information.

Masters collected the sheet of paper and motioned for the door. "Thank you for your cooperation, Mr. McClary. If we have any further questions, we'll contact you."

Without another word, Masters got up and headed out the door. Grady gave Mr. McClary a nod, then quickly followed Masters. The door shut behind them, and Masters grinned.

"Enjoyed yourself, did ya?" Grady asked.

"Perhaps," Masters said. "You never know who is guilty and who is plain ole hiding something."

"Well, he knows nothing. That's obvious."

"We know that now. He's second-guessing his boy, though."

"I don't think he's our guy," Grady admitted.

"Neither do I." Masters shrugged. "But we still need to talk to him. He may know something."

Chapter Nine

Saturday, February 22, 08:30

It wasn't the same type of incision as Nelson," Grady was told. He sat reading over the medical examiner's report for the third time. The ritual began the same, but things took a dramatic detour when they reached the incision point. In Nelson's case, the brachial and femoral veins were severed. With Dale, the perpetrator was more meticulous; they targeted the arteries. The scene itself told the whole story. *Why the difference?*

Grady picked up the scene photos and replayed the evening in his head. He knew something was different the moment he stepped into the room. The copious amount of blood spoke volumes. His notes revealed that, like the first three victims, there was a lack of a chair. Everything else matched the Nelson scene—a partially nude body, the coffee table, and how the perp displayed the body.

"They found Dale's car," Masters burst into the office, startling Grady. Masters' hand was cupping the phone he held. "It's in a field just outside of Newpark. Branson is heading down to take a look." Masters sat at his desk and scribbled in his notebook.

Masters looked up at Grady. He had said *Newpark* like Grady should know where it was. His face must have reflected his ignorance, and Masters' eyes spun again, and his head shook. "Thanks, officer," Masters said to the phone, then was silent for a moment, "No, don't touch anything and compromise my scene. I'm sending a detective to take over. Metro can tow it to the yard once he's finished."

He ended the call with a glare. "I know you're still new, but you really need to get to know your city, Grady. This deer in the headlights will only work for so long."

"Gotcha, boss," Grady said as Carmen's warning regurgitated into his mind.

"Newpark is south along 95, halfway between here and Jacksonville. GSP spotted it and called it in after our BOLO went out." Masters walked to the map of Georgia that was tacked on his office wall. He pointed to Dale's house and followed the highway to where the car was found. "That's about 30 miles from the crime scene."

"Let's hope we have more luck with this one than we did with Nelson's vehicle."

"That's why I'm having Branson handle it," Masters said without looking away from the map. "If it comes up empty, he can't blame you for two cars gone wrong."

"Thanks—I think." Grady wasn't sure what to make of the comment. True, if the suspect was as meticulous as expected, that vehicle would be wiped clean. Grady was surprised that they found it so soon and that it wasn't torched.

"Don't let it get to you. You had a good hunch. It just didn't pan out. Now we know drugs aren't involved. We've closed that door. Now we explore other options."

"I still feel something is staring me in the face. Something obvious. That missing weapon haunts me. I still don't understand how Tanner disposed of it. We went over every inch of that place and found nothing." Grady said, his mind clouding once again. Grady shook his head to clear it.

"New scene, new opportunities," Masters said. Turning to Grady, he adopted a fatherly tone. "Sooner or later, the perp slips up and leaves us a crumb. We follow that crumb until we find another. Eventually, we nail our suspect. Crumbs solve cases. We just need to find them. So, don't let it bother you. We bring Dale's vehicle in and let forensics take over and see what crumbs this bum left behind."

"Yeah, and if Branson finds that evidence, I'll never hear the end of it," Grady said with half a chuckle. He closed the file and tossed it on the desk.

Masters returned the half-hearted laugh. "Probably not. But remember, we're on the same team. We have one murder and an attempted murder on our hands. I've known Branson for years. His pop and I go way back, and I was in a way responsible for bringing him onto the force. I understand he can be overbearing, but he is a brilliant detective. He just has to work on his people skills. So, cut him a little slack as a personal favor?"

"Gotcha, boss," Grady said. *Just don't screw this one up, Grady.*

Not sure what to say next, Grady let the room grow quiet. After Masters sat, he stood and walked over to the map and started to study it. No better time to get to know his city than downtime. After locating the two sites Masters pointed out, he located Forsythe Park, where Nelson lived, then the station house. "Do you have push pins?"

As Grady search for his house, he could hear the screech of Masters' rusted desk opening and miscellaneous objects being rustled around, then the rattling of a box of pins. Grady turned, and Masters tossed the box to him. They were the clear type with the flat head.

"Can you toss me the Wite-Out as well?"

Masters did.

Grady colored the ends of three push pins then placed them in each scene location. He wrote numbers on each pin corresponding with the timeline of events. He then pulled out a fresh notebook from the file cabinet that was next to him. Another eerie screech resounded. He wrote *#1* on the first page, then *Forsythe Park* along with all the notes he could remember about that night. He picked up the file off Masters' desk and copied times and other numerical details. He did the same for *#2, Southside,* and for *#3,* he only wrote *Newpark.*

"You've been through this before," Masters said. It was not a question.

"You could say that. I'm tired of playing catch-up. I like to be organized, and if I get my head back in the game, then I won't stay behind this creep," Grady explained, still looking over the files, making sure he didn't miss anything. He caught a peripheral glance of Masters as he sat. He had a fatherly grin glowing through his stubble.

Grady thumbed through his notes and looked back up at the board.

"So, what do you see." Masters asked.

"I still believe it's all connected—the three, Nelson, and now Dale. I'm even more convinced, but I don't know why. All evidence points to the contrary. Dale matches the first three. Nearly to a tee. If Nelson never entered play, then we would call this a serial, but he did, and that throws everything off." Grady paced, gesturing to the map with his hands. "If Tanner *was* our guy, he's on a slab. So, *who* killed Dale? Better yet, who was able to kill Dale and make it look exactly like the first three? That puts us back to Tanner's not our guy." Grady sat, running his hands through his hair. "It would mean he's a copycat who flubbed things up, which makes sense since Nelson lived."

"I see," Masters said, nodding along. "As was my supposition from the start."

Grady shook his head and exhaled. He leaned over, looking over the photos again. He picked up the officers' statements and read through them. "What do you think Tanner meant by, 'I don't have much time?'"

"Haven't a clue. Maybe he was late for a date?" Masters jested.

"He knew he was about to die." Grady kept reading. "The officers said he kept checking his watch. He was waiting for something."

"For EMS to arrive. That's when he decided to jump in front of four bullets," Masters said.

"It's more than that. Clarke and Ryan's statement reads that Tanner checked his watch when he heard the EMS siren, then he began chanting. That could be important. I need to speak to them again."

"Important for what? So Tanner was itchy about doing what he was about to do. He had a tick that made him check his watch. He was probably high. Have we seen his tox screen?"

"They stated he was calm," Grady said.

"Still, what will checking his watch reveal about why he was killed, let alone who killed Dale?"

"Crumbs," Grady said, looking at Masters dead in his eyes.

"Well, I guess you need to talk to Clarke and Ryan again, don't you?" Masters said again with a fatherly grin.

Saturday, February 22, 13:30

Branson drove back into the lot three hours after finding Dale's vehicle abandoned in a patch of bushes right where Georgia State Patrol said it would be. No one had laid a hand on it other than the first officer on the scene. Even Branson touch the car other than to verify it was William Dale's vehicle and that there were no other bodies or other conspicuous forensic evidence.

While waiting for the tow truck, Branson popped the trunk, and other than two boxes of files, a first aid kit, a suitcase, and what looked like a go-bag, it was clean. There was no evidence of blood, weapons, or disorder to speak of. The backseat had a suit still wrapped in dry-cleaning cellophane hung and a pair of tailored shoes on the floor. He couldn't tell the brand without entering the car. At first glance, if the murderer got away in this car, he cleaned it up.

Branson made sure the tow company was meticulous not to disturb the vehicle in any way other than what their job parameters warranted. "Not a scratch," he told them. He knew that every mark would tell them a story of where that car had been since it had left Southside. It could tell the history of William Dale and perhaps why he was targeted. Maybe those files in his trunk held clues, but highly unlikely—the driver most likely took what they needed.

Fingerprints were what they sought. Hair strands, skin cells, bodily fluids, and the fabulous forensic word, DNA. Foreign to the field operators, but gold to the squints in the lab.

Now back at home base, the lab monkeys could get to work. First things first, they'd hit it with their black powder and Kabuki brushes in search of the fingerprints he already knew weren't there. Other than that oblivious officer, this vehicle would be clean. He would sign the chain of custody form and grab the beer that waited for him in his office fridge. The secret stash that no one but maybe LaCrosse knew of. He almost caught him once. But what was one beer in the middle of the day? It didn't hurt anyone. He earned it. He was a hard worker. Much harder than that rookie Grady.

"Make sure you cover this vehicle bumper to bumper, Glavine," Branson ordered. "We don't want to miss anything. I asked for *you* to be in charge because you're the best forensic scientist we have, and if there is evidence to find I trust you'll uncover it. And when you find it, you can call me on my cell."

"I thought Detective Gradiosa was the contact with this case," Dr. Glavine said with a furrowed brow.

"I am a Senior Detective. You can contact me. I brought the vehicle in, and you will contact me because I asked you to, understood?"

"Yes, sir. My apologies."

"Thank you, Glavine. Small misunderstanding, no apologies needed. You have my number?"

"Yes, sir."

"Wonderful. I'll be up in my office completing paperwork. When you find something, call me." Branson said and left Glavine to his job.

Dr. Glavine walked over to his desk and picked up the phone.

He called in the rest of his team. As Branson had said, he was the best, and there was work to do.

Saturday, February 22, 17:45

"Thank you, officer. Yes. I'll be on time. Monday afternoon, 1 p.m. at the Gino's Diner on 11th and Pine," Grady said into the phone, not knowing where in the world he agreed to meet the two officers. "I appreciate you meeting me. I won't take too much of your time." Grady ended the call and headed back to Carmen's desk.

"Did you finally get hold of Clarke or Ryan?" Carmen asked, looking up from her computer, the glare from the screen hiding her eyes.

"That was Ryan. Meeting them on Monday for an early lunch. I also spoke to Joshua McClary. He'll be back in town on Tuesday for his hearing next week. I meet with him on Wednesday."

"You really think he'll have information?"

"Probably not, but we leave no stone unturned. Crumbs lay everywhere." Grady smiled.

Carmen laughed, aware of Masters' crumby theory. "Hey, he works in a deli, what better place to find crumbs."

"No doubt. Speaking of crumbs, forensics is going over Dale's vehicle downstairs. I'm heading down to see if they found anything."

"Glavine," Carmen said.

"Glavine?"

"Yes, Dr. Dominick Glavine is our lead Forensic Scientist. He and his team have been processing Dale's Mercedes since Branson brought it in. I haven't heard anything yet," Carmen clicked on her keyboard, "and nothing has been entered into the system."

"Well, we didn't expect him to find anything with how clean the past crime scenes have been. I'll check in on him anyway.

Thanks, Carmen." Grady gave her a brotherly grab to the shoulder and buzzed out of the detective unit.

As Grady headed downstairs, he could hear Atwood laying into a couple of officers about keeping their units clean. Half-filled coffee cups and burger wrappers were disrupting her tight ship. It seemed to him that all desk sergeants use traffic duty as a threat to coerce officers into compliance. He couldn't help but laugh to himself.

Another flight down, Grady could see a group of men and women around a silver BMW through a plate glass window. He followed the wall to a door, wondering if the passcard that allowed him entrance to the detective floor would give him access here as well. He swiped his card, and the red light turned green. A buzz told him he could enter. All heads turned in curiosity, and one man started his direction. The man was short with thinning brown hair and wore thin-framed glasses.

"Dr. Glavine?" Grady asked.

"Yes, sir. You must be Detective Gradiosa," Glavine said, extending his hand.

"Please, call me Grady," Grady accepted a firmer shake than he expected.

"Of course, Grady." The doctor turned to look at the vehicle behind him. "She isn't giving up much."

"Yeah, we didn't expect much from it in the—" Grady started.

"Detective Grady, sorry, please let me finish," Glavine's demeanor changed. He began to glow.

"At first, we dusted her head to toe and nothing but the officer's prints. Then, Brody had an idea from a previous case she worked on with the FBI; to check the underside of the door handles. Again, at first, we didn't find anything. Driver side, nothing. Passenger side, not even a partial. Nothing on either rear door. But when we dusted the trunk handle. Bingo! We came up with two nearly clean prints. And index and middle finger. The only prints on the entire vehicle."

"When did you find the prints?" Grady asked.

"About an hour and a half hours ago. As soon as we grabbed them, we began the IAEFS search. If your perpetrator is in there, we hope to get results soon." Glavine, still beaming, headed over to his computer set up and began to type.

"Great work, Doctor," Grady assured.

"Thank me when we get a result," Dr. Glavine's smile grew, and he pushed up his glasses to read the screen. "Here we are. Your prints belong to a man named Stuart Tyler Nelson."

Grady couldn't speak. He almost didn't hear his phone ringing. Doctor Glavine nudged him, bringing him back to reality. "Detective, your phone."

Grady took his phone out of his pocket. It was Masters. "Hey boss, have I got some news for you."

Masters cut him off, "Yeah? Well, it'll have to wait. They've found another body."

Chapter Ten

Saturday, February 22, 20:45

Female, 23 years of age, approximately five feet four, 120 pounds. Name: Andrea Lee Woodson. Parallel incisions to both left and right upper thigh regions through the Sartorius muscle severing the superficial femoral arteries. Incisions also to bicep regions of both arms through the brachial muscle severing the brachial arteries. These injuries caused traumatic bleeding. Exsanguination occurred, in my opinion, within three to four minutes. With a lack of hematoma, in my opinion, the victim was unconscious when incisions were inflicted."

Dr. Henrietta Beltran clicked her recorder off and wrote a few final notes on Ms. Woodson's chart. This was the second case file she had handled in the last 48 hours that matched near identical. She had heard through internal channels that the cop gunshot victim had certain ties to what was going on. Indirectly, but he may have known what's going on. The man he had inflicted similar wounds upon survived. The other side said he was a copycat, and the victim only survived because of the perp's substandard performance.

Dr. Beltran was impressed with the professionalism of the incisions. They were precise and showed all the marks of some-one with medical training. She hated to admit her admiration of a murderer, but she couldn't help herself. Most of the cases that hit her slab were sloppy messes. Arms and legs severed from torsos, decapitations, crushed limbs; there wasn't much she had not seen in her 20-year tenure. To see a clean body lying on her table, looking as if she was sleeping, was a change of pace.

She walked the length of the tray, giving Ms. Woodson a final look over. "You died too young, dearie."

Dr. Beltran covered Andrea Woodson, slid the tray back into the bay, and closed the compartment door. Her staff would make final preparations for the autopsy, to be completed in the next few hours. With as much blood reported at the scene, the cause of death would be most likely as supposed, but her job was to make it official, and that she would do. It's what the state of Georgia paid her to do. But she was tired and needed rest. She had completed William Dale's autopsy just six hours ago and had yet to sleep. If this case was anything like Dale's, and she had no doubt it was, she would be assigning *Exsanguination* as the cause of death. And a two or three-hour nap would not change that outcome.

Grady pushed another push pin into the map, this time one of the eastern islands. Willerten, to be exact. Another place he was unfamiliar with. Another place nearby, but just on the outer rim of their district, drawing another stern warning not to step on toes from Atwood. The case being the part of a potential string, the Addison District was more than happy to allow Masters to take the lead and share resources, but badge courtesy only goes so far, and Grady knew that all too well.

He was looking across the map, searching for a pattern. If there was one, he couldn't see it. Not that two deaths would show anything. There needed to be at least three to reveal any type of locational pattern. With Nelson not being a murder victim himself, you couldn't count his scene technically. But with the new revelation of his prints being on Dale's vehicle, who knew what involvement Nelson had on this case now.

"Have we been able to find Stuart Nelson yet?" Grady could hear Masters asking Carmen in the other room.

"Nothing. Since his release from the hospital, Nelson hasn't shown up for classes, and he hasn't logged into his Uber app in just as long. Mesa and Nettles went to his residence, and he wasn't there. They're sitting on his place and will radio in when he arrives," Carmen said, then went back to clicking away on her keyboard.

"Where's Grady?" Masters asked.

"In your office, going over the crime scene photos again."

"What do you expect to find, detective?" Masters asked, walking into his office.

"Crumbs. Something that will lead us to something, that will lead us to our suspect."

"You don't think two clean prints on the trunk of a dead man's Mercedes is a big enough crumb?"

"There's that," Grady said, picking up the evidence file. Inside were vehicle photos in the brush, the rear before and after dusting, and close-up pics of the prints. Next was a photo of Officer Joshua Brooks, first on the scene. He left several prints peering in the driver's side window before coming to his senses and donning a pair of gloves so he wouldn't further compromise the scene. The next page bore a familiar face of Stuart Allen Nelson. Why his prints were on this vehicle, they didn't know.

"Did we look at Dale's appointment book again? Did we miss something? Was Nelson a client?" Grady asked the air around him.

"That's your job. My job is to scare the bum into confession when we catch him," Masters sat at his desk and picked up their recent case file with the crime scene photos. "She was young."

"Twenty-three," Grady confirmed.

"Someone's daughter. Could've been someone's lover," Masters pondered. "She had her whole life ahead of her. And this bum stole it from her. We need to find him."

"Hopefully, we'll hear from Mesa and Nettles soon. I'm talking to Clarke and Ryan on Monday to get more info about their encounter with Tanner. Maybe they'll remember something that can help. Then I meet with McClary to ask him about Dale. He may know if Nelson was a client or if he bumped into him. It's a long shot, but one worth taking."

"You know, regarding Nelson, there's another possibility," Masters said, looking up from the file. "What if Dale was a fare. That could be the connection. I know it still wouldn't explain how his prints got on Dale's vehicle, but it could explain how they knew each other. Have Carmen see if she can access his Uber account and check his customer charges. See if Dale's name comes up."

"Will do," Grady said. "I'm also thinking of having Glavine take a look at the original three crime scene files. I think a fresh pair of eyes on them may reveal something we've overlooked or missed. I hear he's one of the best down here. Just need your approval."

"Whatever you need to do. We're two bodies down and only one confusing crumb to run with. We could use his help on this," Masters said.

Grady relayed the Uber request to Carmen and picked up the three cold case files on his desk. He made the two-floor trek past a still unrelenting Atwood, handing another pair of undisciplined patrolmen their Traffic Duty assignments. A front just blew through, and it was supposed to be in the lower 50s. Not the best day to be outdoors directing traffic through construction zones or around detours. In a couple of hours, they would understand why you didn't want to pull such an assignment and would think twice before they dared toss a wrapper or leave behind a cup.

Dr. Glavine was sitting at his desk. The sound of keystrokes was the only sound in the empty room. The vehicle that once sat behind him was gone, off to the impound yard awaiting a claiming by the next of kin. "You don't like music, Doctor?" Grady asked.

"Not when I'm in thought, Detective, I lose my rhythm," Dr. Glavine said, laughing at his joke. "What can I do for you? Did those prints help with the investigation?"

"Yes and no," Grady admitted.

"Hmm. Not sure what to make of that," Dr. Glavine's eyes narrowed, and his nose crinkled.

"The prints belonged to a previous victim. It's inconsistent that his prints would be on Dale's Mercedes. We're not sure what to make of it yet."

"I see," Glavine said, now stroking his chin. "I notice you have a stack of cases with you. Are these the other cases you're researching?"

"Yes, Doctor. This is where I need your help. We've gone over these for weeks. They're all cold cases that happened over the last month or so, three total. We, rather I, feel they're connected to the string of murders that are happening now. I've been told you're the best when it comes to Forensic Science, and I'd like you to take a look at these cases and compare them to the cases we have open now."

"Three cases? I thought you had two deaths?"

"Yes, Nelson survived. The prints you found were from the surviving victim. But his injuries were comparable to the other victims. Tanner either screwed up or had some ulterior motive for allowing Nelson to live, again, in my opinion. That's another thing we need your help to figure out."

"I would be honored to help you, Detective. I do love a good cold case." Dr. Glavine accepted the stack of files as if he won the lottery. Grady followed him to a long table where he laid them side by side by order of the date on the file jacket.

"Let's see what we have here," the Doctor continued. He opened up each one to show the first crime scene photo for each victim. All six bodies, and Nelson's empty table, were on full display. "Were photos of Mr. Nelson's body taken at any point?"

"I don't believe so. If there were, I haven't seen them," Grady explained. "It's my understanding their main concern was saving his life, not the chance that this was part of a serial string."

"Too bad," Dr. Glavine said, pursing his lips. "Would've been good for comparison to match either set of photos."

As the doctor paced the floor, pausing at each file, he gave one a thorough look then moved to the next. Occasionally, he would pick one up, then put it down, releasing a curious, "Hmmm," or an "Ahhh." Nothing revealing an epiphany, just sounds of deep thought. After few passes, he moved onto the notes underneath. Beginning at the oldest file, he lowered his thin-framed glasses and read quickly, moving file to file until he was satisfied.

"First impression?"

"The first one was a bit sloppy. It's hard to notice, but you can tell it was the first attempt. The suspect improved their skill over time. By the third, it was perfected. By the sixth, a work of beauty." Dr. Glavine said.

"What we've surmised," Grady said.

"There is just one problem," Dr. Glavine explained.

"What's that?"

Dr. Glavine pointed to the first four folders one by one. "A right-handed perpetrator committed these first three. Based on the direction of blood pooling, I can surmise within reason that a right-handed person could have exacted Mr. Nelson's injuries."

"Why is that a problem?"

"These other two, your new cases, I can say almost certainty, were committed by a left-handed individual," Dr. Glavine said, pointing to the photo of the victim after the medical examiner cleaned the wounds."

"You can tell that by just a photo?"

"You can also tell by the pressure mark on the thigh where the suspect's wrist laid when they made the incision. To be meticulous and keep their hand steady enough to hit the femoral artery without disturbing anything else, they put just enough pressure to leave a mark."

"Impressive. I don't see how we missed that."

"New perspective brings fresh insight."

"Indeed."

"So, we *are* dealing with a copycat. Someone became enamored with the work of the first three cases that they picked up where the first left off. Which means that they're not connected."

"On the contrary. They are very much connected. The *copycat*, so you say, had to have the same set of skills as the first, wouldn't you concur?"

Grady had to admit the doctor made sense. A person couldn't just pick a blade up and start cutting up a person just because they enjoyed the sight of blood and appreciated the handiwork of another criminal. They had to have the same expertise to inflict the same set of injuries. "Do you think this skill was learned? Someone medically-trained?"

"Perhaps. But with the unfortunate advancement of the internet, anyone can learn to make these types of incisions. And as I have stated, the first victim showed hesitation on the part of the perp. That reveals a lack of practice. A formally educated individual would have cadaver practice and wouldn't have had those hesitation earmarks. But that does not mean they do not have some medical training. You did say that Tanner discussed the time Nelson had left. That would require experience and not book knowledge of how long it takes for exsanguination to occur."

"Yes, he did. And Tanner was right-handed." Grady said.

"Yes, his file said so."

"We haven't been able to tie him to the first three."

"Without seeing the lacerations to Nelson, I cannot make speculations either way. Right hand or left hand, there is another remarkable thing about your victim's injuries."

"What's that?" Grady asked.

"They appear to be made with the same *type* of weapon. Again, I cannot say for certain that they are made with the *same* weapon, but the wounds are identical in every way. It would be simple to surmise that they are exacted by the same weapon. If it weren't for the change of hand, I would conclude this is the work of one individual with the same weapon."

"Is that right?" Grady felt his ears warming.

The doctor continued, "Yes. If not the same weapon, definitely the same *type* of weapon. Most likely a surgical scalpel of some sort or perhaps a hobby knife. Thin blade, about inch, inch and a half in length."

It shocked Grady that the same weapon could have been used in all six crimes. It didn't seem possible unless another person was in that room. The suspect simply left before the big showdown. But witness accounts didn't mention another suspect, and there wasn't enough time for anyone to leave the premises between Tanner's chanting and Clarke and Ryan entering the room. *Where was that weapon?*

"Is that all?" Grady eventually asked, snapping out of his internal debate.

"On the weapon? Yes, without delving into further speculation. Photographically, the scenes appear the same, except for the chair, however. Why is the chair here?" Dr. Glavine asked, pointing to the photograph of the Tanner scene.

"Tanner sat in the chair waiting for the officers to arrive." Grady explained Tanner's final moments, his chanting, the two officers ending his life, and the missing weapon he just said was possibly the same in the new homicides.

"Interesting," Dr. Glavine began to squint again, staring at Tanner's crime scene photos and reading over the transcript. "I may have more for you on this later, Detective. I need to conduct further research. I cannot speculate on things without having all the facts, and conjecture would only hinder your investigation. Can I hold on to these two photos for now? And make copies of this transcript?"

"Certainly, Doctor. Whatever you need to help you catch our killer," Grady said.

The doctor ran the sheets through a scanner behind him and reinserted them into the folder but kept the two photos he was interested in. He handed the folder to Grady, the two men said their farewells, and Grady made his trek back up the two floors to his office desk.

Atwood was not at her post, likely gone for the evening; it was after 23:00. He should have been gone himself, home in bed with his wife, who would be asleep by now. Elizabeth was used to his late hours. She understood the law enforcement lifestyle, especially during a case like this. Late hours were a given. Missed dinners were the norm. Unfortunately, criminals were not considerate of family time.

To their benefit, Lizzy accepted that he was doing good in the world and never complained, or worse, grew suspicious that he was ever not where he said he was going to be. Not that she ever had to worry. He loved her and never laid eyes on another woman. He had his chances—and not just with a swinging cougar-wannabe landlady—real chances, but his commitment to his wife and God helped him overcome such temptation. It was at that moment, he realized, he missed his wife and needed to see her. The case was stalled anyhow. He entered an empty squad room, even Masters wasn't in his office. Grady placed the case files on his desk and went home to a warm bed and an even warmer wife.

Chapter Eleven

Monday, February 24, 10:30

Eleventh and Pine was not as hard to find as Grady thought it would be, nor was Gino's diner. Affixed to the front eave was a tall, faded caricature of a grinning Italian holding a skillet in one hand with eggs and bacon and a deep fryer basket in the other overflowing with fries, onion rings, and what looked like cheese sticks. A patrol car sat in front of the establishment. It looked at home, as if it had spent much time in that spot. Grady smiled as he stepped up to the door. A bell sounded as he entered, and the smell of fried foods hit him immediately.

"Over here, Detective," a voice drew his attention. Two officers sat in a rear booth next to a window. One was waving him over.

To Grady's advantage, officers wore nameplates because he couldn't remember who Clarke was and who was Ryan. He walked up to the table, shook hands, and exchanged pleasantries. The waitress stopped by, refilled cups, and gave Grady his.

"Okay, gentlemen, I won't take up too much of your time. I understand that you have a beat to get back to. I appreciate you taking the time to meet with me. I'd like to revisit the Tanner case, if you will."

The officers exchanged glances. Ryan's shoulders sank as his head lowered while his hands started to rotate the cup of coffee on the table. Clarke's attention went to his partner; he placed his hand on his shoulder, then looked back to Grady. "Must we?"

Grady knew the look. Ryan was suffering post-traumatic

emotions from what happened. "I just have a couple of questions, Officer. I promise to stop if you feel uncomfortable."

Clarke looked back at Ryan, who nodded. Clarke responded, "You can ask me, and I'll answer your questions. If Ryan feels he can add any pertinent information, he will speak to you. I just ask that you don't ask him anything directly. He's receiving counseling and dealing with what occurred that night, but let that progress remain between him and the therapist, please."

"I can assure you, and I speak from experience, that his health is my concern as well. I wouldn't want to impede upon that. I promise it's just a couple of clarification questions on our notes," Grady explained.

Clarke nodded. Ryan nodded. Grady nodded.

"In your statement, you said Tanner repeatedly checked his watch."

"Yes, it was like he was waiting for something."

"Or for a specific amount of time to pass?" Grady offered.

Clarke thought about it. "Could be. He did say something like, *'there isn't much time.'*"

"Our forensic doctor stated that our recent victim bled out in a matter of minutes. Nelson was in his state for much longer than that. The reason was that veins were cut instead of arteries. This allowed a slower bleed. Tanner could have known how long to let Nelson bleed. Do you think he was timing that when he was checking his watch? Did it appear to be a count down?"

Clarke again was lost in thought back to the incident. Ryan seemed to be thinking as well, but not as deep as Clarke. "I'm not sure. Could be. In retrospect, he was definitely winding down to that final moment, so yes, it very well could have been a count down to how much time Nelson had left. But the way it all ended, I can't be completely sure."

"The way it ended?"

"His final exit," Clarke said, raising his eyebrows and eyes widening a bit. Grady understood the minute he said it. He was trying to be sensitive to his partner. Grady looked over to Ryan. His eyes were swollen and water-filled.

"He grinned," Ryan said in an indiscernible whisper.

"What was that officer?" Grady asked.

"Tanner. He grinned," Ryan said, wiping his eyes.

Grady hated to push, but this is what he came to ask; the main question he wanted to have answered.

"Did he do anything before he grinned?"

"Tanner was chanting that terrible banter. It grew louder and louder. He raised his hands above his head and held them there. Then he checked his watch again. Then he looked down at us and grinned, shouted, and then went to jab whatever he was supposed to have in his hands into the victim. That's when we shot him… We shot him… We killed him… We killed an unarmed man…." Ryan lost himself to his sobs. Clarke took his partner into his shoulder and let him cry for a good moment.

"I'm… I'm sorry." It was all Ryan could say. He let his partner go and put his arms on the table, head between them, taking deep breaths.

"I didn't mean to—" Grady started.

"Not your fault, Detective," Clarke said, hand on his partner's shoulder.

"If it's any consolation, we're close to making him for three homicides. He most likely wasn't an innocent man. Unarmed at that moment, yes, but far from innocent. There was a reason he was unarmed at that moment. There was a reason he chose to check out the way he did. It isn't your fault, Officer. You did your duty. If you didn't, then Nelson would have died. You saved a life that night. Please see the honor in that," Grady explained.

Ryan regained his composure and took a few deep breaths. After a moment, he looked back up. "I understand about Nelson. And I was unaware of the other homicides. That helps. Thank you for letting me know. Please keep me in the loop of your progress."

"I'm sorry. But, I have to ask again about Tanner checking his watch just before the grin. It may be important. How are you so sure? It's not in your original statement," Grady asked.

"I am sure because I see it in my dreams every night. I'm sure because it's where my focus was that night. I *had* my service weapon trained center mass, but my eyes were on his face. I saw his eyes glance at his watch, then that mustache curled up in that evil way before he bared his teeth and yelled. The second I saw his hands move, I pulled the trigger twice, as I was trained to."

"You didn't see the grin or watch check, Clarke?"

"No, sir. My eyes were on his hands. I was trying to determine what he had in his hands. It was dark in that room. His hands were in a shadow, and I couldn't make anything out for certain. I must've missed the watch check. His wrist could have turned, but I was looking at fingers, not wrists. But like Ryan, the second he screamed and began his assault, I discharged my weapon."

"Thank you, gentlemen. I appreciate you meeting with me. I'm sorry if I have dug up unpleasant memories and deepened wounds. It wasn't my intention." Grady did feel bad, but it was something that needed to be done. He felt closer to an answer.

"No, thank you, Detective. If you hadn't stopped by, I wouldn't know about Tanner's past. Knowing that we took out a fugitive may help me sleep better. Again, keep me in the loop. The moment you know he's tied to these other crimes, I want to be informed," Ryan said with a light in his eyes that wasn't there when Grady entered the restaurant.

"Yes, of course. And you're welcome. Thank you for your continued service. The force needs more officers like you. A blow like that would knock down a lesser man. I'm honored to serve alongside such a serviceman."

Ryan smiled, and they shook hands. Nothing more needed to be said. Ryan joined his partner, who was already at the counter paying. Grady sat sipping his coffee that had been topped off. He called the waitress and asked if it was late enough for lunch. Given the green light, he ordered the fried special of the day; a two-piece dark with onion rings and coleslaw with a side of cobbler. Once full, he headed back to the station to update the file and see if Carmen had any additional information.

Carmen was in her usual Monday afternoon multi-tasking mode: four screens displaying info, two printers spitting out documents, and talking on one phone while the other was ringing. Grady buzzed in and walked to her desk.

"You busy?"

Carmen rolled her eyes and kicked at him.

Grady quickly dodged and laughed out loud.

Carmen nodded her head toward Masters' office, and Grady obliged. Carmen held up one finger for him to wait. "Thank you, Doctor. I'll be looking for those records by the end of the day… you too."

Carmen hung up the phone and turned her attention to Grady. "Okay. That was Dr. Beltran. She completed the Woodson autopsy. Nothing new. Just as we figured, she died of injuries sustained by the incisions. Same as Dale. She'll have the finalized paperwork for us by the end of the day. She also performed the Dale autopsy and said there are no forensic differences that would give us any clues to a suspect."

"Yeah, we figured as much. Did you see my evidence information from Dr. Glavine?"

"About the hand impressions? I glanced over it but wanted you to explain it because you talked to Glavine directly."

"Great. Well, let's go in with Masters, and we can go over it together. I can also fill you in on what I discovered with Clarke and Ryan."

Grady grabbed the file and his notes and followed Carmen into Masters' office. For the next hour, he explained the differences in the cases and what Dr. Glavine had shown him about a right and left-handed perpetrator. He showed them the impression marks that Glavine had shown him which they had missed. Carman and Masters both shook their heads in disbelief. They couldn't unsee them once they saw them; they were apparent.

"'New perspective brings fresh insight,' so says Dr. Glavine. That and he has years of experience looking for these things," Grady said.

"We also talked about these two not being medical students but still having some medical training. At least Tanner may have. Carmen, can you look into Tanner's past? Maybe he served in the military or was an EMS at one point. Anything that would give him access to knowing the timing of a person bleeding out. Clarke confirmed he was habitual about checking his watch. I probed about it being a timing issue. He couldn't agree with it, but it would make sense with Tanner's 'you don't have much time' remark and his demand to call EMS. It seems that he wanted Nelson to live."

"Yeah, I can check for a military record. I only searched criminal history. Never went as far as searching this side of the law," Carmen said.

"And with the change of hands, we know that our present perp didn't commit the first three. Nelson is the transition. And without photos of his incisions, we can't be sure whether Tanner's connected to those first cases. Dr. Glavine wouldn't say for sure, but he said that a right-handed assailant most likely committed Nelson's wounds based on how the blood pooled."

Masters chuckled. "So, in a way, we're still at square one. We know Tanner is the perp for Nelson. We know he's dead and not our suspect for our new victims, and we cannot connect him to the previous four cases."

"Essentially. But we know more about the *how*. I know it makes the *why* more confusing, but we'll figure it out. That's what we do. There is one more thing. Dr. Glavine stated that it appears that all six victims were injured by the same type of weapon, if not the same weapon." Grady looked for reactions.

Carmen nodded. Masters' eyes dimmed and he stroked his chin.

"That would mean there would've been a second suspect in the room with Tanner at some point," Carmen said.

"No witness statements corroborate that statement," Masters defended.

"Right. Lawson was the first officer on the scene, and he canvassed the complex thoroughly because of the reports of the pickup in the alleyway. That vehicle turned out to be a roughneck getting home from work. No ties to Nelson; they had never met. He lived two floors up and was watching the Hawks game. He didn't hear anything until the gunshots. The other neighbors on Nelson's floor didn't report anyone else suspicious, and rumor has it they're a curious bunch. The only person seen entering Nelson's apartment that evening was Tanner," Grady explained.

"Devil's advocate," Carmen began. "If it is the same weapon, that explains why it's missing. That means it's still in the hands of the perp."

"But who other than Tanner had access to that weapon?" Grady asked.

"Nelson," Carmen said matter-of-factly. She looked at both Grady and Masters each in turn. "When you have eliminated the impossible, whatever remains, however improbable, must be the truth."

"I know Sherlock Holmes as well, but how could Nelson inflict his own injuries?" Masters said.

"Oh, I'm not saying he did. We are still speculating that there are other perps," Carmen said. "Tanner is the first, and Nelson is the second. Nelson's prints are on Dale's vehicle, which puts him circumstantially in contact with Dale. My theory is Tanner was working with Nelson, and either they had an agreement or some sort of falling out."

"Agreement? Why would Tanner agree to die?" Masters asked.

"Hey, devil's advocate, remember? However improbable, must be the truth," Carmen repeated.

"Let see if I follow," Grady began. "Tanner and Nelson are somehow connected. Tanner committed the first three murders.

Then at some point, Tanner agrees to commit suicide by cop, inflict a non-lethal injury upon Nelson, which allows Nelson to continue to find victims using the same weapon that Tanner used on the first three victims and himself."

"You got it," Carmen said.

"That's a pretty interesting theory, Carmen." Masters said.

"It's far-fetched, but the only one that makes a lick of sense. It's the only one that explains what happened to the weapon used on Nelson. We can't find it because Nelson had or has it. He and Tanner hid it in a place where only Nelson knew where to find it. When all was clear, Nelson came back and retrieved it."

"Makes sense," Grady said. "However improbable, must be the truth."

"But what's the motive?" Masters asked.

"Does there need to be one? They had a mental illness. The proof is with the chanting gibberish. Who does that if they're right in the head?" Carmen explained.

"We need to find Nelson. Have the twins come up with anything yet?" Grady asked.

"Nothing. Mesa and Nettles sat on his place Saturday night and all day on Sunday. He still hasn't returned to the apartment. His landlady said she hadn't seen him in a few days, but that he's paid up through the end of February. Right now, LaCrosse is sitting on the apartment while they both take the evening off. They will be back first thing in the morning. We could always put a couple of patrol officers on the place if we need to, but if he's our guy, we may want one of us on this case."

"Yes, keep us on it," Masters agreed. "Excellent work, Detective. I know it's speculation, but it makes sense. We'll know more when we find Nelson."

"I do have another concern. Now that we're out of Dale's office, perhaps Nelson is holed up there. If the owner is still out of town, that would be an ideal place to hide out. Someplace the police aren't looking. Just a thought," Grady suggested.

"We have no one to put on it unless we pull a couple of officers," Masters said.

"We can ask Atwood to lend us Clarke and Ryan. They are familiar with the case, and it's just a stakeout. Low probability of Nelson showing up. Just not leaving a stone unturned. Our motto, right?"

"See. He has been paying attention, Masters," Carmen said.

"Make the call," Masters said.

Chapter Twelve

Wednesday, February 26, 10:45

Joshua McClary was good on his word and didn't put up any arguments answering questions. He knew William Dale. He had been his attorney for the past six months and working to keep him out of prison. The younger McClary was open and honest about his past and didn't attempt to hide anything.

"Yes, I've committed past identity theft crimes," he told Grady, eyes meeting his, no sign of deception, "but I'm clean now. It's part of the deal I made with Mr. Dale for him to represent me."

"So, you did mess up. He busted you on it, and then you killed him?" Grady knew the answer but wanted to see his reaction.

"Hell no. I needed him. I've done my time. I don't want to go back there." McClary's eyes widened, his head wagging back and forth. Grady knew that look, the fear of a white-collar man in a blue-collar prison world.

"Do you know of anyone who may have wanted to hurt Mr. Dale?" Grady asked.

"I didn't know any of his clients. We met at the old lady's house. It was his office. She was a relative, I think. Sick too."

"How do you know that?"

"She used cannabis—some sort of cancer. Nothing terminal, but she does have her certificate. Dale told me about it when I asked him about the smell. You can't miss it when you walk in there. She doesn't smoke it. I think she uses oil or something."

"Anyone else? What about Stuart Nelson?"

"Nelson? Nope. Don't think I've heard that name. But I hear so many names with my job. They all sound the same after a while."

"What about Stephen Tanner?"

"Doesn't ring a bell," McClary said, shaking his head. "I've only seen a couple of faces. Never really met anyone to put a name to. You know, attorney-client confidentiality."

Grady pulled out a mug shot of Tanner from his file. McClary looked it over and handed it back. "Haven't seen the guy. Even in the deli. And I see a lot of people. Plus, I would think I'd remember a mustache like that."

"What about this guy," Grady said, setting down Nelson's driver's license photo from his file.

"Okay. Now, this guy I've seen before. It had to be from the deli. I know it wasn't from Mr. Dale's office."

"Do you have a vehicle, or do you use a ridesharing site?"

"Both. One thing my pop taught me was not to drink and drive. I won't get behind the wheel if I've had too much to drink. I'll use Uber or another app if they're backed up."

"Nelson is an Uber driver."

A light went on behind McClary's eyes. He made the connection. "Yeah, I remember now. I guess being a little lit when I met him got me confused. Nice guy. Why are you asking about him? Is he connected? Did he kill Mr. Dale?"

"I can't answer that right now. We're just asking questions and gathering information," Grady said.

"Well, anything I can do to help your investigation. If I see Nelson again, I'll let you know," McClary offered.

"I would appreciate that. Just don't let Nelson know we're looking for him," Grady warned. "Thank you for your time. I'll let you get back to your customers."

"Thank you," McClary shook Grady's hand and headed back to the kitchen.

Grady left the Atlantic shores of the Irish headlands and headed back to the precinct.

LaCrosse was at his desk with his nose in a notebook. Smoke could almost be seen rising from the paper he was writing on.

"Got something good, LaCrosse?" Grady asked.

"I just got off the phone with your Dr. Glavine. He said there might be something to the gibberish that Tanner was spouting. If Clarke or Ryan could remember any of the words he was chanting, the doctor would like to know what they were."

"Well, isn't that the point of the word, *gibberish*? From what they said, it was unintelligible," Grady said. "Honestly, I just don't want to go back and put them through more questioning. Especially Ryan. He is suffering PTSD. I can try to talk to Clarke, but not Ryan."

"He sounded serious—said he's still researching," LaCrosse said.

"Yes, he seemed interested in the photos of the crime scene and Clarke and Ryan's statement. He held on to them. Wonder what Tanner's chanting has to do with it all? It seemed more of a mental state to me, even if Clarke did say he was calm and collected." Grady continued, "So, did you learn anything yesterday on your stakeout?"

"Just that the landlord is a feisty one," LaCrosse said, gritting his teeth.

Grady laughed, remembering Ms. Keppler and her moves on Masters. "She got ahold of you too, then?"

"Too? You?" LaCrosse raised his eyebrows.

"Heck no. Masters."

"Oh, I would've paid to see that," LaCrosse admitted. "How did he react?"

Grady cocked his head. "I'm not sure how to answer that. It was my first time meeting him. I would say that he handled it well. Professional, even."

LaCrosse's shoulders danced with laughter. "That must've been a sight." LaCrosse took a breath and exhaled. "But other than that, it was quiet, meaning no Nelson. The complex was busy, people coming and going all night. I figure he must have moved or is staying somewhere else. He didn't enter through the front, and no lights came on in the apartment. Clarke and Ryan relieved me at 0600, and I went home for some sleep."

"I'm going to call Clarke. It's just a quick question. No need to set up a meeting and pull him off his beat again." Grady said. He tossed his notebook on his desk and grabbed a cup of coffee. Carmen had brought in a box of pastries, *'no doughnuts, we're too sophisticated for doughnuts on the second floor,'* she would say. He picked through what was left, found one that wasn't lemon, and eventually made it back to his desk.

Grady opened his notebook and thumbed back through his notes on his previous meeting with Clarke. Once he was satisfied with what he would ask, and the crumbs were gone from his chin, he picked up the phone. He dialed down to the front desk, and the expected voice answered.

"What can I do for you, Grady?"

"How did you know it was me, Atwood?"

"I know all the internal extensions, Detective," Atwood said in a perfect irritated monotone.

"You have them all memorized?"

"Yes, I have a photographic memory. Now, can we be done with 20 questions and get to what you need? I have a palace to run."

"Sorry. Officer Jason Clarke. I need to reach him. Do you have a number for him? You'd be doing me a gigantic favor."

"What am I, the white pages? Call dispatch," Atwood said and hung up.

Another lesson learned, Grady mused. He succeeded in getting Clarke's number from dispatch. They enjoyed a laugh at his expense when he told them about his blunder, but he supposed he had earned it. New precinct, new rules. Another thing he needed to get used to. The phone buzzed three times before a reluctant voice answered, "Clarke."

"Detective Grady, here. Are you available for a question or two?"

"Make it quick. Ryan is picking up lunch. We're at Southside

End, staking out William Dale's office. I tell ya, sir, he isn't coming back. I request permission to end this assignment," Clarke said, the ache of two days in a sweaty patrol car in his voice.

"I'll see what I can do. As for my questions. You said Tanner was chanting throughout the night up until his suicide. Any chance you remember any words he may have said?"

"No, Detective. It was gibberish, like we said. Even when we were in the room and could hear him clearly, it just didn't make sense. It wasn't English, Spanish, or any other language I'm familiar with. I read a bit of Latin in college, and we've been trained in Arabic and Farsi. It wasn't any of those. I'm sorry, gibberish is the only word I can think of to describe it."

"Do you think Ryan may have heard anything different," Grady asked, biting his lip.

Grady heard a deep exhale and a long pause. "I don't want to ask him, Detective."

"Neither do I. But forensics believes it may be crucial in learning why Tanner did what he did," Grady explained.

"I can't make any promises. Ryan's on edge about that night. He can still serve, and it doesn't affect his abilities in the field. I don't want to give the wrong impression, but I don't want to toe that line too often. However, I will see what I can find out and contact you if he remembers anything."

"Thank you, Officer. Again," Grady said, and the line went dead.

Grady looked up and saw LaCrosse staring at him. "What?"

"Ever been through it?"

"Shooting an unarmed man?" Grady responded.

"Yeah," LaCrosse said, sounding like he had made a point,

"Yes," Grady admitted. "You?"

"It isn't something you forget or get over easily," LaCrosse said, more as a reminder.

"That's one reason why we can handle this better than anyone else," Grady agreed. "We know what it would take for us to set aside our internal pains and get to the answers that will get the case solved."

LaCrosse nodded. "But also remember that all of this is still fresh to him. It just happened in his mind. Ask your questions, yes. But tread lightly. You would've wanted the same treatment after your first incident."

"Understood," Grady said as he picked up the phone and dialed the front desk.

"What is it this time, Grady? Forget where you put your crime scene tape?" Atwood said.

"No, ma'am. It's right next to your trophy for Attitude of the Year," Grady said, grinning ear to ear, throwing caution to the wind.

Silence greeted him, followed by a long, "Ahhhhhhh, Newbie grew a pair since our last talk. I like it. How can I displease you, Detective?"

"Clarke and Ryan. Go ahead and pull them off of Dale's office. It's a dead end. Have them do a drive by at the beginning and end of shift just to be on the safe side, but you can release them to normal patrol."

"How generous. I get to have *my* people back," Atwood said. "They better be undamaged."

"No worse for wear. They're all yours. Thanks again for the lend."

"Not a problem, Detective. I hope you catch the bastard."

"We're on our way," Grady said with full confidence they would do so.

"'Glatchka mondavka insinivicus,' are you sure that's what he said?" Grady confirmed, reading the slip of paper he was handed.

"Ryan said he took a course in phonetics in college, and because he was watching his face, it's as close of an interpretation as he could get. Sounds like a drink you'd order in a Russian pub if you ask me," Clarke said.

"Is Ryan okay? Did you have to press him much?" Grady asked.

"Not at all. I mentioned Tanner in passing, and he dropped the phrase. I didn't even mention you or the investigation. I did ask if I could pass it on to you, he consented without hesitation. Said, *anything to help*. I think he's doing much better after finding out Tanner was more of a criminal than he thought he was."

"That's good to hear, Officer. Thanks for the update. I appreciate it."

"Not a problem," Clarke said and left.

Grady looked at the unintelligible phrase again. *Glatchka mondavka insinivicus.* Somewhere in some dictionary, it had a definition. One that Dr. Glavine would sure to have. Grady took a photo of the paper and texted it to Glavine. Then he dialed his number.

The phone rang a few times, and an excited voice answered the line. "Detective, I just received your text. This will help tremendously. Where did you find this?"

"One of the officers who was present remembered the phrase," Grady said. "Hope I have the spelling accurate."

"I am sure it's close enough. I will get right on this and will give you an update as soon as I have something," Glavine said and hung up.

Grady felt encouraged. The tone in Glavine's voice was enough to have him believe they were at the door of a major breakthrough.

Chapter Thirteen

Friday, February 28, 00:35

This can't be happening again. Another one?" Masters asked. "We need to catch this bastard."

"Is it Nelson?" LaCrosse asked, swiping his card at the gate, entering the pen.

"We're not sure yet, but the M.O. is identical. The officers on-scene are calling it that. Mesa and Nettles are en route. I'm about to head out if you want to join me," Grady said. "Branson is 30 out."

"Vic info?" LaCrosse asked now at his desk, grabbing his gun and a clip from his top desk drawer.

"Sketchy. Mid-thirties. Female. That's about it, for now," Grady said. "We'll know more when we get there," Grady grabbed a coat and beanie from the top of his desk.

"Right behind you," LaCrosse said, following behind Grady.

They headed down into the quiet lobby, not even Atwood was in this late. A burly lieutenant was stationed, looking half asleep. A couple of officers lingered. The Lieu was giving them their station for the evening, graveyard duty from the sound of it, literally. He had wondered about what that would be like in this town. Every city had its stories about pulling their graveyard tours. Punishment, obviously. Must've been late to roll call one too many times or spoke ill of the Captain's prized pup. But every stationhouse needed someone to cover that neck of the woods. Grady knew the receiving end of that punishment all too well.

"So, what do you think?" LaCrosse asked as they passed the reception desk, snapping Grady out of his trance.

"I'll know more when we get there. I still haven't heard from Glavine about an interpretation of the gibberish Tanner was spouting. I want to know if it's connected somehow. Otherwise, we are just walking into another scene we're all too familiar with."

"Nelson could always make another mistake and leave us a clue this time around. He did leave behind that fingerprint on the BMW," LaCrosse said.

"*If* this is Nelson. I want to be positive it's him too. But you know as well as I do, Masters will have our necks if we start jumping to conclusions before having the facts. Until we find something concrete, we continue to investigate the facts and never assume," Grady said.

LaCrosse smiled. It peered through his mustache. "Yes, sir."

"Did I say something wrong?"

"Not at all. You just sound like the boss. Guess that's a good thing. It means you are thinking straight. Not letting this perp get to you."

"I'll take that as a compliment," Grady said.

They found LaCrosse's run-down Chevy and got in. LaCrosse revved the engine. "Okay, boss, where we headed?"

"Gordsten Park. Small neighborhood to the east. Just a few miles off Central office," Grady grinned as he read from a slip of paper where he had written the address down.

"This guy is getting bold keeping it so close to home." LaCrosse backed up and headed out of the lot.

"Yeah, especially when Nelson was just around the block from Central itself."

"Guess he thinks our focus is on the lawyer and the outer perimeter," LaCrosse said, making a left down a dark road that looked like all the others.

Grady laughed. "He's right. Our eyes and minds are thinking he's trying to get away, so he closes the perimeter and moves in closer." Grady folded his arms and tapped his chin. "He has no intention of trying to leave. He wants to stick around. Almost like he *wants* to be caught."

"Didn't you say that about Tanner? That Clarke said the perp acted like he wanted to be caught?"

"Not so much wanted to, but was comfortable with the thought," Grady said. "Clarke said Tanner's mannerisms gave the conclusion that getting caught was part of his plan. It didn't make sense because it would mean that Tanner's death was part of the plan. Even Carmen was speculating that. But who willingly goes into a job with death being the endgame? That doesn't make sense." Grady flapped his hands in his lap. "This whole thing doesn't make sense."

"In reality, though, when does the mind of a perp make sense? I understand that their ultimate motive is to get away with a crime. But if they're criminally insane, then wouldn't freedom take sanity off the plate?" LaCrosse questioned.

Grady sighed. "I've thought over that with Tanner. From what the officers say, he was too calm to be insane; he was calculating. Can a criminal that far-gone be right-minded and rational enough to perform delicate surgery? I don't know. Maybe the experts have it wrong. Maybe Tanner wasn't insane at all. Maybe there was some purpose behind this that was rational to only himself. I wasn't there. All I have to go on is what our officers saw. The experts only see the chanting and the refusal of verbal commands to stop his actions. That's enough for them to label Tanner insane. All I know is that our officers saw something different."

"I don't know. The drugs in his system didn't help," LaCrosse said. "I saw his tox-screen. It wasn't much, but it was enough to impair judgment."

"He was smoking a Camel," Grady said in defense and pointing to the left where the police lights were lighting up the surrounding homes. "Paperwork versus reality. Whatever he had entered his system before he committed the crime, not during. Perhaps hours before."

LaCrosse raised his arm in defense. "Okay, okay. I'll give you that. I'm just saying he wasn't innocent."

"I'm not saying he was. I am saying that he knew what he was doing and was not under the influence or impaired while he was doing it. My point is that I have a feeling there was a specific purpose to his actions. Something calculated, thus the repeated checking of his watch. That's what the good doctor thinks the chanting is about."

"Interesting theory," LaCrosse said as he put the Chevy in park. Mesa and Nettles were exiting the single-story home. It was indiscernible of color amidst the red and blue flashing lights.

"At least we know what to expect," LaCrosse said, then pointed to the two officers. "Look at Nettles' face."

"She didn't go into the Dale scene," Grady said.

"I know, neither of them did. Nettles may have gotten a peek before they bagged Dale." They both watched Nettles step off the final step and lose whatever snack she came to work with in the hedge next to the walkway. "It's strange, though, right? Little mutilation, but just the overabundance of blood can be overwhelming sometimes."

"I suppose. I don't remember how I handled my first real bloody scene," Grady said, but that wasn't the truth. He remembered. Double homicide by a highly jealous lover; need he say more? He shook the memory from his head, and LaCrosse just smiled. He knew all too well the false statement. Not another word was said.

"Yeah, we all push those memories far back—no need to rehash them. Let's see what our perp left for us this time. If we're lucky, Nelson made a mistake this time," LaCrosse exited the vehicle, and it made the all too familiar Caprice creak and slam. Even the newer models adopted the patented door squeak as they aged. Grady had to chuckle as his door echoed LaCrosse's, and they slowly approached their partners.

"What we got?" LaCrosse asked as if he didn't know.

"Female. Mid-thirties. Wounds to her upper arms and thighs.

Too much blood to positively identify where, but they seemed identical to what we've seen in the photographs. It's—" Mesa choked back for a second. Even he seemed a bit overwhelmed. "It's much different in person than in the photos. There is just so much blood for so little damage to the body. I have seen homicides before, but not like this. It's eerie."

"I've seen it. Twice. I agree. You can hack up a body and not see as much blood," Grady explained. "Dr. Glavine says it was because there is no tissue to soak up the blood, so it spills everywhere else. Of course, he has his technical jargon to explain it, but that's what it sums up to." Grady paused in case he was making Mesa uncomfortable. "You okay?"

"Oh, me? Yeah. I'm good to go. Just Nettles was shaken up. Said she was fine but then tossed her corn nuts the moment we hit fresh air," he explained.

"How many inside?"

"One body. Two officers, two forensics monkeys, one of them may be Glavine. He introduced himself, but I was busy with the body. Short, thin hair and glasses, mild accent."

"Yeah, that's Glavine. Guess he had his ears on. Wonder if he has info on that Tanner phrase?" Grady asked aloud.

"Dunno about that. But he was anxious to get his hands on what is there. I told him he needed clearance because I was unaware of forensics being called yet. He seemed pleased when I mentioned your name."

"You okay, Nettles? You're usually on point," LaCrosse said as Nettles approached their group.

Nettles took a breath and smiled. She met LaCrosse's gaze. "Yes, sir. I'm good to go. Sorry, I was taking in the surroundings and not paying too much attention to the squint. My bad."

"I have water in a cooler in my trunk. Go get a bottle," LaCrosse offered.

"Thank you, sir," Nettles said and headed to LaCrosse's unit.

LaCrosse then focused on Mesa. "Give me a run-down," he asked to get Mesa's mind flowing.

"Clean house. You could smell freshener if it weren't for the acidic scent of blood. Vic is in a side room back and to the left. Media room, relatively expensive equipment, not top of the line, but she didn't go to Wal-Mart for her purchases. Interesting a female having a man cave, though. There are little signs of this being a male domicile and her being a visitor—too many female-themed items. That is until you enter the media room. The room itself is slightly rearranged. The coffee table is moved out a bit to the middle of the room, and recliners are pushed back," Mesa explained. His speech centering him back to the usual detective tone Grady had heard days before.

"Thank you, detective," LaCrosse said. "Go get a water and tend to your partner. If we have further questions, we will follow up. Man the perimeter and keep an eye out for anyone extra interested in case our perp is a watcher. We already know that he prefers to stay local and is unafraid of striking less than three miles from headquarters. He may be bold enough to show his mug."

"What are we looking for?" Mesa asked.

"Our best guess right now?" Grady began. "You remember Nelson's driver's license photo?"

"Yes, sir."

"You see his face, you grab that bum," Grady said, then clarified. "Quietly if you can. Don't need him slipping away."

"10-4," Mesa said. "We'll run the perimeter and give you updates."

Grady and LaCrosse walked up the stairs and into the house, knowing what they were about to see. They had witnessed it before at the Dale crime scene. Both had their badges ready for the green-faced officer at the door. Grady just shook his head. *Too many rookies out here,* he thought. He never could understand how the sight of blood, even an overabundance of it, could turn a stomach. *Am I hardened to it? No, I don't think so; it just never really bothered me.* He had to chuckle. *What does that say about me?*

"This way, detectives," a voice called from down a hallway. Grady guessed their entry had been radioed back to the scene.

"Like the Dale scene. Back of the residence," LaCrosse said.

"We'll see. Dale had an office in the back. That was the reason he was back there. This could be just a coincidence," Grady replied.

The house was not similar by any means. Not older like Mrs. Perkins. It was not even ten years old, by Grady's guess. There were no knick-knacks, no hutches or armoires, and no pot smell. As LaCrosse had mentioned, the only similarity was the murder was toward the rear of the residence. They both followed the activity, and Grady soon heard the excited tenor of a familiar voice followed by the flash of a captured photograph.

"Doctor, don't you have enough photos yet? We need to process this scene and get this body out of here," a voice questioned.

"Just a couple more, Officer. We need to make sure we have every angle. We need to compare it with the other crime scenes. Has Detective Grady arrived yet?"

"I don't know who—" the officer began, but Grady cut him off.

"Right here, Doctor," Grady said, entering the room with his hand extended.

Dr. Glavine received it and shook firmly as his eyes hid behind his smile. He turned and nearly stumbled over the victim's shoes on the floor as he walked toward the body. "You must see this, Detective Grady."

"I've seen it, Doctor. Twice. This is our third victim. It has all been the same so far. Incisions to the femoral and brachial arteries where the victim bleeds out. It looks the same from here. And Doc, this is Detective LaCrosse. Not sure if you've met before since I'm the newbie here."

"No, I have not had the pleasure. Good to meet you, Detective. Now come, let me show you something here. It is one thing to see the scene in a myriad of photos. It is quite another to see live and in person."

Dr. Glavine seemed to dance around the body, making careful calculations with every step. Grady could tell it was not his first crime scene. He was not just a lab monkey, as one of his colleagues had called him. He had seen his share of real-world situations. However, he was confident that Glavine didn't get out to crime scenes very often. He was good enough to be able to see a photo and tell you what happened. *That's the curse of being that good. You lose real-world exposure*, Grady thought. *So, in a sense, Glavine is reliving the old days of being a field agent, and his excitement is showing.*

"Look over here." Grady followed Glavine to the body. "As I expected. Your perpetrator is left-handed. See this blood flow, how it pulls to the right side of the body. That is the direction of the cut. Only a left-handed person would cut in that fashion. Well, a right-handed *could,* but it would be uncomfortable."

"How's that, Doctor?" LaCrosse asked.

"Ever try and cut your steak with your opposing hand, Detective?"

LaCrosse raised his hands and air cut a steak. "Eh, I could do it if I tried."

"Yeah, maybe. But with the precision that our perpetrator has exacted here?"

LaCrosse looked down at the victim.

"Remember the photos too, LaCrosse. Straight line. No mistakes or shakes," Grady added.

LaCrosse shook his head, "I suppose not."

"Your perpetrator is left-handed. This is the same person who exacted the cuts as the photos you showed me. I'd bet my lab on it."

"Not to rain on your victory lap, Doc, but we sort of figured that," LaCrosse said.

"Ahh, but did you figure that I decoded the Tanner phrase?" Dr. Glavine said, his eyes glittering.

"You what?" both Grady and LaCrosse say in almost unison, jaws agape.

"I know what 'Glatchka mondavka insinivicus' means. Moreover, I know *why* Tanner said it."

Chapter Fourteen

Saturday, February 29, 08:30

The alarm was buzzing louder than he wanted it to, and Grady rushed from the bathroom to shut it off.

"Do you have to go in today, James?" Elizabeth asked from her side of the bed, still curled up under the covers. "I want to spend some time with you. The Melbourne property is stalled in paperwork, and I don't need to meet with them until Monday."

"I really wish I could, Lizzy. Masters messaged, and we have a tip we need to check out," he explained.

"Can't someone else go?" Elizabeth asked, knowing that someone else couldn't. She had been a cop's wife long enough to understand she married the lifestyle. She not only married the man, she married the entire city he served.

"He's my partner. And boss. There's someone out there hurting people. It's part of my job to protect them. And who knows, that person whose life we save could be *your* next client. Wouldn't want to keep work from you, heaven forbid."

That comment made her chuckle. "Just be careful out there, Grade. I worry about you."

"I know you do, love. I am and will." Grady sat on the edge of the bed and kissed his wife's cheek. It was warm with sleep. He wished he could get back into bed and share the passion husbands and wives share, but his city called, and she was a jealous lover.

"We just had a big break and are ready to close this case. Once this one is behind us, I will have more time, promise," Grady said, grabbing his jacket, trying to remember the temperature outside. Putting it on, he blew a kiss and headed out.

It was not as cool as Grady thought. He tossed his coat in the back seat and drove the half-hour to the station. Thoughts were swimming through his head of all Dr. Glavine had covered with him and LaCrosse. The interpretation of an unintelligible ramble of a crazy man now was some sort of manifesto with a clear purpose. What that purpose was was yet to be determined.

Glatchka Mondavka Insinivicus ended up meaning, *Transformation Purification Invulnerability*. A forgotten tribal language that Dr. Glavine discovered through his research. The good doctor had a crazy theory of what that meant—theories that, according to most of the team, were pulled from horror movies and works of fiction, not what happens in small cities on the east coast.

Glavine explained an ancient tribe's belief that the spirit didn't go to heaven or hell as the contemporary Western mind understood those concepts. These ancient people believed that after death the inner spirit rambled depending on the good or bad the individual had done while alive. Their spirit guides would determine the soul's destination, hopefully ushering the departed into peace with their ancestors who had passed before. They also believed these spirit guides could be influenced by those on this side of the living. The entire ancient religion existed to usher people into their ultimate resting place.

"This is where things get interesting," Glavine had explained. "There was a forbidden sect of that religion that believed one was not required to enter the land of the dead. They believed a spirit could remain among the living if that spirit had a host to join with. The ancients believed both the person dying and the host had to be alive at the time of the transference. The ceremony had to occur at the precise moment when both souls were leaving the body. The soul of the one performing the ritual could then enter the body of the dying person."

The entire ceremony made Grady sick to his stomach. Forcing one to die so another could live was murder, no other way to explain it.

Grady thought back to each scene. The only one where Dr. Glavine's theory made sense was the Nelson case. It was now clear why Tanner behaved the way he did. Many of his actions could now be explained. The description Clarke and Ryan gave of their encounter made sense. *All but the watch check. That still needs explaining,* Grady thought. He would have to review his notes, maybe something that he missed.

There were the three scenes before Nelson. They needed revisiting, namely the cut location, the chair, and the fact that they all died. *Did the incantation play into those scenes?* he mused. *Three victims before, three after. Is it a pattern? Do the numbers mean something? Will there be more victims? Moreover, is Nelson committing these crimes? Was he part of some ritual performed by Tanner, as Carmen suggested?* Grady's mind was still swimming when he pulled into the lot at the station. He parked next to LaCrosse's coupe and headed upstairs.

Grady paid no attention to Atwood or any other officer on the main floor. He ascended, pulled out his card, and buzzed the gate. Everyone was huddled around Carmen's desk—even Branson. With everyone present, something was up. Carmen's head was first to turn. She waved him over, which drew Branson's attention. Their eyes met, his nose turned with displeasure. *We're on the same side, man.* Grady couldn't help but roll his eyes.

"Get over here, Grady. We have something," Carmen said, continuing to wave. "Security video. It's Nelson outside Janice Blevins' residence. Well, two houses down, but close and clear enough to identify him."

Carmen pulled up the feed and clicked her mouse. It was dark, and a figure walked across a darkened lawn. "Well, you can't—"

"Just watch," Carmen said. "The feed switches through five

angles around the property. This homeowner either has serious property to protect or was paranoid."

Just as she stated, the feed filtered through five angles; front door, side of the property, back door, garage, and an angle that looked like a slab of concrete from a central point about eye level. That angle had an overhead light that spilled over the slab.

"Watch the slab," Carmen instructed, a grin in her voice.

After a couple of cycles, that dark figure from the first pass appeared on the slab of concrete. He walked under the light. Clear as day and unmistakable—it was Stuart Nelson. He was dressed in dark clothing, from black jeans to dark blue sweatshirt and ballcap, but it was him. "This camera is remarkable. How did we get this feed?"

"The homeowner turned it over without hesitation. Mr. Howell said he had a break-in two years ago and lost two computers, a big screen television, and other valuables, and the perp was never apprehended. He said, and I quote, *I'll be damned if I am going to let that crap happen to me again.*" So, after he replaced his belongings with the insurance money, he purchased a top-of-the-line security system. This is the result."

"God bless technology," Mesa said.

"Amen," Nettles replied as she and her partner high-fived.

"Great work, Carmen," Grady said.

"But," Carmen began.

"Yes," Grady interrupted, "I know, all circumstantial. Unless we can pull his fingerprints or something else from Blevins' home, we cannot tie him to her murder."

"What?" Mesa questioned.

"He's an Uber driver," Carmen began. "All he has to say is 'Your Honor, I was in the neighborhood to pick up a fare and got mixed up on the address.' Gavel Slam! Case closed."

"Give me a few minutes with this bum. He'll be singing," LaCrosse chimed in.

The room erupted in laughter. "Relax, Detective," Masters said, patting him on the shoulder. "We'll get this guy. He's made his mistake. We have confirmation of his identity. Now let's find him. Retrace his steps. Mesa. Nettles. Go back to his apartment, see if he's been there."

"We're on it, boss," Mesa said, looking to Nettles, who nodded, and they headed out of the squad room.

"LaCrosse. Branson. Head back over to the Blevins scene and look for additional clues. Walk around the area as well. Start from Mr. Howell's residence. Backtrack to the intersections, then to Ms. Blevins' address. Look for anything—cigarette butts, pocket lint, overturned leaves—anything out of the ordinary that Nelson may have left behind. Remember, he has made mistakes in the past. He will make mistakes in the future."

"10-4," LaCrosse said. Branson said nothing but followed LaCrosse out the gate and downstairs.

"What's our assignment, Lieu?" Grady asked.

"Wait to hear back from each team. If they find anything, we act. Until then, we review the files and see if there is anything we missed."

For the next three hours, Masters and Grady combed the files from the first case to Blevins. They'd toss an occasional name or location over to Carmen to run a detailed search or fact check now and then. Most would add a sheet of paper or two into the files that already existed, no actual leads, just tying up loose ends.

"One thing that Glavine has gone to great lengths to research is that there is no connection between any of our victims," Grady began. "We already know they didn't bank or shop at the same locations. He thought he could find something deeper. He figured there was always a pattern that serials like to follow, something that connects their victims. But he found nothing. He couldn't even connect Tanner and Nelson. Other than Tanner was in Nelson's apartment that night. We don't even know how the two of them met. Doc just figures, like us, they met through the Uber connection."

"That's what we figure with all of Nelson's victims from that point on. Puts hell on his alibi, if each victim was also a service call. But then again, we've determined from his boss he's been off duty since his attack," Masters said.

"Doesn't mean he isn't picking up fares," Grady considered. "We never towed his vehicle, right?"

"No, I never saw the need. It would've taken more than gum wrappers to tow the vehicle," Masters explained. "So, he still has it. If he is picking up fares, we can find him."

Grady smiled. "We know he has turned off his Uber Service device, but if he hasn't disabled his vehicle GPS, then we can find him. Or should I say, Carmen can find him."

Carmen smiled. "You assume much. I'll see if I have that information in my records. We did pull a warrant for his vehicle. It will be expired, but the information for his GPS signal should still be valid if it is there. I'll call a judge and get an immediate warrant to use the GPS info to locate Mr. Nelson."

With that, she went to typing on her keyboard, the glow of the screen reflecting off her large, rimmed glasses. "Yes, his GPS info is here." She looked at both Grady and Masters. "Don't look. In fact, don't you have some work in your office that needs finalizing?"

Grady and Masters exchanged glances. Masters gave the managerial stare, and Grady took the hint. "I do have those photos of the Blevins scene I need you to review for the files," Masters explained.

"Right, I'm on your six."

Grady followed Masters into his office and shut the door while Carmen eyed them the entire way. In the silence, Grady could hear the clicking and clacking of Carmen's keyboard, jumping the gun of the judge's order, giving them the head start they needed to get ahead of the game Nelson was playing.

"Is she—" Grady began.

"Don't say it. If you don't say it, she's not doing it," Masters said.

"Gotcha. So how about them Hawks? You think it's their year?"

Saturday, February 29, 19:15

"You two take the rear entrance. We don't need Nelson sneaking out or in," Masters ordered LaCrosse and Branson, his gun in hand. "Mesa. Nettles. You remain in the lobby and keep your eyes peeled. Report anything out of the ordinary. If you see Nelson, don't spook him. Take him quietly."

"What are the chances—" Branson spewed.

"Slim to none," Masters cut him off. "But the landlady did say he's been here within the last week, and he's paid up through today. The lights are on, so if he's gonna be here, now is as good of a time as any."

Grady rolled his eyes, tired of Branson's negativity. *He's only acting this way because it's my case.* Then it occurred to him that this could be the way Branson always was. It made him shudder and not looking forward to future cases with such a bitter colleague.

"We have a key. Grady and I will head upstairs and into the apartment. If he is there, we will apprehend him. If not, we'll call down and sit on the place, depending on what we find in the apartment. Chances are, on his last visit, he was cleaning out the last of his belongings. We'll see. Now take your positions."

The team broke, and Grady and Masters headed up the narrow hallway, Masters in the lead, ducking his head as he had done that first evening. The only difference was that Ms. Keppler had the lighting replaced, and the stairwell was well lit. The stairs still creaked under their weight, and Masters lowered his hand to Grady in a stop signal. Grady waited as instructed, and Masters completed his ascension in silence. Once near the top, Grady proceeded, weapon against his shoulder, within the tight stairwell.

Nelson's apartment was to the left from the top of the stairs. Masters looked down at him and signaled—he was going straight and hug the door jam. Grady was to go left toward the hallway. This put each of them on either side of Nelson's door. There was no neighbor activity down the hallway, no sounds behind Nelson's door, just the sound of the two men breathing and their footfalls on the flooring beneath them.

Both officers approached the door from their respective sides. Masters pointed to himself, to his ear, then to the door. He listened, rapped on the door lightly, and listened again. Nothing.

Grady stuck out his bottom lip and shrugged.

Masters reached for the knob and turned it slowly. It gave. The door was unlocked. Masters used his eyes this time to direct their approach. Remembering their first time in the room, Grady was to go to the right while Masters was to head straight and to the floor. Both men planted their feet and firmed their grips on their weapons. Masters dug his shoulder into the door and pushed hard.

"Savannah P.D. Executing a warrant," Masters shouted and went to his knees. Grady followed the plan and hugged the wall to his right, sweeping the room with his eyes, weapon extended.

The living area was empty—not just of people, of everything. No furniture, no trash, nothing; just the vacant room echo of Masters' warning cry. Still, both men swept each room, taking appropriate precautions but with the same result; the apartment was cleaned out.

"What do you make of this?" Grady asked. "I thought these apartments came furnished?"

Masters stood with his gun facing the ground and free hand running through his hair. "Damnedest thing."

"This place has been cleaned," Grady said. "Professionally. We need to talk to Miss Keppler. As far as we know, he hadn't moved out yet."

Masters pulled out his notebook, found the number and dialed. "Ms. Keppler? Detective Masters." Masters rolled his eyes at the reception he received. "Ma'am. I apologize. I don't have the time for small talk. We are up in Mr. Nelson's apartment. When did he move out, ma'am? … Is that right? … I see … Well, thank you for that information … No, I'm sorry. I don't have the time for coffee. I'll contact you soon with more questions if I need to.

Thank you for your assistance … Mmm, hmm. You too." Masters hung up with another eye roll.

"She said he never spoke to her about completing his move out or gave her the keys. But that doesn't mean anything. He still has until midnight to do so. But she said she's pretty lenient about keys since she changes locks after a tenant moves out."

"You didn't tell her about the furniture," Grady said.

"If you want to call her back, be my guest," Masters said.

Grady laughed, then exhaled. "This place is pretty clean for someone who just skipped out," he said, walking through what was once a crime scene. The whole place was clean, but the bloodstains were still apparent. He looked around the room. The nakedness of it gave much more clarity. Grady's mind's eye could still see where the coffee table was with Nelson's body strewn across it, where the chair was, and where his epiphany first hit him. Then, something caught his attention. The air vent seemed slightly askew.

"Look at that," Grady said, pointing at the vent.

Masters looked to where Grady's attention had drawn him. "Mmmpf. It looks as if it has been removed and replaced. We need a ladder." Masters redialed Ms. Keppler, and minutes later, a maintenance man was in the apartment with a kitchen step stool.

"This is it?"

"It's late. It's all I could find on such short notice," the half-asleep caretaker said.

"Thank you," Masters said. "We'll leave it here when we are done and lock the door on our way out."

Without a word, the maintenance man shrugged and left.

Masters looked at the tiny step ladder, then sized up their physiques. "I'll let you do the honors."

Grady laughed, "Yes, sir," and unfolded the step stool. Using his pocket knife, he removed the plate and looked inside. "Looks empty. Can't really see. You got a light?"

"Nope. It's in the unit." Masters said.

"Wait a minute," Grady said. He and pulled out his phone and turned on the flashlight app. "Sometimes, these things are a life saver." Grady lit up the inside of the vent and let out a whistle.

"What?"

"Dried blood. Not much, but whatever was here contained enough blood to leave residual traces. I bet this is why we never found the weapon. Tanner hid it here." Grady said.

"*Tanner* hid it?"

"Well, it's not like Nelson was in any position to."

"You're saying that Tanner hid the weapon, got himself killed by cop, then Nelson came back to get the weapon and is now out killing people with it?" Masters asked.

"That's exactly what I'm saying," Grady said.

"But why?"

"That's now the million-dollar question. I would assume it has something to do with the mantra Tanner was spewing, *Glatchka Mondavka Insinivicus*. Glavine's research says it means, *Transference Purification Invulnerability*. What that means to us, we don't know yet, but the two are connected," Grady said.

"Transference?" Masters said, walking toward the bloodstains embedded in the carpeting. "That doesn't sound pleasant."

"Somehow this *transference* is causing Nelson to commit these murders now instead of Tanner."

"But how?"

"I'm not sure. I need to talk to Dr. Glavine again."

Chapter Fifteen

Sunday, March 1, 10:45

Grady spent Sunday morning at church with his wife by his side. The spiritual aspect of their marriage was one thing they had decided early on was most important. Without it, the ins and outs of the life he led would take their toll. Elizabeth understood his passion for his job when she married him, and he knew that he would have to make it up to her when he was around. Their faith strengthened them to face his absence. And since the move, he had let that slip; this case had been taking priority. Today was the day to get things back on track.

Elizabeth had her career landmines as well. Her job brought them to Savannah in the first place, and she had to keep pace or risk losing what she had worked for. So, the empty home was not only on him. There had been times he would beat her home and on more than one occasion Elizabeth would have a late meeting or showing across town. Either way, both of them were busy. Distance was a given for an ordinary couple. They were anything but ordinary.

Sunday morning had been a different deal, however. Church was always mandatory. No meetings, no warrant executions. If they were lucky, lunch at home or a restaurant was included. Then a quick kiss, and back to work. The church they had chosen was large enough to have two services—an early 9 a.m. and an afternoon. Today, they caught the early bird. Grady had his phone by his side in case he needed to act quickly.

Masters wasn't happy about it but figured they'd be just sitting around the office waiting. He compromised and, at Grady's suggestion, began to place team members in different areas of the field to be ready in case something broke, and they received word of Nelson's location. It was better to be everywhere than nowhere when anything happened, which, according to Dr. Glavine, could happen tomorrow around 3 p.m. They just didn't know the *who* or *where*.

Glavine had broken the code on the language Tanner used, which gave them the timing of each victim. It was based on the lunar cycle, thus the reason why Tanner kept checking his watch. He had been waiting for the peak of the quarter moon. The final piece of the puzzle was still missing—the *why*.

So far it was just speculation. Clarke and Ryan didn't see anything *happen*. But Glavine theorized there was a spiritual transference between Tanner and Nelson. His research indicated there more to the mantra that Clarke and Ryan didn't hear—likely a ritual performed before the officers arrived. The transference ceremony was completed with the final three words Nelson uttered. "As Nelson's soul left his body, Tanner's entered it," Glavine had explained.

Grady shuddered at the thought, and it brought him back to his church pew and the final benediction song, "How Great Thou Art." With so much information swimming in his head, he couldn't say what Pastor DeMarcus preached to save his life. He kept reaching for his phone to check for missed calls. It had been his idea to spread officers out across the city, but he had his doubts the plan would be effective. If Glavine was right, Nelson wouldn't make his move until three tomorrow, but that thought was of little comfort. The only consolation with the new theory was that the next victim wouldn't die. Nelson needed them to live.

"What are you doing?" Elizabeth asked again with narrowed eyes.

Grady knew that look; it spoke volumes. "Waiting for the call."

"Unless you're talking about a higher calling, then put that phone away right now mister," she whispered through pursed lips.

Elizabeth's glare made Grady put the phone back in his jacket pocket. He didn't touch it again through the final prayer and pleasantries exiting the building.

"Wonderful service, Pastor. Really spoke to me," Grady said, shaking the Pastor's hand.

"Thank you, Mr. Gradiosa," said the Pastor. "Thought I lost you there a couple of times."

"Tough week at work. I apologize. I was with you most of the time, though," Grady said through a half-hearted smile.

"Wonderful. So glad to have you as part of our church. Seek you next week?"

"Most definitely."

Grady and Elizabeth left the church and were just entering the parking lot when Grady's pocket began to buzz.

Monday, March 2, 09:30

Sunday had been filled with a myriad of false Nelson sightings. The first was after church service, which left a scowl on Elizabeth's face. Grady dropped her off at home and left to track down the lead just a few miles from their neighborhood. He did not reveal that information to Elizabeth, though. *Bad idea to let your spouse in on that a ritual seriel killer might be holed up around the block from home,* he mused. Grady did find a man fitting Nelson's description driving an Uber vehicle, but it was not Nelson.

Grady phoned in after the two-hour search. "Carmen, this lead was a no-go. It's not Nelson. Whatever happened to the GPS in his vehicle?"

"We lost that signal not too long after we went into his place the other night," Carmen said. "Sorry, Grady."

The rest of Sunday was filled with the team chasing their tails. LaCrosse speculated that Nelson was keeping them on edge so they wouldn't react appropriately when the real deal was called in.

Come Monday morning, Grady was running on two hours of sleep, and he could see the team didn't have much left in their tanks. Everyone was present, minus Branson. Masters was looking over a sheet of paper he had been given coming up the stairs, presumably from Atwood.

"Okay, everyone. Here are the areas we're going to target today. We're out of time. The victim is running out of time. According to Dr. Glavine, this one is intended to survive, but we hope not to let it get that far. We want to end this before it begins," Masters said, without looking up from his sheet of paper.

"Boss, you really believe this hooey?" Mesa asked.

"Does it matter, Detective?" Masters asked. "There is a victim out there who needs our help."

"If the victim is going to live, and the perp is going to off himself, then why should we worry about it?" Mesa continued.

"Because there is the chance that the victim may not make it. You want that on your conscience, Mesa?"

"No. I see what you mean. We're on it, Lieu."

"You and Nettles take the Westside, LaCrosse and Branson will take the North. Grady, you and I will take the South and cover what there is of the East—don't think he'll go near the coast though, nowhere to run," Masters instructed.

"What's on the sheet, boss?" LaCrosse asked, nodding toward the list.

"More leads. I'll get a breakdown by sector. Probably more dead ends, but it won't hurt to be aware, and we can check each out while we wait. But remember our 2:57 p.m. deadline. Be on your toes and keep your ears and eyes open."

"Gotcha."

After Carmen separated the list and made copies, the team split up and headed downstairs, and each vehicle headed out of the lot.

"Where to genius?" Masters handed Grady the list with they two addresses they had been assigned then started the car.

"Is this a test?"

"Damn right. I told you to get to know your city. I've seen you studying my map. Let's see if all that ogling has paid off."

"Get onto the Parkway South, head toward Georgetown. These are in the area where the Dale vehicle dump was."

"Very good." Masters said, turning on the radio, "LaCrosse, have you left the station?"

The radio beeped. "We're here. Found Branson. He was downstairs with Atwood. We're on the road now, heading just southeast of the airport. After checking them, we'll set up off the highway at a diner Branson knows of."

"10-4," Masters confirmed. "Mesa? Nettles?"

"We're here. We are headed just south of the 95/16 Cloverleaf. It has access to the highway. The addresses on our list are near the golf course there. May just go a few rounds afterward," Mesa replied. Grady could hear Nettles laugh and an unintelligible response in the background.

"We're headed south, down near where the Dale vehicle was dumped. If you see anything suspicious, radio in. But we're all in place for when the radio call goes out. We are trusting in our city now. Let's hope they are vigilant," Masters said.

Each car responded with a trusted, "10-4."

The two addresses Grady and Masters were given had been quiet with no activity. No vehicles were parked at either location nor was there a blue Prius anywhere to be seen. After an hour of scouring both locations, they came up empty. It was just after 11:00 when they pulled into a service station with easy access to the I-95/204 interchange. They parked and waited.

"Somewhere in the world, it's getting dark, and the moon is nearing its quarter phase," Grady said.

Masters looked out the window at the cloud-filled sky. "Only you wouldn't know it. You really believe this hogwash?"

"I don't know. Seems too coincidental not to be accurate," Grady said, checking his watch. "Glavine seems to be sure of himself."

Masters snickered. "Squints are always sure of themselves. They speak, and their tone is dead balls accurate, but more often than not they're off to the left or right."

"True, but we have no other lead or reasoning to explain what's going on here. And if we allow another life to be lost because we overlooked a lead, it'll be our heads on a platter. You want to answer to Captain Lawson that we let this slip through because we didn't listen to a lead?"

"Of course not. We're just putting a lot of faith in something so far-fetched. I don't know what to believe when a doctor says that there is a spiritual force behind these slayings," Masters said.

"I can understand that. But things are going on behind the scenes that we can't explain. Good versus evil. God versus Satan. Just like we really don't know what's going on here. But these things *do* happen, whether we believe them or not," Grady explained.

The car was silent for a long moment. The two men let the words stew in the air. Grady knew he had an opportunity, but he was nervous to continue. He had always had that pause when it came to talking to other people about his faith. It was a fault he wished he could overcome. He was about to speak when the radio bleeped. It was Mesa.

"So, what do we do when the call comes, boss?"

"We move into action, Mesa."

"Yeah, I get that. But what exactly does that mean?"

Grady could see the pause in Masters' face. He hadn't thought that far in advance. "When we arrive on-scene, we react according to the situation presented to us. If it's a hostage situation, we proceed with caution and do not attempt to apprehend suspect until it is necessary."

"10-4," replied the still unassured voice.

Grady could tell even Masters was not sure of his reply. Questions swirled in his mind. At what point must they use deadly force? Should they even try take him alive? Was he Nelson, or Tanner, as Dr. Glavine surmised? When does this *transference* officially occur, and what was the point of no return?

"Carmen put the APB out for his vehicle, right?" Masters asked.

"Yes, in our county and all surrounding counties," Grady said. "What is our response time like?"

"I had Carmen place each of us within 30 minutes of anywhere in the city. Since we are south, we can expect the same, as long as we remain 35 minutes from the city's center."

"Which we are right now," Grady looked at his watch again—11:30. "We're running out of time."

"I know," Masters shifted his seat, glancing in his rearview mirror and then the two side views. Grady had not seen his senior nervous before. He felt he should say something, but he was coming up empty.

"Did you catch the game yesterday?" Grady finally asked. *When all else fails, talk sports,* he told himself.

"What?" Masters asked, coming back to the vehicle.

"The Hawks? Did you see them play?"

"Naw. Missed it. Was in the office all day. Carmen and I were reading over leads and trying to find patterns," Masters said, then paused. "But you already know that."

"Yeah, I guess. Just trying to get your mind off whatever it's on," Grady said. "You look nervous."

"I'm just pissed off. I'm tired of this jerkoff getting by in my city. And I'm tired of sitting around waiting for him to do whatever he's going to do. I hate sitting around. I hate sitting in this piece of crap vehicle—" Masters jumped at his phone ringing.

"What you got, Atwood?"

"First, I'm not your answering service, but I just got a phone call from a lady. She sounded pretty upset with you."

"Alright," Masters said. "And why couldn't this be summed up in a note?"

"Lady said her name was Sophia Thoran, and she asked for you directly. She said, *It's time.* So, I asked her, *Time for what?* She just hung up. Figured you'd want to know."

Chapter Sixteen

Monday, March 2, 11:45

Masters paced the parking lot, knowing time was against them. He dialed his phone again and conversed with Carmen. No update. "We need a trace on that number, Carmen, let me know the moment you have anything."

Leaving did no good. They could drive and hope to get closer to Sophia Thoran to save her life, but she could be in the neighborhood behind the service station where they were parked and leaving could doom her. The same could be said of any one of their counterparts. "Tell everyone to stay where they're at," Masters barked into the vehicle where Grady sat.

Grady conveyed Masters' orders to the team, and they echoed their compliance.

"We already have an APB on Nelson's Prius, but we haven't heard anything today on the hotline. I will check again," Grady said. He remembered his manners when calling Atwood for a vehicle update. She responded in kind.

"Nothing on the Prius," Grady said.

Grady closed his eyes and started to replay the scene Clarke and Ryan experienced. Where was Nelson in his process with Sophia Thoran? Grady looked at his watch. It was ten minutes before noon. According to the timeline, they had three hours to go. It was a female this go-around. Grady hated to be chauvinistic, but he was sure a female voice would carry much further than a male. It was just a matter of time before they began to receive calls of a domestic disturbance. He turned up the radio and waited for the inevitable.

"You know, I was thinking, we should've brought Clarke and Ryan in on this. They have experience with Nelson," Grady said.

"Too late now," Masters said.

"Maybe not," Grady said. He found Clarke's number and hit dial.

After several rings, a not-glad-to-hear-you voice answered. "Detective, what can I do for you?"

"Clarke, I don't have much time. Are you on duty? If so, what's your 20?" Grady asked

"Ryan and I are just leaving the motor pool now. About to gas up. Why? What's wrong?"

"We need your help. We believe we're about three hours away from Nelson committing the same act that Tanner committed on him. We're not sure of his location, but it'll most likely be within the city somewhere. We have our detectives spread throughout the area and need an extra set of hands and the situation handled professionally. You and Ryan are the only officers who understand what we're dealing with. Short version, we need you to intervene as you did with Tanner and Nelson. We believe he's about to perform the same ceremony. Those words Ryan heard mean something. We need to stop that ceremony, but don't use deadly force. Our sources believe deadly force completes the transference. We can't explain how—it's just what Dr. Glavine believes. Do you understand?"

There was silence on the line for a long moment.

"Officer?" Grady asked.

"I'm here. Ryan figured it was something strange like this. He heard and wanted to help. So do I. What do we need to do?"

Grady was relieved. "After you fill up, stand by. Sit in the motor pool lot and wait for further instructions. We're waiting on a location. Be ready, though. We'll need to move at a moment's notice. But proceed 10-40, got that? We don't want to spook him. Not that we will, he may be expecting a grand show. You know that. You were there the first time."

"Understood," Clarke said.

"And Clarke," Grady said, hushing his voice. "Keep an eye on your partner. Who knows what this may bring back for him?"

"10-4."

Grady disconnected and watched his partner continue to circle the vehicle, rubbing the stubble on his face.

"Where are you, you bastard?" Masters said to the air, then to Grady, "Sit-rep?"

Grady picked up the radio, "Anyone see anything in their area?"

"Nothing."

"Nope."

"Nada."

Grady dialed the station. "Atwood, this is Gradiosa."

"Yes, Detective," she answered, hushing the background noises. "I'm still pounding away. What do you need?"

"Any updates, Sergeant?"

"Nothing yet. I have my entire team on alert, and I'm answering every call myself."

"10-4. Keep me posted."

"10-4."

Masters stopped pacing and leaned back on the hood. "He's out there, Grady. *She's* out there, right now, most likely suffering by now."

Grady rechecked his watch. 12:15 p.m.

"Sit-rep." Masters asked.

"We just—" Grady was cut off.

"Just humor me."

Grady squawked the radio, "How are we looking, team?"

"Nothing."

"Nope."

"Nada."

They sat in silence with just the passing traffic noise to keep them company. Their radio's occasional squelch would turn Masters' head, but it was just the typical police radio notification to another team in the field. Then an 18-wheeler's Jake Brake would drown out all sound. Realizing his partner's concern,

Grady shook his head, letting him know there was no news at that moment.

Hours seemed to be passing, but it only had been minutes, and even Grady began to feel on edge. He, too, wanted this to end. The anticipation building was unlike anything he had experienced as an officer. He had been through stakeouts and takedowns, but before they always had a target; always knew exactly where they were going and at what time. There was always a plan in place before they acted. Here they were clueless about everything but the who. Grady knew this was dangerous. Lives were lost without a clear, executable plan. But Nelson gave them little choice.

"Time?" Masters asked.

"1:35," Grady said, ignoring that Masters wore a watch on his left wrist that gave him the same time he had. "We have an hour and 22 minutes."

"Sit-rep?" Masters said, looking up at the sky.

"Branson. LaCrosse. Sit-Rep." Grady followed into the mic.

"Nothing over here. Traffic is picking up. A couple of Priuses, but nothing blue."

"Nettles? Mesa?"

"Same here. Traffic is heavier than earlier, but no blue Priuses. Glad this guy drives a distinguishable vehicle."

"Clarke? You and Ryan still in position?"

"Yes, sir. Awaiting your orders."

"Stand by. Remain on this channel."

"10-4."

"I still would like to have my head in the morning, and she would call if she heard anything, so if you want to hear anything from Atwood, you call her," Grady said.

For the first time in the last few hours, Masters cracked a smile, but it quickly faded. "Yeah, she would. Atwood may be irritated easily, but she knows when it matters."

Grady's phone buzzed, and the station's number displayed. It was Atwood. Grady answered it on speakerphone and keyed his radio. "I have one for you, Grady. 1040 East Palmwood Drive. Westside, near Birmingdale. Any of your team near there? Domestic disturbance call. Not sure if it's your guy. Report of a woman screaming."

"That's us," Mesa replied. "We're five miles south. Seven minutes out."

"Remember, everyone move in silently. No sirens," Masters said into the radio. "Atwood, remind any blue and white's you send that way the same. Tell them not to enter until we arrive. No one is to breach but us."

"10-4," replied Atwood.

"All units, head that way. 1040 Palmwood Drive. We will meet up before we proceed. Masters out," Masters dropped the mic and sped out of the lot toward the highway.

"You think this is it?" Grady asked.

"Do we have a choice?"

Masters took a sharp turn onto the highway, which reminded Grady that he wasn't buckled in. He repositioned himself and corrected the oversight.

"Well, navigator, which way would get us there faster?" Masters asked.

"Stay on 95. It's a straight shot to Route 80," Grady said without pulling up his map.

Masters looked over to his partner. "You sure about that?"

"Yes, sir. 95 to 80 West to Birmingdale," Grady said confidently. Maps came easily to him. They always did. It was like a photographic memory to a book reader; only he could do it with maps. He could recall them in his head. It worked the same way with crime scenes. It was how he saw the differences with the chair. While sometimes it took a minute to register, he always saw differences. It was probably a reason why growing up he loved the back cover of *Highlights Magazine*. The "What's Wrong" theme would always appeal to his meticulous nature.

"I think we could use lights and siren this far out with the speed we're using, Masters," Grady said.

Masters looked in his rearview mirror as yet another vehicle blew its horn at him as he jetted past it. Grady could only assume the gesture that would accompany such displeasure. "Yeah, I suppose your right."

Grady flipped the switches, the dashboard lit up, and the patented scream of an emergency vehicle caused more than one pair of brake lights to brighten ahead. Grady smiled at the sudden respect for the speed limit. They also heard no more horns as the sea of vehicles parted ways for them, and Masters was able to resume his foot-to-floor speed with no further hindrance.

"These damn things are never fast enough," Masters said, blowing between two semis, the siren echoing between the two trailers. "Time?"

"2:05."

"Damn."

Grady was watching his partner swerve in and around every vehicle on the highway. In and around a construction zone that brought it down to two lanes where he used the breakdown lane. Luckily, it was only about two miles, and the traffic quickly thinned out.

"We should have heard something by now. Mesa should be on the scene by now," Masters said.

"Mesa. Nettles. Report?" Grady called into the radio.

Nothing.

"Nettles. Sit-rep."

Silence.

"Damn," Masters said.

"Mesa. Are you on-scene? Respond."

Silence.

"LaCrosse. Branson. What's your 20?"

"Five minutes out," Branson said.

"10-4. Take caution as you approach," Grady warned.

"10-4. We'll apprise you of the situation when we arrive on-scene. Branson out."

"Mesa. Nettles. What is your location?" Grady asked.

Nothing.

Silence.

Masters made the turn from the interstate onto the parkway when the radio squealed. It was Nettles. "This isn't the right location. This isn't Nelson. We have the wrong address. It's just a domestic dispute. Stop wherever you are at, Lieutenant. Nelson is still out there."

Masters pulled into the breakdown lane and stared out the windshield. Grady flipped off the switch on the emergency tones, and silence surrounded the two stunned men. The only sound came from the clicking turn signal indicator and passing vehicles, which rocked the vehicle. Masters put it into park, picked up his phone and dialed. "Atwood. Please, tell me you have something else."

"Sorry, Lieutenant. I have nothing," Atwood said.

"Thank you, Sergeant," Masters said, tossing his phone to the dash.

Grady dialed Carmen. "Hey, do you have anything on the number used to make the call?"

"I may have something. Another call just came in. Give me a second," Grady could hear her keyboard clicking. "Okay. This number has a Skidaway Island prefix. I can see if I can narrow it down."

"Thanks. Call me when you have more," Grady said and hung up. "Skidaway Island," he told Masters.

Masters slid the column into drive and peeled out into traffic. They hit the turnaround and headed back the way they came. Grady grabbed the talker from the floorboard.

"All units, Grady here. We believe we have a location on our suspect—Head toward Skidaway Island. We don't have an address yet. Just head in that direction. When you cross a bridge, radio in. Grady out."

"Time," Masters asked.

Grady checked his watch. "You don't want to know."

"Grady!"

"2:15."

"Damn!"

"Well, quit swearing and get us there, Lieu," Grady said, flipping the siren switch.

"What do you suggest, navigator? That's across the city. We have 30 minutes."

"Stay on the major highways. Get back on 95, then cut over on 16 till you hit 516 to the parkway. Fastest way. Really the only way."

Masters was halfway smiling. "You have been studying. Glad you're able to perform under pressure, Grady. Because this is when it counts."

Grady had to smile over the compliment, but now wasn't the time to revel in the moment; there was a job to do. He radioed the team and requested ETAs.

Each had been just as far out as they were, except for Clarke and Ryan. They were 20 minutes away from Skidaway Island compared to everyone's 30–40.

"Once you cross the bridge, find a stopping point and wait for further instruction. We don't have an address at this point," Grady said.

"10-4," Clarke replied.

"You do realize that 240 is a two-way from the parkway to the Vernon and into Skidaway, right?" Masters asked.

Grady had a blank stare.

"That's okay. You know the roads, that's commendable, can't expect you to know the width of them. It will add time to our drive, though."

Grady's phone rang. "We have an address. 1240 Golden Bluff Lane. It's the Southeast part of the island. Sending it to you now with a map drop. I will send it to everyone else as well."

"Great. Can you also send it to Officer Sean Clarke? I'll send you his number when we hang up. He is closest to the scene."

"Yes, definitely."

All was in place. They were on their way and about to capture a fugitive. Grady had been responsible for arresting criminals, but none like this. He could hardly sit still. He could feel his heart hammering inside his chest, and his mind was running through a hundred different scenarios. All they had been working on the last few weeks was finally coming to a head. Grady knew he had to get himself in check because an officer who acted on impulse was a dangerous one. He took a deep breath and exhaled.

"You alright?" Masters asked.

"Yeah. Guess I'm feeling the moment."

"Yeah, I know what you mean. I'm ready to catch this bastard."

Grady picked up the radio, "Alright, gentlemen, and lady, we have an address. Carmen is sending it to you. Proceed with caution. Again, proceed silently. I know he is most likely expecting us, but we don't want to spook him. Clarke and Ryan will be first on the scene. They will be in uniform and a block down from the address. We will proceed up to the home and coordinate from there to enter. We're on borrowed time. As a reminder, 240 going into Skidaway is a two-way. Be careful. Grady out."

As before, a trio of "10-4s" showered Grady.

"Time?"

"2:25."

"Damn."

Chapter Seventeen

Tuesday, March 2, 14:50

Grady and Masters reached Highway 240 in record time. Now it was just a matter of getting through the two-lane traffic. It appeared light from a distance, but Grady knew from experience every road was different once the traffic really picked up, and once on the two-lane portion of 240, there was no stopping or turning around—unless you wanted to take a swim in the Skidaway.

Grady looked up at the sky, then checked his watch. "Seven minutes."

"We're not going to make it," Masters said.

Grady picked up the radio mic, "Anyone on the island?"

"Mesa here. We're. We are parked here with Clarke and Ryan."

"We're right behind you, Grady," Branson responded.

Grady looked behind him. LaCrosse flashed his brights.

"We should allow Mesa to proceed with Clarke and Ryan to the location," Grady offered to Masters. "But to enter with caution. If this is anything like before, Clark and Ryan know how to handle it. Wouldn't hurt to radio for an ambulance now. Chances are he's already waiting. They need to stop whatever is happening up there and take Nelson alive and not allow this transference ceremony to occur."

Masters nodded in agreement, and Grady conveyed the instructions. The team went into action as Masters weaved through any opening he found in the traffic, which was few and far between. His shadow did the same. His lights and siren did little to help.

"Check-in when you get to the location and give frequent status updates."

"10-4," Nettles replied.

Four minutes passed, and the radio popped, "Dammit. You are not going to believe this."

"What's wrong," Grady asked.

"Two blue and whites are on the scene," Nettles replied.

"I thought we were the only officers on this case?"

"Wait. I don't know if it's us. May be local security."

"Are they armed?"

"I'm not sure. I don't know enough about island municipal security," Nettles said.

"Masters. You know about these guys?" Grady asked.

Masters shook his head, eyes still focused on the road, trying to not get them killed, swerving around another 18-wheeler.

"Proceed with caution. If these guys are armed, you don't want to spook them. They have no clue what's going on here. You need to get in there now before something bad happens."

"10-4, we are on our way—"

The sound of distant gunfire cut Nettles off.

"Nettles, what's going on? Was that what I think it was?"

"Stand by. We're going in."

Although Masters was already going as fast as he could, he seemed to muster more speed out of the Caprice and found extra space on the road. He finally reached the end of the two-lane and the side streets that led to Golden Bluff Lane. He found the two other sedans like his and jammed on the brakes behind them.

Grady saw what their companions saw: two blue and white security vehicles dressed up as the SPD police vehicles on the highway. Each Detective pulled their service weapon and approached the home. As they drew closer to the 1240 address, they could hear the barking of commands. It was Mesa. The sound of an approaching EMS vehicle quickly downed him out. Grady found it playing out just as Clarke had described it in his report. He could only imagine how it felt to them. And what Ryan must be going through right now.

"Be ready," Grady said to no one in particular. He knew that they knew what to expect.

They approached the side gate to the home from where the voices had been echoing. "Mesa?" Masters called out.

"Back here, boss," Mesa called and continued as they entered the room, pointing at each victim for emphasis. "We have one down. It's Nelson. One critical. Female, in her 30s. I can only assume it's Sophia Thoran. Two clueless security dumbasses shot Nelson without phoning in SPD. We need that EMS back here ASAP."

Right on cue, two EMTs entered the home, and both stopped in place. "Don't you need the coroner?" The taller of the two said.

"No," replied Mesa. "Not for her. She has a weak pulse but is alive. Get her to the nearest hospital immediately."

The two paramedics lowered Nelson to the floor and placed a sheet over him. The taller one unpacked their bag while the other began to tend to Sophia Thoran's wounds. Grady looked the scene over; Thoran laid on a coffee table in just a tank top, workout shorts, and tennis shoes. Nelson was sprawled over her with the four exit wounds to his back. A chair sat next to the table; there was no weapon in sight. Grady was taken back to the first scene. Like the former, the blood loss was not as copious as any of the murder scenes. This scene looked identical to the Tanner's.

"Clarke. Ryan. A moment." Grady asked. Both officers joined him at the body.

"You okay, Ryan?" Grady asked.

"Fine, sir," Ryan said, and he looked it. "I'm over what happened, sir. I can continue."

"Good. Does this resemble what you saw with the Tanner scene? I know I saw the aftermath as well, but I would like confirmation."

Both men examined the scene. Except for the presence of

Nelson's body, they confirmed it looked identical to what they experienced at Forsythe Park.

The paramedics finished securing Sophia Thoran's wounds and announced they were ready to transport her. They propped up the gurney and wheeled her out of the house.

"Are you comfortable with guarding Sophia Thoran until our team can meet you there? I need her under 24-hour guard. She's not to leave your sight or be discharged. This is important. Do you understand?"

"We copy," Clarke said.

"Does this have to do with 'Glatchka Mondavka Insinivicus'?" Ryan asked, eyes locked with Grady.

Grady gave a blank stare, then looked to the side. He didn't want to lie. He looked back to Ryan. "Yes, it does. But we don't have time to get into that right now. Just don't let her leave your sight. One of us will relieve you once we complete our search here. I'll explain when I meet you at the hospital. Again, don't let her leave your sight. Understood?"

Then Clarke and a much stronger Ryan said, "10-4. Understood."

Clarke and Ryan followed the EMS unit, both with lights and sirens. Grady only wished he had more time to explain the circumstances of who or what Sophia Thoran could be—to explain that she could be Nelson, or perhaps even Tanner. He wasn't sure if the transference took place. But if they did their job and kept her under watch, they would be safe for the moment. Now was the time to find the weapon. And with the clues found in Nelson's apartment, they had a good idea of where in Sophia's home Nelson hid the knife.

Monday, March 2, 2020, 18:25

"This is impossible," Nettles whispered as the fourth hour passed with nothing to show from their search. "This is a 1,200 square foot home. Nelson's place was a tiny apartment."

"We still need to comb it top to bottom, Detective," Masters scolded, checking the inside of the fireplace. "No stone unturned, remember?"

"Yes, Lieu," Nettles said, with a deep breath to regain her focus.

The team first searched the air vents. They didn't want to be bitten twice by the same snake. But it seemed Nelson had received the same memo because there were no loose vent covers, nor was there anything hiding in the entire ventilation system.

"He learns quick. Or has a pattern of not using the same location twice," LaCrosse offered, entering the room.

"Keep searching. It's here somewhere," Masters said.

"It has to be. But it's a big house. Lots of places to hide," LaCrosse said

"That's why we're still here," Nettles said, almost mocking.

"10-4," LaCrosse said and headed back to the kitchen. "If we only knew exactly what we're looking for."

"Grady said it would resemble a surgical scalpel or a hobby knife. Thin. The blade would be about an inch and a half in length. The handle would be longer so the hand can steady it."

"Needle in a haystack," came a voice from the hallway. Branson entered the living room. "You know how small those things are?"

"Relax, Daryl," said Masters. "This is coming from Dr. Glavine, not Grady. He's the one *you* asked to personally handle this case, remember?"

Branson gave a blank stare and exited the room, caught in his behind-the-back discussion with Dr. Glavine.

"What was that about?" LaCrosse asked.

"Nothing," Masters said. "Just someone who's not too happy about someone taking a case and running with it and acting on hunches and being right."

"Hmm," LaCrosse said and left the room with a chuckle. "The kitchen is clean. I inventoried the knives, as we did before, just in case. But nothing like what you described. I'll check the bathrooms now. Plenty of hiding places there."

"10-4."

Grady entered the house from the back door. "The only location he could have placed it is in the garage. I've lost daylight, and that porch light isn't providing enough light anymore. The patio seems to be clean, so does the car, which is registered to Sophia Thoran. No knife. So many hiding places, though, and the size of the knife, it could be anywhere." Grady ran his hand through his hair and looked around the room.

"Yes," Masters said, with a defeated tone. "I don't want to go through what we did with Nelson."

"Yeah. Sitting across the street and waiting for her to come back," Grady shook his head. "Heck, no. We did that before, and look what it got us. Three innocent lives are now dead."

"Have you heard from the hospital?" Masters asked.

"Not yet."

"It's been hours. Maybe you should check on our officers. They may be expecting you. You did tell them you'd relieve them."

"I'm on it."

Grady stepped into the cooling night. A front must've moved in, or perhaps the island was just closer to the ocean, either way, there was a noticeable temperature change. The chill gave Grady a shiver. It made him think of Elizabeth. She hated the cold and would scold him when he'd allow the chill to enter the house. He missed her. This case had taken him away from her. He could tell she felt neglected, and he knew that he must do something about it soon. But now wasn't the time.

Grady was able to give both Clarke and Ryan the information he failed to provide them before they left with the ambulance. They assured Grady that Thoran/Tanner wouldn't leave their sight. They would do what they needed to do to keep their eyes on her at every moment, for their safety and the safety of the doctor and nurses.

"Clarke, I'm sorry about the delay. Do you have a status update?"

"Thoran just got out of surgery. They stopped the bleeding, repaired the veins, and are replenishing her fluids. The doctors expect she'll make a full recovery. She's sedated right now," Clarke explained.

"Remember, stay on her. Sedated or not, don't let her leave your sight. Until we're proven otherwise, she is extremely dangerous," Grady said.

"Understood."

"Where's Ryan?"

"He's getting coffee right now. But we're not leaving our post unmanned."

"Just as long as one of you is there. Don't let the doctors take her anywhere without one, or better yet, both, of you accompanying them. Remember, she could be Nelson because of the transference."

"Understood," Clarke said.

Grady disconnected. "They're getting tired. They've been up just as long as we have and aren't used to long stakeouts."

"Send Mesa and Nettles to relieve them," Masters said. "We aren't finding anything here. Another hour or so, and we'll be out of here anyway."

"10-4."

"I don't know what to tell you, Masters. There's nothing here." Branson said, motioning back at the house. "It would be too small to find, even if it were here. We'd need days to scour this place."

"You're right, Branson. It's dark and going on nine. Plus, we let Nettles and Mesa go two hours ago. I say we wrap it up and come back when it's daylight," Grady suggested looking at Masters, halfway trying to appease Branson.

Masters was looking around the garage they had been sifting through. Grady shared the defeated weight. The knife wasn't in the garage. He knew it wasn't. He felt it. But he didn't want to leave it at that. The motto 'no stone unturned' wasn't going to allow him to quit.

To their benefit, Sophia Thoran was a neat freak. Everything had its place, and the garage was immaculate. Which was the main reason to conclude the knife wasn't going to be there; it was too clean, not a drop of blood anywhere.

"Okay. We're done here," Masters said after a defeated exhale. "Wrap things up and bring the evidence we've collected. We'll take it to Dr. Glavine for examination."

"10-4," Branson said. "I'll inform the team."

"This is a waste of time," Masters said when Branson left ear range. "No one was out here. Unless Nelson cleaned up, came out here, boxed the knife up, and then went back inside."

"Can we put it past him to do such a thing?" Grady said.

Masters gave him a half-joking, half-dirty look. "Unfortunately, no. If he was willing to pull out a screwdriver and put it in an air duct, he can put it in the bottom of a box and clean up. That's why we keep digging."

Grady's phone rang, its tone echoing in the hollowness of the garage. He didn't recognize the number. "Detective Gradiosa."

"Detective. This is Nurse Allen over at Mercy General. I'm afraid I have some terrible news."

"Go ahead, Nurse," Grady said, motioning to Masters.

"Oh heavens, where do I begin. First, your Detective Nettles is okay. She's in surgery as we speak. If she weren't already in a hospital, things would be different. I wish I could say the same for Detective Mesa. He suffered a laceration to the carotid artery and expired before we found him. The patient they were watching, Sophia Thoran, we cannot find her. We aren't even sure how she got past the desk clerk. That floor is normally crowded."

"She escaped? How long ago?"

"About ten minutes ago. We would have called you sooner, but we didn't have a number. I found your card in Detective Mesa's wallet. It was lying on the floor under a chair."

Grady's mind swam back to the day he handed that card to Mesa, proud to finally have something to tie him to his Savannah PD team. He remembered Mesa's laugh and reply that not even he had one of those. Now he was gone.

"We called the local police. They are here, and they sealed off the building. They're searching for her now. But they say it is doubtful she's still in the building. Too much time had passed between the time we found the detectives and the time we called it in. They say she had plenty of time to exit the building."

"Thank you—" Grady said, forgetting the nurse's name.

"Nurse Allen. Janice Allen."

"Thank you, Nurse Allen. We're on our way. Please tell your security division to isolate the security tapes from two hours before you found them until right now. We'll be there shortly."

"Yes, Detective. And I am sorry for your loss."

"Thank you, Nurse."

Grady hung up and broke the news to Masters, who took the news better than expected. There was pain behind his eyes, but it didn't show in his actions. He just nodded in acceptance and agreed they needed to go to the hospital and check the video-tapes for evidence of where Thoran went. She was still injured and would need medical attention soon. If they were to catch her, now would be the time she would most likely slip up. They just need to be watching and listening.

Chapter Eighteen

Tuesday, March 3, 01:30

Grady and Masters were in the security office reviewing the video feed of Thoran leaving the hospital. It was a hobbled but a quick exit. She had found a set of workout clothing on the Rehab floor where patients change from their therapy sessions. From there, she was indistinguishable from a patient with a late appointment and aching from her treatment. Exiting the building didn't warrant a second look.

They tracked her to the Rehab wing from the attack on Mesa and Nettles. Neither of them had seen it coming.

Thoran wasn't seen because the desk clerk had stepped away for some reason. That's when she made her move into the next room and took the clothing from her neighbor to exit the floor. She was clever and timed it perfectly. Why the neighbor didn't raise the alarm was anyone's guess. Most likely asleep. He may have been threatened, that would come to light with follow-up questioning.

"I'm sorry, Masters," Grady said.

"Mmmmph," Masters grumbled, eyes glued to the screen.

"Have you ever lost a brother like this?"

Masters' eyes went misty, then distant. He had.

"I'm sorry."

"Now's not the time to mourn, kid," Masters said. "We have to find Thoran. Or whoever is out there right now." The camera's cycled through a few more times. "There!" Masters pointed.

The parking lot cams picked up Thoran getting into a cab. Most likely having the money to pay from Mesa's empty wallet.

Masters smiled when he saw the footage. "We have our first lead. We need to get this footage to Carmen. We need that cab number."

Grady looked at the screen. While the image was pixelated, it was almost legible. That was a job for Carmen and a job she did well. The cab company would have records of the driver having been at the hospital at that time and where the fare went.

"Where are your tapes?" Grady asked the security officer.

"Tapes? Everything is digital now. Where have you been?" The officer chuckled, his partner followed suit.

"Even better. Are you able to make copies?"

"I can make you a CD or flash drive copy. Which do you prefer?"

"Flash drive would be great. Can you email from here?"

"Of course, we're not in the stone age, you know," the other said.

"Alright, guys," Masters said. "We can do without the wise-cracks. Just get what we need, and we will be out of your hair."

One security officer pulled out a thumb drive and plugged it into the server to his left. He makes a few clicks on the screen and looked up at Grady with raised eyebrows.

Grady turns to Masters. "How much do you want?"

Masters looked to the floor. "The whole thing. Do you really need to ask?"

"No. I suppose not."

Grady turned back to the officer. "Ten minutes before the suspect gets out of the bed until the cab she gets into leaves the premises."

"Alright," said the first. "Should take about five minutes."

"This will get all cameras and all angles?"

"Yes," said the second. "With this drive, you will be able to check individual angles when you go to review the file."

"It will be just like you were watching it here," said the first.

The screen flashed back to a live view. Doctors and nurses were going about their daily business of treating patients. The ill were examined, and tests were being run. Some were getting good news, while others were facing the uphill battle of an unfavorable diagnosis. Two of their own were above their heads at this very moment. One life had ended; the other was battling for hers. Nettles' surgery had been successful. She had gotten lucky. In Thoran's haste, she had not cut entirely through the artery, and the way Nettles fell kept enough pressure on it to save her life.

The second's clearing of his throat brought Grady back to the present. The security officer's hand was in the air with the flash drive. Grady took it. "Thank you, officer. If we have any additional questions, we'll contact your department."

Masters was standing by the door, looking through the one-way glass. It viewed the lobby that not too long ago Sophia Thoran crossed as she exited the building.

"How did she get that blade?" Masters asked the window.

The question hit Grady. "Maybe it was in the room? In one of the drawers?"

Grady and Master exchange glances.

"Guys, we need you to pull up the videos again. Begin with where you started recording for us. We need to backtrack from there," Grady instructed.

A volley of grunts came from behind them, but they did as they were told. Within seconds Mesa was alive again, and Thoran was back in the hospital bed lying still. Mesa was sitting in a chair outside the room in a chair. Nettles was stretching her back, then pacing the hall. The video captured Thoran standing from her bed and leaning over to the dresser next to the bed. She reached in and pulled something out. It looked like a shoe. The image's graininess made it hard to tell what she was doing, but she put the shoe back in the drawer and laid back down. She must have made a sound because that brought Mesa into the room and his demise.

"Do we have this part on our video?"

The security officer looked at the time stamp and looked at the record of what he burned for Grady, "Yes, it's on there."

"Thanks," Grady said, turning to Masters and holding the thumb drive in the air. "We'll find her, Masters. This is the key. Let's get back to the station. Carmen needs to get started on this."

"It will take a few hours to clean up, but I have the program that'll do it," Carmen said. "A few sweeps, and we will have something that's at least legible. Until then, I'll phone the cab company and see if they can check info on cars in the area at that time."

"Thanks, Carmen," Grady said. He looked up and saw Masters' office door shut. He looked back to Carmen.

"Let him be," she said. "He needs to gather himself. He understands we're pressed for time. But we can't act until I come up with a lead. So, give him that time."

"I think he blames himself," Grady said. "He's the one who sent them to the hospital to replace Clarke and Ryan."

"He was just doing his job," Carmen said.

"Yes, but…" Grady trailed off.

"But what?"

"I was the one who convinced him to send them over. I explained that Clarke and Ryan were overworked and needed the relief. If I had just let them—"

"Then we would be mourning two dead officers," Carmen said. "Regardless, this would've happened."

"I understand—"

"I'm not saying their lives don't matter as much, but I am saying that both Nettles and Mesa would say their sacrifice was worth the risk. That they were just doing their job," Carmen began. "You're doing exactly what the boss is doing in his office right now. Kicking yourself and second-guessing. Don't let it get the best of you. At that moment, you did what you thought was best. Given that situation again, you would do the same thing. Don't second guess yourself. Second-guessing is what gets you dead."

"I can see why he trusts you," Grady said.

"Your darn right, he trusts me. He better. I'm the only one here with common sense," Carmen said with half a smile. She sat down and made a couple of clicks on the computer screen. A frozen image of the cab came up. A sweeping light bar came across it from left to right, then top to bottom. It repeated. "Okay, we're in business. Hopefully, that will clean up the image enough to read those numbers. But I'm hoping to have better luck with phone calls before the image. Now scoot while I do my magic. Go talk to our boss. He's had enough time to sulk."

"Thank you, Carmen," Grady said. He headed to the office door, knocked gently, and walked in.

The room was dark; only the desk lamp lit the room. Masters hadn't turned on the overhead fluorescent light.

"May I come in?"

"It's a free country," Masters replied.

"Carmen is working on the cab footage. She's calling the company now to try and track down the cabbie while the software does its magic. We should have something soon."

"Let me know the second she has something."

"I will," Grady said but didn't leave the office.

"Is there anything else?" Masters said, not looking up from the desk or the coffee cup he was nursing.

"You can't blame yourself, Masters. You had no idea this was going to happen. Hell, it was my idea to send them down there. If you blame anyone, blame me," Grady said.

Masters looked up and met Grady's stare. "I don't blame anyone. I know we were doing our job. Yeah, I may have blamed myself at first, but if we blamed ourselves for every decision that went south, we would second guess everything, and that kind of hesitation only does more harm."

Grady swallowed hard. "Yeah. I guess I've been doing my share of self-wallowing."

"Well, stop it. That's an order," Masters said. "And turn on the damned light."

Grady did as requested, and the men squinted in the sudden brightness. He noticed the full decanter and poured himself a cup of coffee.

"How long on the cab ID?" Masters asked.

"A few hours," Grady said. "But Carmen hopes to have better luck with the cab company directly. Unless he's a gypsy."

"Those gypsies love the hospitals," Masters said. "People willing to pay to get out of Dodge."

"Well, let's hope that the cabbie wasn't one."

"She couldn't have gone far. She's still recovering, and surgical wounds don't heal instantly. I'm surprised she woke up so soon, anyhow. You'd think they'd have her sedated heavier than they did."

"They kept me sedated for hours after my hernia operation," Grady said. "Although I was ten, and that was on a more delicate part of the body. And I was sick as a dog coming off the anesthesia and going onto the pain meds."

"And you were ten," Masters reminded with a small laugh.

"I know this is different. My point is she won't go too far. We know it's doubtful she'll go home, but we still should put someone on her residence. I can call Clarke and Ryan to run out there. They should be well-rested. Or we can just rely on the neighborhood goon patrol. But I think they're still in shock over what happened with Nelson."

"No, use our guys. Clarke and Ryan are fine. Radio them," Masters said.

"10-4. All we're waiting for then is a report from the cab company or a sighting to call in," Grady said.

Grady exited the office with a coffee cup in hand. He looked over Carmen's shoulder, and the pixels on the screen seemed to be clearing up, but not by much. She was making headway on the cab companies. Instead of a blur, she could see the contrast between grey and white. It was either a Liberty Cab Service or an All-ways Cab. Both had a red and blue motif.

"Even though I have it down to those two, the day operators don't have information on who was driving the night shifts. It could also be that they don't want to give up information on a driver who could be working off the books and get them inadvertently in hot water. Cabbies have their own code, much like we do. Operators stick tight to their drivers. So, we probably won't have much till that crew comes on at 8:00 tonight."

Grady looked up at the clock. It was just after 8:30 a.m.—they had pulled an all-nighter. A sudden wave of tiredness hit him, and the awareness of missing his wife tugged at his heart.

"I'm sure Masters would agree. There's nothing we can do until we get information from the cabbie. Go home and get some sleep. You'll be nothing to him dead on your feet. I'm sure Elizabeth would be glad to see you as well."

Grady looked back at the office. As if he had radar, Masters yelled in reply, "She's right, kid—"

Grady mouthed the word, *kid*, with wrinkled eyebrows. Carmen just grinned and went back to her flashing screens.

"Go get some rest. I don't need you falling out on our way to catch this bastard. If I do hear anything, you're my first call, so keep your phone charged and close by," Carmen said.

"10-4, boss. I'm out of here," Grady said. He was too tired to say otherwise. He said goodbye to Carmen and ensured he would be first on the list to call if she found anything. Better to be on his way by the time Masters heard than just waking up. He buzzed the gate and headed out of the station to his wife, who was probably already on her way to her office, which would be his first stop before heading home.

Grady pulled up to her office just in time to see Elizabeth walking to her car, a briefcase in one hand and a box balancing in the other. He edged up beside her and rolled down his window. "Headed out?"

"Yes. I have a viewing across town in an hour. Sorry," she said. "Wish I had time to talk. You okay?"

"Yeah, just tired." Grady parked and grabbed the box for her. "Headed home to get some sleep. Been up since...." Grady couldn't remember the last time he had slept.

"You don't know when," Elizabeth completed his sentence.

She knew the line well. It was common for Grady the Detective.

"Yeah," he said. "Sorry. We were close this time. We lost a detective yesterday."

Elizabeth's demeanor changed. She knew how quickly officers bonded in the field. She had witnessed it in Atlanta when Grady lost fellow officers in the past. "I'm sorry, James. Who was the officer? A detective?"

"Yes," Grady leaned back against her car. "He was guarding a suspect we arrested. She overpowered him and escaped."

"Oh my. She?"

"Long story," Grady said. "Don't worry. She has serious injuries and is probably holed up somewhere away from here. We have officers looking for her." Grady yawned and rubbed his eyes, "I haven't slept in two days, so I was on my way home to get some rest while Carmen runs a search for the vehicle she was last seen in."

"Well, if you are hungry, there is some Chicken Salad in the fridge. I made it last night," Elizabeth leaned back next to him and looked up with a crooked grin. She knew that was one of Grady's favorites, and it would always put a dent in whatever funk he would be in. Wives' intuition.

"Thanks, Lizzy," Grady said.

She placed her leather briefcase through the open window into the backseat and moved closer to him. "I love you, Grade. Go home and get some rest." She smiled again and kissed him on his stubbled cheek.

He wasn't sure if he ever told Elizabeth what those kisses still did to him. Those soft kisses sent him into another world that would curl his toes, even after ten years. Despite the weight he was carrying and heavy eyelids, his spirit was lifted. That one kiss steered the car back to the place they called home.

Chapter Nineteen

Hello?" Grady said in a muffled tone. The phone awakened him in what seemed like minutes after he closed his eyes. The clock told him it had been six hours.

"We got her. Well, not got her-got her, but we found where the cab took her," Carmen said in a half-whisper. "Get your ass up. I'm about to take the info into Masters now. Get down here. Better yet, head over toward Gosserton. You know where that is?"

Grady snapped up. It was just miles from his neighborhood. "Yes, it's 10 miles from my home."

"Really?" Carmen said. "Standby." Carmen put Grady on hold, and he knew why. No officer acts alone. She was notifying Masters and putting him on a conference call. The line beeped twice. "Okay, Grady. I have Masters on the line."

"First, Detective, I don't appreciate you getting the drop on new information. But I do like the proactive action. Good job. Second, do not move until you have backup. Understood?"

"Understood," Grady said.

"We all carry the same frustration over Mesa. We don't need a loose cannon acting in retaliation. That will only cause further casualties. You're the one who's constantly reminding us to use our heads here. Don't lose yours."

"Yes, sir. I understand."

"I'll conact LaCrosse and Branson, and I'll head that way myself. You're at your home, correct?"

"Yes, sir," Grady said.

"Both LaCrosse and Branson are as well. But they're coming from the Airport area. I have a bunk here at the station, so that's where I'm at. I'll be near you in 30. I can pick you up, or we can meet. You're in Wilton Estates, correct?"

"Yes. Just North of the University," Grady confirmed. "I have a car. I can meet you."

"That'll work. You know the loop that heads into Gosserton?"

"No, but I can find it." Masters had found one area Grady had yet to research.

"You can't miss it. It's a huge wrap-around off the 204 going into Gosserton. There is a service station to your right once you hit the straightaway. I'll be there in 30 minutes."

"Alright, I know where you're talking about. See you then."

Grady knew that it had been at least two days since his body had any kind of water applied to it, so a shower was a must. He let the water run while selecting a fresh pair of clothes. He took the quickest shower known to man but was careful with the shave, not wanting to give his boss reason to throw any jabs. After deodorant, burning aftershave, and his apparel of jeans, long sleeve t-shirt, and boots, he was ready for the day. Grady faced the mirror and ran his fingers through his dark shaggy hair; it was about the best it was going to get.

He was out the door in 20 minutes flat. *New record?* No time to eat this morning, or was it afternoon? The clock and the setting sun confirmed it almost supper time, nearly six. "This job, sometimes," Grady muttered. He was out of the driveway seconds later and on his way to meet Masters.

To his benefit, Wednesday evening traffic was not too hectic. He was only a few minutes late. Like the morning they met, Masters was leaning on the hood of his car, only this time he was the one with coffee in hand. A bag sat on his hood.

"Thirsty, aren't we?"

"This one's for you, smart-ass," Masters said, hand extended with steam coming out of the lid spout. Drink and eat up— Donuts in the bag. We need to get rolling. Who knows how long she'll remain hidden?"

Grady grabbed a glazed from the bag, took a bite, and

mumbled the first few words, "She isn't going anywhere. I would assume. She's injured and needs to heal before she even tries to kill again. Wherever she is, she's staying put. Thoran barely got out of the hospital in one piece. If she did reopen any of her stitches, she would need medical attention before looking to kill again. First, we call Carmen and put an APB at all area hospitals and med-clinics. Just in case she shows up."

Masters leaned back on his hood and took a bite of his donut followed by a long drag of his coffee. "Did they teach you all that up in Atlanta?"

"Not all of it," Grady said, matching the pose and the sip. "I would like to think that some of your expertise has rubbed off on me during my short tenure."

Masters didn't respond. He looked up at Grady, then to the ground, then stared into the distance.

"Again, good work," Masters said, eyes still locked far away—another bite and sip. "I'm still half-cocked. I've known Mesa for a long time. He came to me as a rookie, wet behind the ears," Masters said, wiggling his ear with a finger. "A patrolman thinking he knew it all. Almost got us both killed on our second assignment. He walked into a meth lab without securing the perimeter..." Masters trailed off—another long sip. He took a deep breath and let it out, "I can't get that hospital video out of my head. It's one thing when it is a room full of perps. No effect. But seeing him just drop. He never saw it coming."

"Maybe that was best. He didn't suffer," Grady said, doing his best to console.

"That's what I keep telling myself," Masters said. Again he was silent. "Do you want to know what I was doing in the office earlier? I wasn't sulking. You must know that. I never sulk."

"So, what *were* you doing?" Now Grady was curious.

"Mesa was pretty much an orphan. His parents were killed in a car wreck when he was 12. His aunt in Albuquerque raised him. He went to the Academy there and took his first post as an SPD officer before transferring upstairs five years ago. I was on the phone with his aunt giving her the news." Masters said with his distant stare, watching the traffic merging onto the highway. He looked to Grady with the setting sun glowing in his misty eyes.

"I'm sorry. I didn't know," Grady said.

"How could you. You've been here ten minutes."

"Nettles will take it hard when she finds out. How long have you known her?"

"Just two years. She's the newest next to you," Masters said, pointing his cup at Grady.

"You could tell they were close. They even dressed alike. It was almost eerie," Grady admitted. "I thought I had double vision the first time I saw them. If it hadn't been for their dominant hand difference."

Masters laughed, "Yeah. They slowly morphed into one after about a year. Branson rode them for about a month until Nettles let him have it one morning."

"Nettles?"

"Yep."

"Wow," Grady said, picking up his jaw off the floor.

"She can be vocal when she needs to be. And she was. He shut up after that morning," Masters said with a memory jogged twinkle in his eye.

"Is that what I need to do? Get in his face?"

"Who, Branson? I don't know. Maybe," Masters said. "It's different with you. He feels threatened by you. It's defensive. He knows you have more years on the force than he does. Not much, but every inch of seniority matters. Especially when that seniority comes from Rampart."

"Rampart? Really?" Grady asked.

"Rampart district is respected down here. They train well up there. It raised Chief's eyebrows when they heard that a Rampart detective was joining the team. I have to admit. It boosted my faith in you. And you've lived up to those expectations."

Carmen's voice whispered over his shoulder again, *Just don't screw this one up, Grady.*

"Now, you're exceeding his ability. Getting in his face would likely get a fist in yours. In case you haven't noticed, he's tried to go behind your back with Dr. Glavine to get information before you."

"Yes. I know," Grady admitted.

"He didn't know I knew, though," Masters said, draining and crumpling his empty cup. He jump-shot it into the trash bin. "How did you know?"

"Dr. Glavine admitted as much." Grady finished his cup, squared up, and matched the shot. "That and I saw the signatures he left behind. For-his-eyes-only signatures. Paperwork that, if it were to reach his hands first, would never have seen the light of day otherwise. Guess he figured if he got the break, he could take over the lead?"

"Perhaps," Masters said, leaning back against the hood.

The sun eclipsed behind the horizon, and the parking lot lights took the job of illuminating the two men. A breeze brought in the coolness of the evening, and sounds from the highway hid the gravity of the moment. They both knew they needed to get moving, regardless of what Branson had been up to or if they needed a tie-breaker shot to determine who would drive to Thoran's suspected hideout.

"Ready?" Grady said, breaking the silence.

"I'll drive. You couldn't find the area with GPS and a helo spotlight," Masters said, pulling out his keys.

Grady laughed as he locked up his car. The familiar creak of Masters' Caprice door greeted him.

Grady picked up the mic. "Branson. LaCrosse. You out there?"

"We're here," said a monotone voice.

"Branson," the two men say in unison.

"Hey, Branson. What's your 20?" Grady replied.

"240. About four miles from the Gosserton exit," Branson said.

"We're at the service station just off that exit on the right. We're heading out now. We'll be about five minutes in front of you. We will radio when we reach the neighborhood."

"10-4."

Masters drove through the neighborhood at a quick pace—that *I know where I am going, I live here* pace—past the address that the cabbie said he dropped the fare at. He described her as the "hobbling grouchy missus." She paid in cash, which she produced from a wallet from the jacket she was wearing. He said he found it odd that a woman would be carrying a man's wallet, but he was getting paid, so it made no difference to him. Not his business. He also recalled that she paid too much. The fare was high for that long of a ride, but even then, she paid $40 more than needed. She got out and shut the door. No good-bye or thank you. The cabbie told Carmen he was used to rude customers, so he just left, thankful for her inattention to her payment.

"The house looks empty," Grady commented.

"Looks can be deceiving," Masters said. "We've been on teams that have entered residences that appeared emptier than that only to find four or five living inside with full drug labs. And the neighbors had no clue. So one woman on the lam could be a ghost, especially if she didn't want to be noticed."

Masters drove around the block and out of the neighborhood. He pulled into the elementary school's parking lot, and Grady informed LaCrosse of their position.

"She had to have picked that house for a reason," Masters said.

"It's too empty to be lived in. It can't be a friend. The same goes for Nelson," Grady said. He reconsidered the drug aspect that had gone flat. "Safehouse?"

"But for whom?" Masters asked.

"Well, if this entire Dr. Glavine theory has any teeth, then Thoran is Nelson, who is Tanner. Who was Tanner?" Grady asked.

Grady dialed Carmen's number.

"You got the questions; I have the answers. Go."

"Hey, Carmen. That address you gave us. It appears to be

an empty residence. Are you able to run a tenant history? The quicker, the better. We're around the corner, and we could use the information when we approach."

"It's late, but I can make a couple of calls. Maybe I can run a search or two that will pull up a history. Give me a few, and I'll get back to you."

"Thanks," Grady said and disconnected the line.

A set of headlights rounded the corner and headed their way. The elliptical nature told them it was LaCrosse and Branson. *Only Caprices had those styles of headlights,* Grady thought. *They must have done something special with those types of vehicles to tip-off drivers. They are close to the standard wraparound, but something is different about them that screamed 'po-po.'* Masters flashed them, even though they saw the same set of headlights, and LaCrosse pulled in and beside them.

"Nice evening for a stroll in the park," LaCrosse said.

"I left my parasol at home," Masters replied.

"Too bad. I brought the breadcrumbs to feed the ducks."

"We'll have to settle for possessed criminals instead."

"I can settle for that. What are we looking at?" LaCrosse asked.

"Waiting to hear back from Carmen. She's getting info on the address Thoran is holed up in," Masters explained.

Right on cue, Grady's phone chirped. Stepping out of the car, he answered the phone. "What ya got, Carmen."

"Tax records show that address belongs to Joshua Connors, 33-year-old banker. He was current until the year before last."

"Connors? Why does that name sound familiar?" Grady said, pacing the length of the vehicle.

"Let me run DMV on him. Give me one second. His record is clean. Or was clean. He's deceased. He was—oh hell—" Carmen's voice trailed off.

"What?" Grady said.

"I know why that name is familiar," Carmen said. "Joshua Connors was one of the first three victims murdered by our unidentified perp. The one we assume to be Tanner."

"He was number three. I remember now," Grady said, recalling the file.

"How in the world did she know to go there?" Carmen asked. "That murder was in Alabama."

"That's your job, tech genius. Have you come across anything linking Connors to Thoran?"

Carmen went silent. Grady could hear keyboard clicking. "He was a banker. Customer perhaps?"

"That's pretty thin. How many bankers work out of state?" Grady countered.

"Lovers? They're roughly the same age. Met at the bank, started a relationship. He died, and now she's fleeing to a safe place. A vacation home perhaps?"

"Still thin. Attacked by the same perpetrator, yes. But to be attacked by the two different unlinked perpetrators, that's tissue paper thin."

"Just throwing around ideas. I don't like to think about Dr. Glavine's idea being correct. Those scenarios creep me out," Carmen admitted.

"I hear ya. But Dr. Glavine would tell us that her coming here makes perfect sense. He'd say that Thoran knows about this place because she's been here, only not as Thoran. She was here as Stephen Tanner when Tanner murdered Joshua Connors two months ago."

The line went quiet. Grady assumed that Carmen was experiencing the shudders he was feeling. The dark spiritual was uncomfortable for Grady even to consider. His pastor never preached that part of God. His sermons usually contained the positive aspect of who God is. He would occasionally address the world as a dark place, and that evil forces existed, but Grady never saw it in a practical sense like what he was experiencing right now.

"We really don't think that's what's going on here, do we?" Carmen finally said.

"I don't know, Carmen. It's out there, but Dr. Glavine's

transference theory is the only explanation that makes sense right now. And until other evidence proves otherwise, we have to proceed with that notion and extreme caution."

"10-4. I'll see what I can pull up on that residence since Mr. Connors' passing. Oh, I have something else on Sophia Thoran. Something of use. She's a nurse. Well, a nurse's aide. So she may not be as injured as you expect her to be or in as much pain. Her job could have given her access to pain killers and the experience to mend herself up."

"Understood. Get back to us the second you hear anything more. We're standing by." Grady hung up and headed back to the car.

The door screech announced Grady's return. "You won't believe this. That house was owned by one of Tanner's victims. His name was Joshua Connors."

"I remember that name. Some sort of banker," Masters said.

"Yeah, that's the one."

"Interesting," Masters said. Grady could see him piecing together and coming to the same conclusion he and Carmen had. "I don't like the looks of this."

"Relax. There could be several reasons that Thoran knew Connors. Bankers know many people."

"But not dead bankers and those who could have killed them," Masters said.

"Carmen is looking into ties that could put them together and what has happened with the residence since Connors passing."

"As it has been my experience, no one wants to move into a home where a homicide has occurred. Chances are that the house will always be vacant. Full disclosure is the law," Masters explained with half a grin.

"Is that so? How do you know so much about housing law?"

"My apartment was the site of a double homicide. The housing authority wouldn't allow it to be rented without telling the tenant. No one wanted to rent it. I was able to negotiate it for almost half the going rate."

"Very nice. So that could be the case here. And Thoran knows this. So, she squats, knowing no one will be visiting the place anytime soon."

"What's going on over there," LaCrosse shouted over to them.

"Looks like our perp has a history with the former owner of the house she's in," Masters answered.

"Former?"

"Yeah, seems that she may have killed him too in a previous life," Masters said.

The darkness couldn't reveal the expression on LaCrosse's face. "Well, that can't be good."

Masters started his engine. "We'll pull up three houses back and approach on foot. Stay close behind and once we round the corner, cut your headlights. We don't want to tip her off. Don't take her injuries for granted. She's dangerous. We've seen the video of her taking out two of our own. Use your head and watch each other's backs. Let's go."

Masters drove out of the parking lot and around the corner back the way he had entered the community. He parked and shut off the engine as he said he would. He looked over to Grady and took a deep breath. "Ready?"

Grady echoed the statement, and both men exited the vehicle.

Chapter Twenty

Tuesday, March 3, 20:45

You two watch the front. Grady and I will cover the rear," Masters instructed.

All the blinds were drawn on the single-story home, but there were no apparent signs of security measures. Grady double-checked the gate for tripwires or motion detectors that would alert someone inside to their presence. After his hand made a second pass, Grady felt they were safe to enter the backyard.

Only a pull string and a latch protected the gate, then a narrow walkway led to a backyard that was larger than he expected. It was overgrown, but unless the tall grass swallowed whatever was there, it appeared empty. The moonlight shone through the patio trellis and cast an evil shadow. Masters, in the lead, peeked around the corner and held up a fist—*Stop*. He turned around and pointed toward the gate they entered. Both men toed their way out of the yard.

"What's up?" Grady mouthed.

"Rear sliding glass door is open," Masters whispered. "Music is playing. Soft, but you can hear it. Someone's in there. Or left the music playing when they left."

"Think they heard us?"

"Doubt it, but we need a plan," Masters said.

"10-4. Let's regroup with LaCrosse and Branson."

LaCrosse and Branson had been on the other side of the house. They had heard the music too but were hidden in a shadow cast by a neighbor's tree. "Tsk. Tsk," one of them called.

"Regroup," Masters whispered and started to pace toward their vehicles.

"What now?" LaCrosse asked when the four of them were a safe distance away.

"Well, now we know someone's there."

"Or was there," Branson said. "Just because we heard noises doesn't mean someone's in there. Could be a decoy, or they could've stepped out."

"I agree. Going in there could be a trap waiting to be sprung. Thoran is dangerous," Grady said, still wanting to try and appease Branson. Despite Branson's rudeness, he was trying to remember Nettles' reminder that no team member's suggestion goes unheard, and all ideas are open to discussion. "However, it could also be dangerous to wait because we're giving Thoran time to prepare her attack. Or time to slip away."

Branson's tight jaw revealed that he was not happy about his plan of getting under Grady's skin was not working. But for Grady, it was getting simpler to overlook Branson's jabs. In fact, since his talk with Masters, he had chosen just to let them go and let Branson deal with whatever he had to deal with. Either he would eventually accept him as an equal or get so upset he'd resign. Grady had chosen not to give it another thought. His job was to focus on solving this case and not let petty things like tension between officers take his mind off the case.

"Either way, we shouldn't be acting rashly," he retorted.

"I agree. What do you suggest?" Masters said, throwing the ball in his court.

The look on Branson's face went from contempt to confusion. The truth was he had no clue what to do. "Im just saying we can't burst in their guns blazing."

"Neither is Grady," Masters said. "How should we proceed, Detective?"

Branson looked to Grady, then to LaCrosse and Masters. "We need eyes inside the place. I don't think we should proceed without knowing if Thoran is inside or not. We also need to know her condition and whether she is armed or not."

Masters smiled. "Very good, Branson. I agree. While we know she left the hospital alone, we don't know if she's in there alone now. So far, we have signs someone may be in the home. Now we need confirmation. If it's her, we need to know her status."

"What about calling for a delivery. Pizza?" LaCrosse suggested.

"No. If she's stocked up, a delivery could spook her. She may not order delivery. Even a wrong address could spook her and could endanger the life of the driver. Can't take the risk." Masters said.

"What's behind her. On the fence line? Is it a neighbor?" Grady asked.

"Not sure."

"We may be able to get a better view of that back door and even into the room. We know the door is open. If the blinds are open or even cracked, it may be just enough to sneak a peek."

"We'll take a drive. It's most likely back-to-back. Don't think this neighborhood has alleyways," LaCrosse said, pointing to the garage, which was at the front of the house. He and Branson got into their vehicle and drove off around the corner.

"We need to move soon. Just sitting out here like this will draw the attention of a neighborhood watch if they have one. We don't need local police out here. We know what happened last time they got involved," Grady reminded.

LaCrosse drove around and returned a couple of minutes later. "No alleyway. The houses are back-to-back. And we're in luck. The house behind this one is also vacant."

"Either luck or the tenants moved out when all hell broke loose here," Masters said.

"Yeah, but either way, it's empty. We can pull up, park, and go into the backyard unnoticed."

"Okay. Head back and wait for our signal. Stay silent. Don't alert neighbors," Masters warned.

"10-4," LaCrosse said and drove off.

"Should we stay here or follow them?" Grady asked.

"I think we should stay put and let them be our eyes," Masters said.

"You approach from the right. I'll hop the fence and come in from the left?"

"Damn. I wish we had Mesa and Nettles," Masters said, starting to walk back toward the house.

"We could always call in Clarke and Ryan," Grady whispered.

"No. If Thoran isn't here, then she could be headed back to her home. Can't risk that."

"True. You ready?"

"Yeah." Masters took out his radio. "LaCrosse. Branson. You copy?"

"We're in position. I can confirm the window is open, and the blinds are partially pulled. Someone is inside. They've passed the window twice. I cannot confirm if it's Thoran."

"Understood. We're in position as well. Ready for positive ID on Thoran. Anyone else inside the residence?" Masters said.

"As far as I can tell, that's a negative. Other rooms are dark. But I can confirm our subject is female." LaCrosse said. "Although, she is moving awfully fluid for someone who's injured."

"Understood."

"Grady. Are you in position?"

"Affirmative. Just on the other side of your position."

"Remain there until we can confirm the subject is alone."

"10-4," Grady said. He wasn't feeling right about this one. Fluid movement. Alone. Maybe they received bad information. Maybe Thoran was here, but not alone. She could be knocked out from the medication, and this was a partner of hers. What would happen if Thoran got the drop on them? Grady saw the surveillance video replay in his mind again.

"Masters," Grady whispered into the radio. "Something's not right. We need to stand down."

"What are you talking about, Gradiosa?" Branson said into his radio a bit too loud. It drew a reaction from the individual inside.

The music suddenly went quiet. Even Branson realized his error.

A face appeared at the back door and looked both ways into the darkness. The dark-haired woman was in a parted silken robe. Underneath were a tank top and short shorts. Her legs revealed no evidence of recent surgery or that she was the victim of a sadistic suicidal maniac. It wasn't Sophia Thoran.

"Are you sure you have the information on the residential history accurate, Carmen?" Grady asked.

"No one lives at that address, Grady. Not since Connors' homicide. I show no record of it. The county has it up for auction in May. I see they've had it cleaned twice, and another crew is set to go through it again the last week of April. I'm looking at the order now. The house is supposed to be vacant," Carmen said.

"10-4. Thanks. Can you check for any known accomplices of Tanner or Thoran who would be about 5'9, dark hair, approximately 180?"

"Gotcha. That shouldn't take long. Give me 15 minutes. I'll run all databases."

"Thanks," Grady said and hung up.

Grady walked back to Masters' car. They had retreated to the school. The group of men was in a circle near the rear of the vehicle. Despite the darkness, Grady could see Branson's face a dark red color. Anger, embarrassment, he couldn't tell. But he remained silent. It didn't matter. His flub might have saved his and Masters' lives if Thoran was still inside the home.

Masters was the first to speak. It was the same thing that was on his mind. "Just because someone else was at that window doesn't mean Thoran isn't inside. We need a new approach. Suggestions?"

No one said a word for a while. The fact was, their cover may have been blown already. If the robe-clad lady had any sense, she would've reported what she thought she heard, and Thoran would either be long gone or on high alert. But none of them got that impression from her, so the plan was to go back.

"The wrong address pizza idea," LaCrosse said. "I know it was shot down before, but we are running low on options."

"It's too late for that now. Already going on 22:00 and a Tuesday," Masters said. "It's a decent idea, just beyond the window to use it."

"Uber driver?" Branson chimed in. "They work odd hours. Just announce it with the knock. Excuse for the knock would be a dead phone battery."

"No one here is young enough for them to believe such a notion," LaCrosse said.

"But you have the 'stache for it," Masters said, grooming his upper lip and chin. He looked over at Grady with a wink. "The Crowne Vic fits the role too."

"What? You don't like my mustache?" LaCrosse said, eyebrows raised.

"Hey. You know that I love it. It is distinguished," Masters said. "One of the reasons I keep you on this unit."

"And I thought it was my arrest record."

"Let's get moving. It's already late enough," Branson said.

"For once, I agree," Grady said with a grin, which gained an eye roll from Branson. "We can man-crush over LaCrosse's mustache when this is over."

"No one is answering," LaCrosse whispered towards the open mic he was wearing. He knocked again and shouted at the door. "Uber driver. I'm here, Mr. Furgeson."

Nothing.

"This is Jack. I'm your Uber driver, Mr. Furgeson," LaCrosse said again. "Is this 245 Laguna Way? I don't see any numbers outside?"

LaCrosse knocked again. He could see movement through the frosted glass on the door. "Stand by," he whispered. "I think someone is coming to the door."

The padlock made a click, and the handle turned. The door opened enough to allow the chain to catch. The same face that appeared at the back door peeked through the crack. "I'm sorry, sir—"

"The name's Jack," LaCrosse said with a smile.

"I'm sorry, Jack. You have the wrong address. This is 243. 245 is next door. But I think that their last name is Williams."

"Really?" LaCrosse said, pulling a folded piece of paper out of his back pocket. He pretended to read it. "Oh hell. It must be my Dyslexia. I'm looking for 542. My apologies. I didn't mean to frighten you, ma'am. I know what it's like. I have a daughter about your age who lives alone. Wouldn't want a big scary-looking man to stroll upon their house in the middle of the night."

"That's okay. No worries. Simple mistake. And I don't live alone. My husband Derrick is in the other room asleep. I don't like answering the door to strangers, but I was afraid you'd wake him up."

"Well, that's good. Again, I apologize for the confusion. I better get going. Don't want Mr. Furgeson to miss his flight. I'm late enough as it is. Good evening missus."

"Good night," she said and closed the door.

LaCrosse returned to his car and drove back around to where Masters and Grady were waiting down the block.

"Impressions?" Masters asked.

"Someone else is inside, but I don't have to tell you it's not male," LaCrosse said.

"How can you tell?"

"When she closed the door, I could hear voices. Two female. Raised whispers, could've been arguing."

"Yeah. She shouldn't have answered the door. Blew their cover," Grady suggested.

"Most likely. If anything were to happen, it would be now," LaCrosse said.

"Branson. Still have eyes on the house?" Masters said into his radio.

"10-4. No movement in front of the back door."

"Don't move from your position. If anything were to happen, we expect it at any time."

"Copy that," Branson said.

Grady pulled up a map of the area on his phone. "There aren't many ways out of here. It's all one big circle. Can we pull a couple of units to guard entry points?"

"We don't have a vehicle description. Not only that, it's an assumption that Thoran is inside the residence. This could just be a drug stash house, and they are concerned about a raid. Until we have positive ID on Thoran, we can't pull any resources," Masters said.

"Understood," Grady said. "Either way, we need to move on the house. We need to know. Sitting here is wasting time. Thoran is either in the house or out there. If she is out there, she's getting further away."

"I agree. It's time," LaCrosse said. "I have a good feeling there are only two in the house. Female. We need to move before they have the chance to prepare or call in reinforcement."

"Agreed," Masters said. He spoke to his radio, "Status report, Branson."

"No update… stand by… I see one female, the same as before. She just passed the open sliding door," Branson said. Then to himself, *C'mon girl. Where are you? Show yourself.*

"We need to move into position, just in case we need to act quickly," Grady suggested.

"LaCrosse, take a position at the front of the residence. Grady, back up LaCrosse at the side near the fence just in case she decides to jump. I"ll go around the side as before. Maintain radio silence unless you need assistance. I will give the go to move in."

All officers gave their copy, then moved in unison. Branson watched from his perch through the fence. "She's there. I see her. Thoran is there. Female with surgical padding on both legs, upper thigh region. If it's not her, serious coincidence. I'm moving in."

"Negative, Branson. Wait for backup," Masters answered.

"She's right there. Injured and harmless. I can apprehend her."

"Branson. Negative. Stand down," Masters said.

No response.

"Branson. Don't do it. Remember Mesa," Grady said. Not that his voice would calm him down.

"Branson," Masters said. "Respond."

Branson did not reply.

"What the hell were you thinking, Branson?" Masters said, walking under the crime scene tape around 245 Laguna Way.

"I had her," Branson said, allowing the paramedic to bandage the gash across his arm.

"You're damn lucky to be alive," Masters said.

"Did we get the accomplice?" Branson asked.

"Yes. LaCrosse is taking her to headquarters now."

"Take me there too. I want to be there for interrogation."

"Hell no. You're going to the hospital. Then you are taking a leave of absence," Masters said.

"What for?" Branson said, drawing the attention of the second EMS attendee.

"Do I need to make a list?"

"Because I'm doing my job?"

"Oh, come on, Daryl, you know why you did what you did. This is about Grady, not the job. You've been on him from day one. All you want to do is get the better of him. Even if it means placing yourself in danger. You thought if you were to arrest Thoran, it would give you the one up on Grady. Just like you thought telling Glavine only to contact you with the information on Nelson's vehicle—"

"I didn't—"

"Don't bother lying to me," Masters said. "I've known you too long. I know how you work. You put your life in danger tonight. You put your whole team in danger."

Branson broke eye contact.

"So now you need to think about that. I hate to put you on the bench over this because we need you. You're an important part of our team. But after tonight, you're more of a liability than an asset. Once you get over your big head and can work as a team again, give me a call. No! You know what, give *Grady* a call. *He* is the lead on this case. You call *him* and tell him you are ready to work again. Now go to the hospital and have that arm looked at."

Masters stepped out of the ambulance. The EMS attendee shut the doors and drove off.

Chapter Twenty-One

Wednesday, March 4, 10:45

"Clarke and Ryan are back on duty watching Thoran's residence. We had a blue and white on the house overnight. They and security patrol watched the area until relief arrived," Grady informed what was left of the team. "We have no word on where Thoran could be. She fled on foot. With her hobble, she couldn't have gotten far."

"So, you believe she's still in the Gosserton area?" Masters asked.

"That neighborhood is a loop cut off in a loop," Grady said. "It would be difficult to get out of there without a ride. We should consider the possibility of her still being in the neighborhood."

"I can look into other vacant residences in the area," Carmen said. "We could also go door to door. Check with the neighborhood watch."

"We need to talk to *Mrs. Derrick*. Maybe she has information. She's looking at 10 to 20 for drug possession and intent to distribute with what we found in that home," LaCrosse said. "Cut a deal. Maybe she'll sing."

"Where is she now?" Grady asked.

"Central holding. If she hasn't been arraigned on the drug charges yet. We'll have to speak to Atwood," Masters said. "Our guest claims she doesn't know who Thoran is. That they always get people passing through who need somewhere to lay low for a few days. And hiding out always comes with a *no questions asked* policy. She says it's better that way. Stay out of a person's business, and you don't have to answer questions later."

"Seems like a decent policy amongst thieves," Carmen said. "Don't ask. Don't tell. No responsibilities later."

"Do you believe her?" LaCrosse asked.

"Yeah. Makes sense." Masters said.

"No honor amongst thieves," Grady said. "Stick to yourself and don't ask questions. Untrustworthy. So, mind your own business, and I'll leave you alone to yours."

"Maybe she saw something, though. Certainly the scars raised questions that prompted discussion. Women do talk," Carmen said.

"You're forgetting," Grady said, "Thoran may not be Thoran. She may be Tanner. Tanner was a male."

"Ugh. I keep forgetting that part. I'm hating this case more and more by the minute," Carmen said, rubbing her temple.

"Talk to *Mrs. Derrick*, her legal name is Mandy Romano. And no, there is no, Mr. Romano," Grady said, handing LaCrosse the file.

"Got it. I'm heading down now," LaCrosse said.

"Just watch your back, LaCrosse. We've taken too many chances on this case already."

"10-4, boss." LaCrosse buzzed the gate and headed downstairs.

Surprised, muffled voices came from the stairs, and one of them was female. The gate buzzed again. The unintelligible voice belonged to Nettles. She was dressed and ready for work. Smiling like her old self but with a minor hobble, only slightly the worse for wear. "I heard you could use an extra set of hands."

Masters' eyes squinted and looked Nettles over. "You up to it, kid?"

"More than you know, boss," Nettles said.

"Then let's get to it. You'll need to be brought up to speed. Grady can do that. I just need to make a couple of calls." Masters headed toward his office, then paused. "We're glad to have you back, Nettles. Don't overexert yourself, please. We know you just came through major surgery and an equally exhausting ordeal."

"I'm okay, boss. Really, I am. I can't sit in a hospital room and do nothing. I feel fine. Great even. I'm better to you on the street, catching this perp," Nettles said.

Masters grinned with pride. "Glad to have you back." He slapped her on the shoulder and continued to his office.

"He blames himself," Grady said.

"I know," she said, looking toward the office door, then to Grady. "So do you. Stop it. You made the right decision sending us to guard Thoran. We were doing our job, Grady. There was no way either of you could have seen this coming. So whatever self-loathing you are feeling, knock it off, alright?"

"Yes, ma'am," Grady said. Seeing Nettles alive and well had eased his *self-loathing*, as she had put it. He would have to live with Mesa's loss but seeing her standing there, with her grin and the same attitude she always had, gave him some relief and a boost of confidence in the case. "I'm relieved you came through this."

"Docs say another centimeter, and I would've been a goner. I'm glad I have good peripheral vision. I saw her coming and was able to react. Looks like it saved my life."

"Yeah," Grady said, his mind slipping back to Mesa. He was glad Mesa didn't have a wife and kids. They wouldn't have to experience the dreaded sidewalk walk. Masters had already made the long-distance call. Next of kin notification was always complicated.

Nettles must have noticed his uncomfortable stare into space. She quickly changed the subject. "So what's our next step, Grady? What are we looking for?"

Grady took a deep breath and picked up the papers in front of him. Grady explained all that had occurred since Thoran's attack, from escaping in civilian clothes to attacking Branson the evening before. "Branson is alright. Just a deep gash to his arm and a bruised ego. He's in recovery on the sidelines until he heals. Now that you're up to speed, let's talk with Carmen. We'll see if she has found anything on Thoran's location.

"Okay, Carmen. Status report."

"Good to have you back, Nettles. Not much difference, Grady," Carmen said. "We still need to find out if Thoran made it out of the community. LaCrosse is on his way down to interview Mandy Romano to see if she's willing to talk about Thoran. Ryan and Clarke are still on Thoran's former residence. We also have a blue and white at Laguna Way. No activity at either location."

"Thanks. We should head out and take a look at Laguna Way. It was the last place Thoran was at. She left in a hurry. Perhaps she left clues behind," Grady said, then to Nettles, "You up for some fieldwork?"

"You know it," Nettles said. "I need my piece and shield."

"Masters' office," Carmen said. "Should still be on his desk."

"10-4," Nettles disappeared into the office.

"You think she's ready?" Grady asked, second-guessing himself.

"Hell yeah," Carmen said. "Don't let her size or experience fool you. She is ten times stronger than you would think. Her being here should tell you something. If Masters trusts her, so should you. Remember your journey, Grady. She has been through it too. Give her the courtesy that you want to be given. That's all she wants right now."

"Understood," Grady said with a nod. "I should've known. If Nettles wasn't ready to be back, Masters would've shut her down when he was here."

"Now you're using your head. You get your gold star, Detective."

Nettles returned with watery eyes; her badge wasn't the only one she found on Masters' desk. "Let's get going, Grady. We have a case to solve."

Grady grabbed his keys and caught up to Nettles at the gate.

"Where to first?" Grady asked, more as a tension breaker.

"You said we should hit Laguna Way since it would carry more clues," Nettles said.

"Right. You up for driving. I know you still have a little bit of a limp," Grady said, feeling guilty and like an imbecile the moment he said it.

"I drove down here. I'm good to go, Grady. I took a cab to my place, showered, changed, then drove my personal vehicle here. I'm fine. Treat me like a baby again, and I'll have to kick your ass the way I would Mesa when he challenged me. I'm not your little sister or an invalid." The tight jaw and narrow eyes said it all. She was ready, and he better not question her ability again.

"Got it. So, am I driving, or do you want the wheel?" Grady said, holding up the keys, not sure if she had agreed to or not.

"You are senior officer, Detective. I drive," Nettle said with an outstretched hand.

"Just make sure we get there in one piece. I've heard a thing or two about your driving," Grady said, holding the key back for a second.

"Oh please, that was one time. And I can't believe Mesa told you about that," Nettles said, swiping the keys from Grady's hand.

"Just making sure—*Nitrous Nettles*."

That drew a laugh as they settled into Grady's cruiser. Grady could see why Mesa enjoyed riding with her. She was pleasant and infectious. It reminded him how much he missed Elizabeth. With what happened with Thoran and the hours he was pulling, he had few opportunities to spend with her. Last night he crashed the minute he got home. They barely shared two words and a kiss. It wasn't so much a lack of desire to spend time with her but the inability to keep his eyes open. The grateful thing was that she understood his job's demand. She had accepted it long ago.

"Where to, boss?" Nettles asked, snapping Grady from his daze.

"Out of the lot and take a left. Then out to Gosserton. Jump on 16, then 516, and head South to the Parkway. Unless you know of a faster way."

"10-4," Nettles said. "About as good a route as any."

Grady watched her as she turned the wheel and pulled out of the lot. If she was in pain, she was doing an excellent job of hiding it. He was satisfied.

"You can ask questions. I'm okay now," Nettles said.

"What?" Grady asked. She must have felt his stare. "I don't want to pry."

"I almost died, Grady. Yes, I know. But I'm fine, really. The doctors wouldn't have let me leave the hospital if I weren't. Okay, I'll be honest, they did say to take it easy, but I can't do that with so much left to be done. I want to get this bastard just as much as anyone. Probably more, especially after Mesa."

"But we can handle that. If you were to get hurt again, we, especially Masters, would be more upset than he already is," Grady said.

"I realize that, but it isn't his call. I'm part of this team. Mesa's death affected us all, and being on the sidelines is not an option. I know you've only been with us a short time, but would you want to sit this one out?"

"I guess not," Grady said.

Nettles was right. He would want to storm the castle just as she did. Who was he to try and stop her? At the same time, he would have her back all the same.

"Nettles, I want to ask you another question. It's a bit personal," Grady said, thinking back to what had been bothering him watching the videos.

"Let me guess. Do I know Christ? What's the condition of my soul?" Nettles asked in a deepening voice.

The subject surprised Grady. He had never heard her mention religion but was grateful that she mentioned it instead of him.

"Yes. How did you know I was going to ask that?"

"It's no secret that you're a Christian, Grady. We all know it. And we respect it. Truth is, we all are kinda surprised that you aren't more open about it. Mesa and I talked about it all the time. Meaning you aren't in our faces telling us that we need to *turn or burn*. It's no wonder that you would feel a need to bring it up now that *life* has been the subject matter."

"And are you?"

"Yes. I'm a Christian. I'm not active, but I go now and then.

Work keeps me pretty busy, as you well know. But I go when I can."

Grady wanted to ask about Mesa but felt it would be crossing a line and bringing up a tough subject if that answer were to be *no*.

"That's good to hear," Grady said and let the subject end there. They drove a bit more in silence. When they hit the highway, Grady flipped on the radio. "What do you like?"

"Whatever, I'm not picky."

Grady, wanting to lighten the mood, rolled the station over to a heavy metal station and left it there for a moment. It did the trick.

Nettles smiled. "Okay, not that open-minded," she shouted over the noise.

Grady laughed. He switched it over to a less screechy guitar and drum-driven station that made them both happy, and the conversation moved into the music genre they grew up with. As Grady expected, Nettles preferred a pop-rock style of music being a child of the '00s. Grady was more of a '90s rock fanatic. They met in the middle of liking some older '70s and '80s music. She even knew many of the Christian bands that Grady mentioned.

Grady learned that Nettles was from South Carolina and was supposed to go back after college but joined the SPD instead. She had initially attended school to study Criminology in hopes of one day becoming a lawyer, but her mindset changed after a recruiter visited her campus. "I soon envisioned myself in uniform, making a difference in the field. So, I took the field tests, passed, and went off to the academy," Nettles explained.

"How did you end up under Masters," Grady asked.

"Ha! That's another story in itself," Nettles said. "Let's say that I made a name for myself in the field. Somehow I came to Masters' attention, and within a year, I was upstairs as a detective."

"That must be some story to impress Masters. I hear he is unimpressible," Grady said.

"You must not be too shabby yourself," Nettles said. "You come from Rampart. They don't promote too easily up there, I hear. To carry a detective badge there means something. Much less a senior detective badge."

"That's what they keep telling me," Grady said.

"Well, that makes both of us special then. Both of us have impressed Masters to a point where he holds us in high regard. Let's not let him down. We need to find Thoran again. Hopefully, we will find some clues at Gosserton," Nettles said.

"I hope you're right. If history tells us anything, it won't be long before Thoran begins her cycle. We're almost five days into the month. We already know that her fourth victim won't be until April 1st, the next quarter moon. She still has her cycle of murders to complete between now and then, all in 27 days. She must already be searching for victim one, but we have no idea of who or where. Our only way of stopping her is to find her."

Chapter Twenty-Two

Wednesday, March 4, 16:30

C'mon, Sarge. When will I get to see Ms. Romano? It's been two hours. How long does it take a couple of blues to bring her from Central Holding?" LaCrosse sat in an office area behind Atwood's desk. Usually, anyone waiting for anything from the Desk Sergeant would be sitting on the lobby hardwoods. He was uncomfortable but grateful to be granted the privilege of a desk chair.

"Losing your patience, Detective?" Atwood said, not looking up from the front desk where she was perched. She scribbled on a document in front of her. "I can always downgrade your accommodations."

LaCrosse grunted; Atwood grinned.

"Are you still upset I beat you at poker last time we played?"

Atwood put down her pen and swivel her chair around to face LaCrosse. "If I were still upset, you'd be waiting for Ms. Romano in holding. The lobby benches would be too good for you. I got over that weeks ago. Even if I were still upset that you cheated your way to that full house."

LaCrosse raised his hands with a smile. "I stand corrected. My bad. Or should I say, your bad, *bad beat*, that is?"

Atwood threw a pad of sticky notes at him. "I just can't with you, Detective."

"Detective, now is it?" LaCrosse said. "Can't call me by my name in the office?"

Atwood looked around. The couple sitting in the lobby waiting for their son's release for Drunk and Disorderly was keeping to themselves. One officer was texting, but he was off to the side near the hallway side exit. Another officer was by the outer door, but she didn't seem interested in entering the building at the moment. Atwood looked back. "What difference does it make if I address you by your given name? We're in the squad room anyhow. It's how it should be."

"Gotcha, Laurie," LaCrosse said, with a smile and corner mustache raise.

Laurie Atwood blushed. "Stop it." She looked around. "Quit it. Okay, Antony."

Antony LaCrosse sat back in his chair, extended his legs with his arms behind his head. "Now was that so hard, Laurie?"

"No, I suppose, it wasn't," she said, then the smile just as soon vanished. "Now that will be enough, or you'll be evicted from my office. Is that clear, Detective?"

"Yes, Sarge," LaCrosse said. "So, where is my perp?"

Atwood rolled her eyes as the front doors opened, and two officers walked in with a brown-haired female in her late 20s in a tan jumpsuit between them. "Here's your friend now," she said to LaCrosse, then to the two officers, "Interview Room Two."

"Understood," said the one on the left. She nodded, and the other officer followed directions, the two disappearing down the hall.

"Let them get her situated, and then you may speak with her," Atwood said.

"I won't be long. I just have a few routine questions. Chances are, she knows nothing. But with a little bit of luck, Thoran got cocky and revealed a thing or two," LaCrosse shrugged.

"Well, she wasn't in too much of a talking mood when she came in earlier. It took running her prints to get a name. Even then, she didn't confirm her identity."

"I guess she has been processed then. Already at Belton?"

"Huh? Oh, the suit. No. Officers brought her in wearing only a T-shirt and short shorts. I couldn't let her parade around in that.

We had a couple of jumpsuits, so I let her change into one. She hasn't been processed yet. We still have her in holding. Masters said to keep her here because she could be the key to finding Thoran. But he needs to be reminded of due process." Atwood exhaled and looked at LaCrosse. Her earlier jollier demeanor now serious. "We have to begin the process of filing these drug charges against her. I'm skating on thin ice for his behind, again. You tell him that. Suppose Lawson gets wind of this? It'll be *my* ass, not his. And I won't cover for him again. Not when it comes to the Cap."

"Alright, alright," LaCrosse said, again raising his hands. "I'll tell him. I'm sure he knows. In fact, I'm sure things will be resolved after I speak with Romano. I'll let you know after my interview."

The two officers came back into the lobby. "Where can we wait?"

"Squad room." Atwood thumbed to her left. "Follow the hall here. It will turn to the right. Second open door on the left. You can't miss it. There are a couple of vending machines and coffee there."

"Copy that," the female officer said and nodded the other officer in that direction as she had done earlier. "Just let us know when you're through."

"There is a phone with an intercom there. I'll page you when Detective LaCrosse is done with his interview."

"Thank you," the female officer said, and they exited.

"Well, I better get over to Ms. Romano before—" then he stopped mid-step. "You said she kept quiet. Didn't say a word."

"Yeah," Atwood said.

"Where was she?"

"Here for a bit. But she was taken to Central Holding not too long after."

"She didn't say a word here?"

"Not a peep."

"Hmm," LaCrosse said, sitting down in a chair behind Atwood.

He grabbed a magazine that was on the corner of Atwood's desk and began thumbing through it.

"Don't you have a customer to attend to?"

"In a moment. In a moment. Gonna let her stew for a moment." LaCrosse looked up at the AC vent. "Where is that controlled?"

"That one? My office."

"And the one for the holding rooms?"

"Not sure. I know there is a control panel in the hall between Holding One and Two," Atwood said, then grinned. "You planning to sweat her out?"

"Maybe not sweat, but for sure making her uncomfortable," LaCrosse said. He set the magazine down and walked the hallway, disappearing around the corner. He was gone for a few seconds, then returned to the room. "You said that she was silent. The point is to get her talking. Even if it is swearing at me to cool the room down, that's talking. A talking person is easier to deal with."

"Not bad, Detective. I can see why Masters keeps you around," Atwood said.

"That and my good looks," LaCrosse raised his eyebrows and winked. He looked at his watch. "Ten minutes should about do."

"What did you set it at?"

"Eighty."

"Heavens, LaCrosse. I hope that vent doesn't go into Caps office."

LaCrosse looked down the hall, then up to the ceiling, "He's on the second floor. I doubt it."

"For your sake, I hope not. If I'm not sticking up for Masters, I sure as heck don't have your back."

LaCrosse laughed and checked his watch. He picked up the magazine again. "You would think you'd have better material for a guy to read, Sarge." He thumbed through it for several minutes and tossed it back on the desk after a couple of sections.

"I'm remodeling my kitchen, if you don't mind."

"Okay. It's about time." LaCrosse stood and removed his jacket.

"Won't be needing this. Okay. Wish me luck." He smiled again and headed down the hall.

LaCrosse entered the adjoining viewing room. Romano was sitting with her cuffed hands folded and attached to the table in front of her. Her face was contorted, and sweat was evident along her dark hairline. He never got a look at her earlier. She was not an unattractive woman. Not the typical junkie who was thinner than a pencil with beady eyes that shifted everywhere. Romano had a rather calm demeanor, other than the sweat beads and stains forming on her forehead and shirt.

LaCrosse stood and watched, studying her for clues that would give him an idea of what could break her.

Romano licked her lips. That was her first mistake. She was thirsty.

LaCrosse looked over at a small fridge that was in the corner of the viewing room. He opened it, and there were a few bottles of water with names written on them. He chuckled at the possessiveness of some people. *Guess folks aren't that into sharing.* He grabbed two of them without a second thought and shut the door.

He studied her for a few more moments, seeing if she would give away any other secrets. Romano began shifting in her seat. LaCrosse smiled. That was the sign he was looking for. She wanted out of that room. Now was the time to strike. He opened the file and gave it a once-over. "Here we go."

LaCrosse opened the door to the holding room, and Romano jumped.

"Oh, I'm sorry, Ms. Romano. I didn't mean to startle you. I'm Detective LaCrosse," he said, sitting in the chair across from her. He placed the water bottles on the edge of the table but out of her reach. Then he sat and opened the file and began to look it over like he had not read it before.

"Mandy Romano. Age 24. You are from Houston. Hmm. That's

a nice city. I've been there a couple of times. Great baseball team. Altuve is a decent player." LaCrosse lowered the file. "Do you like baseball?"

Mandy Romano was trying to keep her eyes focused. But her sweat was making it difficult. It was now dripping down her cheeks and to her top making spots. She didn't reply.

"Not a baseball fan?" LaCrosse said. "Well, that's okay. Let's move on." He raised the file. "The file says that you've lived a few places since Texas. St. Louis, Nashville, Knoxville, Tallahassee, back to Ft. Worth, then here. Seems you've been all over the South, haven't you, Ms. Romano?" He lowered the file again but caught her eyes looking up to him from the water bottles.

No response.

"I can help you, Ms. Romano. Mandy. Can I call you Mandy?"

Her eyes didn't leave his. But he could see she was suffering.

LaCrosse looked up to the ceiling. Then around the room. "Man, it's warm in here. I'm sorry, I didn't realize how bad it was. Are you hot?"

Mandy said nothing. She wanted to. She licked her lips again. And quickly realized she shouldn't have.

"Are you thirsty?" LaCrosse said. "I have a couple of water bottles here. You can have one if you'd like."

Mandy's eyes shifted to the water bottles as a sweat bead dropped to the table.

"All you have to do is ask," LaCrosse said.

"C-c-can I have one, p-p-please?" Mandy said.

"Of course," LaCrosse said. He picked up a bottle and put it in front of her, then made a face. "Oh, hell. What am I thinking? That won't do." He reached in his pocket, pulled out a set of keys, and unlocked the cuff on her wrist. He reattached it to her wrist after it was free of the table's hook.

Mandy took the bottle, opened it, and emptied the bottle in one drink.

"Better?"

Mandy nodded.

"Now, let's see what we can do about the heat," LaCrosse opened the door and looked both ways, and hollered to no one about the temperature situation. He needed to keep something in his favor. Then re-entered the room.

"Let's hope they can get whatever is broken fixed. Because I don't want to be in here anymore than you do." LaCrosse had learned a couple of things in this type of situation. The first was to give them something they wanted. *Water—Done.* The second was to put himself in the same situation as the offender if he want to gain their trust. "But I have a job to do, and they won't let me out of here until I do my job. So, we are both stuck in this sweatbox until we both accomplish what I was sent in here to do. Whether they send us air or not."

Mandy nodded.

That's a good sign. She's communicating.

"Okay," LaCrosse looked at the file again, then set it down. "So, Do you like the Astros?"

Mandy's eyes went narrow with confusion for a second, then she caught up and smiled. "No. I don't like baseball. I don't even know who, Altoovah is."

LaCrosse laughed. "Altuve. Great, see we're communicating. And which city did you like best of those you've lived in?"

Mandy's eyes glossed over in thought. "It's not so much of *which* city as so much of just being."

"How do you mean?"

"I'm a traveler," Mandy began, slow at first, but her speech picked up its cadence. "As your little booklet on my life tells you, Detective. I move around a lot. I work here and there. I do jobs for people, and then I move on."

"Jobs. Like drugs."

Mandy's face puckered with a shoulder shrug. "If that's what it takes. I can't stand the stuff, nor do I touch it. I like having control of my brain. But if selling it is what it takes to get me to the next place, I'll do it. I tell you, though. It pays well." Mandy grinned.

"They don't get mad when you leave?"

"Eh. Now that I'm in here, perhaps. But these guys are small time. Pot mostly. But don't think I'm going to tell you anything about their business. I value my life. Small doesn't mean they can't get to me."

"They aren't who we are interested in," LaCrosse said, seeing his opening.

"What is that supposed to mean," Mandy said, eyebrows raised. "What, the scared chick?"

"Yes. What's her story?"

Mandy puckered again and shrugged, "Not really sure. She shows up one night, and as I said before, people are wanderers. It's really sort of a safe house. People come in and lay low for a bit and then move on. No questions asked. I don't know if these travelers pay my bosses for their hospitality; that's their business. I just keep the house tidy and the deliveries coming in and going out."

"She didn't say anything to you. At all?"

"Nope," Mandy shook her head. But not with complete confidence.

"Not a word about where she had been or what she was up to?"

"Nada," again not meeting LaCrosse's eyes.

"You didn't ask her about her scars?"

Mandy was silent for a moment. LaCrosse could see that she was trying to remember how to answer correctly.

"This is important. Lives are at stake here, Mandy."

She looked up and exhaled. "She did mention that she recently had surgery. But she didn't go into much detail about it. I know better than to pry into details or to ask a bunch of questions. Criminals don't react well to questions. They either think you are interested or a narc. I don't need either."

"I see," LaCrosse said. "I heard you arguing with her after I left. What was that about."

"She was pissed that I answered the door. When you kept knocking, she went upstairs to get a better look around the neighborhood to see if there was anyone else around. I knew you weren't who you said you were. You reeked *the law*. But I told her the story you gave me. But she was so wound up, I figured if she had answered, you'd be dead."

"So, you did get bad vibes from her?" LaCrosse asked.

"I suppose," Mandy looked down at the empty water bottle in her hands. She began to roll it around. "There was something not right about her."

"Like what?"

"I don't know." Mandy shifted in her seat. "I can't explain it. I've seen criminals before. But she was different. She went lit when I heard the first noise in the backyard. Was that you guys as well?"

"Yes. That was us," LaCrosse admitted.

"I knew something was up. I guess she sensed it too." Mandy put the water bottle down—it was making crackling noises and increasing her tension. "It was making her uneasy. Her…"

"What?"

Mandy shifted again and shook her head. "I can't explain it. It's too weird."

"Explain it in your own words." LaCrosse pushed the other water bottle in front of her.

Mandy took it, slowly unscrewed the top, and took a sip.

"It was not so much what she said but how she said it."

"Go on."

"It wasn't Sophie anymore," Mandy stopped speaking, and took another sip. She looked into the distance.

"Keep going."

"Her voice became deeper. Like a man. Not demonic or any-thing. But like she was another person." Mandy shook her head. "Like I said, I don't know what I was hearing. She had been smoking that night. Maybe she was smoking some weird blunt, and I got a whiff of it and was hallucinating. I don't know."

LaCrosse figured now would be the time to go in for the kill, "Did she say anything to you about where she was going?"

"No. In fact, I didn't even know she had left until you guys came back and tore the door off the place," Mandy rolled her eyes. "My employers are going to love that one. Guess I'm out of a job and not getting my last paycheck."

"You aren't worried about where you're going now?"

"Not really. I don't have a criminal past. This is my first offense. Not that I was doing anything wrong. I never touched or sold the stuff. I was basically a house sitter. I figure I'll see a judge and walk after arraignment," Mandy said. "The only thing I have to worry about is getting out of town before my current employer finds me. That's if he chooses to place the blame on me. If not, I'm free either way."

"If you don't have a past, then why the stone wall?"

"If I had told you from the get-go that I was innocent, what would you have said?"

"I would've called you a liar and thrown the book at you."

"Exactly. So I chose to remain quiet and let you do the work at finding out who I am. Then you can draw your own conclusions based on the facts."

"One more question. Did Tanner, I'm sorry, Sophie ever mention the name Stephen Tanner or Stuart Nelson to you?"

"No. No, I don't think she did."

"What about in the other voice you heard?" LaCrosse asked, hoping for some sort of reaction.

"While it did sound like a male voice, it never said or used a name. I'm sorry."

"That's okay," LaCrosse consoled.

""Wait. The smoke rings. Those crazy smoke rings. Remember when I told you about her getting upset and the voice. That night she began looking through the drawers. She found a pack of cigarettes and lit one. Then she sat at the kitchen counter smoking. That's when she exhaled and growled like a man; she took a deep drag and blew smoke rings in the air. I don't know if that helps any. But you said anything unusual I could remember."

"I'll take note of it," LaCrosse said and added it to his file. "Thank you for your help, Mandy. I'll see you are taken back to Central for your arraignment."

Chapter Twenty-Three

Thursday, March 5, 10:15

Grady and Nettles compared notes from their trip to Gosserton. The Laguna Way home had been well processed and carried no new information they didn't already know. The three hours they spent there only rewarded them with a few new gauze wrappers and the knowledge that someone in the home liked Tic Tacs.

During their previous search, they discovered the runners hiding spaces and cubby-holes—some were occupied, most were empty. The less they found, the better off Mandy Romano would be in court and less of a target on the drug runner radar. Still, finding product allowed charges to be filed and made Mandy Romano a patsy if the judge saw it fit to do so. With her clean record, it was all dependent on the judge's mood that morning.

To her luck, Judge Dean believed in second chances. He looked over the case and the notes provided by the well-respected Detective LaCrosse that stated she was not a threat and should be treated with leniency. The judge called the case, read the notes, asked Mandy Romano a couple of questions about her future, then released her without bail; own recognizance. She would have to appear at a hearing in a couple of weeks to dismiss the case against her. Of course, if she were to commit another crime, then that would void everything. Miss Romano agreed and was released a couple of hours later.

After the morning roll call, Grady called down to evidence and inquired about what they had pulled out of the home and found they had confiscated all the clothing. He arranged for Romano's items to be brought up to the office.

The office gate buzzed, and LaCrosse entered the floor. "Mornin' team."

"LaCrosse. I made arrangements for Romano's personal effects to be brought out of holding. I think she's being released today. It would be a shame to have just a t-shirt and shorts and nowhere to live. At least she can have her clothing."

"Cash she has," LaCrosse said. "It was her personal items that were lost. Thank you."

"I only found clothing. If she had anything of value, she would have to file a petition to get any of that back."

"Understood. Thanks, Grady," LaCrosse said and sat at his desk. "Where's the boss?"

"Not in yet."

"Branson?"

Grady shot a *you-know-the-answer* look at him.

"Right. Right. Forget I asked."

The gate buzzed, and Masters entered with two flats of coffee. "Get it while it's hot, ladies and gentlemen. We have a lot to get done."

"I see you've been busy, boss," LaCrosse said.

"We both have," Masters said, nodding over to Carmen, who was clicking away on her keyboard. "Not all of us have the luxury of getting 12 hours sleep."

"Hey, it was only ten last night," LaCrosse said, throwing a paperclip at Carmen. "I had to shower."

"You wouldn't know it," Grady said with a cringed grin.

"Ahhh," Carmen said. "Newbie is getting comfortable."

LaCrosse took a step toward Grady and lifted his fists. "You wants some of this?"

Grady took a defensive posture, raising his fists."I can take you, old man."

After another step, LaCrosse raised his hands higher and pulled Grady into his armpit. "Smell it! It's clean, I tell you."

"Alright, Alright. We have a vanishing villain to find. LaCrosse's bathing habits can wait," Masters said, heading to Carmen's station with a cup in his hand. "What do we know, Carmen?"

She accepted it and began drinking. "I still haven't picked up any video surveillance of Sophia leaving the area. If she got out on foot, we didn't pick it up. Doesn't mean she didn't get out in a vehicle. There were too many of those to count and no way of tracking any of them.

"I searched for homes in the area that were vacant or in a similar situation to the Laguna Way location. You would be surprised how many homes are in foreclosure or some sort of legal status over estate holdings."

"Couldn't be too many in this small area," Grady said, retucking his shirt as he and LaCrosse joined them.

"Eight."

"Eight in Gosserton?" Masters asked.

"Yes. I double-checked. Where I lucked out was that only five of them are vacant. One of them is ours. That leaves us with four possibilities if Thoran is shopping for a vacant hideout in the area matching the same criteria as what she came from. If we expand to just vacant homes, then we move into two dozen homes."

"That's *if* she stayed. We could be spinning our wheels if she's left the area," LaCrosse said.

The gate behind them buzzed. "If? Now, who is sounding like Branson," Nettles said, entering the floor.

"Shut it, rookie. I can still put you in your place. Just ask Grady here."

"Hey now." Both Grady and Nettles laughed.

"So, what's the plan with checking all those addresses and not stumbling upon her by accident and end up getting dead?" Grady asked.

"That's the problem. We can't," Masters said.

"So, what? We wait and see? Wait for Thoran to expose herself and be ready to make the arrest?" LaCrosse speculated.

"We know it isn't that simple," Masters said.

"So, what *is* the plan?" LaCrosse said.

"What we need to know is where she plans to go next," Nettles said. "Have we uncovered any patterns to the type of victims?"

"All ages. Both sexes. No specific demographic, social, or economic status. The individuals have been random in all ways," Grady said, thumbing the file folders.

Grady ran down each case, beginning with Tanner's first alleged victim. He highlighted name, age, and other features, ending with Thoran. "As you can see, every one of them is different. They share nothing other than they all have this case in common."

"Wait," said Nettles. "What are the names of the survivors again. Those who go on to continue the pattern?"

"It began with Stephen Tanner, then to Stuart Nelson. Now we're dealing with Sophia Thoran," Grady said.

"Woah," Nettles said.

"That's interesting," LaCrosse said. "Their names are similar. "Initials are close. S and T. Just no 'T' in Nelson."

"Get this," Grady said. "Stuart Nelson's middle name is Taylor."

"So, we have three separate cases of murderers, all with similar initials?" Nettles asked.

"Stephen Allen Tanner, Stuart Taylor Nelson, and Sophia Anne Thoran. Not quite. But we're close. We have taken a bigger step in the right direction," Grady said.

"There is just one problem," Masters said. "While this is good info, it only helps us with the fourth victim. It does nothing for the three victims between now and then. As far as we know, they have no connection to the alphabet or names. We need to figure out a way to help them right now. It's a great job, but how will it help us find who victim one is for Thoran?"

The buzzer sounded, and everyone turned in unison toward the gate. Branson shut the gate slowly. He was in plain clothes, even more plain than he would be a detective's uniform. His head was low, and his eyes were everywhere but meeting anyone in the room. He stopped short with his hands folded behind him and looked up to Grady. "Can we talk?"

"Sure," Grady said, nodding to Master's office.

His head still ducked, looking like a punished dog, Branson disappeared into the office.

Masters shrugged, and everyone else went back to work as if nothing happened. *Wise choice,* he thought. Grady stopped at the door and looked back at Masters, who dustpan-waived him into the room and mouthed, "Go ahead."

Grady entered Masters' office and closed the door behind him. Branson was looking up at the map Grady had created. It had a couple of dozen pins with labels marking event locations throughout the city.

"How's the arm?" Grady asked.

"Healing," Branson said, lifting his arm showing the scar.

"Glad you're okay."

"Thanks," Branson said. He turned his head, noticing the map. He walked to it, following each point, putting his finger on the location where Dale's car was located. "You did all this?"

"Yeah. Each pin marks a location of significance. The colors differentiate what's going on. Blues are where we have current activity. Whites—"

"You're a good detective, Grady," Branson interrupted. He wasn't there to talk push pins.

"Thank you, Branson," Grady said.

"I want to apologize for what I've done. You didn't deserve me treating you the way I did."

"I accept your apology."

"If I had known how serious this case was going to turn out, I wouldn't have acted the way I did. You must understand that. I never meant to hurt anyone."

"I understand."

"Now our suspect has gotten away because of my stupidity. Mesa's killer is still out there, and it's my fault. I need to rectify that, and you're the best officer to lead us in getting that done." Branson turned and extended his hand. Grady accepted it.

There was a knock at the door, and LaCrosse called out, "You two done making out in there? We have a case to solve."

Branson laughed. Grady was sure it was the first time he had heard him do that, much less seen a smile on his face. "Let's get with Carmen and bring you up to speed."

It didn't take long for Grady and Carmen to take Branson through the new file additions. They had been at a standstill for the last 48 hours. The only real progress was LaCrosse's interview with Mandy Romano. LaCrosse had discussed it with the team that morning and mentioned the strange voice Thoran used with Romano. Grady was reviewing the file when he read the notes LaCrosse had made at the bottom of the file. *Ms. Thoran blew smoke rings into the air—'*

Grady stood from his chair, "What the—LaCrosse!"

LaCrosse came out of Masters' office. "What?"

"What is this about smoke circles in your notes?" Grady said, handing LaCrosse the file. "You never said anything about Thoran smoking?"

"Mandy Romano stated that Thoran lit up a smoke that night. She sat at their kitchen table and blew rings into the air. So, what's the big deal?"

Masters must've heard because he hollered from his office, "Because we know of a dead criminal who did just that before he took four in the chest from Clarke and Ryan."

"You mean undead criminal," Grady said. "Or rather transferred undead dead criminal. Transferred into Nelson. Who may now be in Thoran."

Carmen shook her head and rubbed her temple. "Have I ever told you guys how much I am hating this case?"

"We have an idea," Masters said from his office.

"We need to find Thoran," Grady said.

The gate buzzed. It was Atwood. "You say you're looking for Thoran?" she said as the gate closed behind her.

"Yeah. You have a beat on her?" Grady asked.

"You're not going to like it." Atwood handed him an index card with a handwritten address.

"We have a case?" Grady handed it to Masters, who had come out of his office.

"A body?" Masters asked.

"Yes. Just received a call-in about a body. It matches the description of our previous bodies. I'm sorry."

"Where?"

"Port Wendle. Northeast, near the airport. I have Clarke and Ryan en route," Atwood said. "I told them the cavalry was on its way. I explained that no one touches anything until you arrive."

"You live up in that area, right, LaCrosse?"

"Not too far, yeah."

"You and Branson head up there. Give us fresh eyes on it," Masters said. "Grady and I will hang back in case we receive reports of her surfacing down here at one of the two locations. Once you get there, take over the scene and have them report in. Atwood, send Clarke and Ryan to Skidaway Island for a once over. Put a plain wrapper on Laguna Way until we can get there. Satellite the place, do not approach."

Atwood raised her eyebrows but didn't retort, "Understood. *Lieu.*"

Masters realized his tone and grinned, "My apologies. Thank you, Sergeant. I appreciate your help," he said with a wink to Atwood, who turned and headed downstairs. He then focused his attention on his team.

"The biggest thing for us is to stay on point. We knew this was coming. It was unavoidable. We need to find any clues left behind that may lead us to where Thoran is. Report anything to Grady or myself. Understood?"

A cloud of affirmation filled the room, and everyone left to their assignments.

Grady stood behind Carmen as she pulled up the address they were given. Port Wendle was a small community just northeast of the airport. Not much different than the previous neighborhoods were like on the map. Small but complex to drive around. From what he saw on screen, this one didn't appear to have a security perimeter as Thoran's did. But that wouldn't be known until LaCrosse and Branson arrive.

"What is Clarke and Ryan's ETA to Skidaway?"

"Fifteen," Carmen said.

"That two-way is brutal," Nettles said. "More like 20 to 25."

"They'll call in when they arrive," Carmen reassured.

"Our undercover at Laguna?" Grady asked.

"They're in place. No activity."

"Have them report in hourly or with any activity, however small," Grady said.

"Understood."

"What are you thinking?" Masters asks Grady.

"If she's as good as Nelson, she's a ghost by now," Grady said. "She won't show up at any familiar location. The only reason Nelson returned to the first scene was to retrieve the knife that was hidden in the vent. Thoran has it with her this time around."

"That's a safe assumption," Masters said.

"The question is, where will she feel safest to lay low? Does she have somewhere to hide that we don't know about? Since she is Tanner, that opens the door to his known associates. Joshua Connors was one of Tanner's victims. But Connors resided in Alabama, his address here was a rental property. So, given that information, we need to revisit the victim list, check those names for any connections to Savannah."

"I thought of that," Carmen said, clicking on her keyboard. "The first victim lived alone; she had no ties to Georgia whatsoever. Connors was his second, we know about him. Tanner's third victim, owns a second residence in another state, not just in Georgia."

"That's pretty thorough," Masters said.

"That's what you pay me for, boss."

"Known associates?" Grady asked.

"Tanner's?" Carmen asked. "No, I haven't gone that deep yet. It took me long enough to dig through the legal mumbo jumbo of the housing info. I'm on that next."

"Since Thoran is Tanner, with the hint of the smoke rings, I think we can safely assume here that he is in charge. Let's run with his history. Let's also run through every person he contacted through his stint in prison. We also need to discover why he seemed to go straight."

"Go straight?" Carmen asked.

Grady grabbed his file and handed it to Carmen.

"For a long time, Tanner was getting himself into trouble. He was a rather poor criminal. But right here," Grady pointed to the notes in his file, "he turned around. For almost a year, his file is clean. Not one arrest. Not one incident on his record. Something happened. Then all of a sudden, he pulls this stunt? Homicide and suicide? But we now discover that he's responsible for three unsolved homicides prior to it? How does he go from petty theft to three homicides to suicide by cop? All with this twist of this *transference* ritual. Remember Stephen Tanner is now Sophia Thoran."

Carmen rubbed her temple again. "Have I ever told you guys how much I am hating this case?"

Chapter Twenty-Four

Thursday, March 5, 14:15

S he's as good as the others," LaCrosse said to Grady through the phone.

"It's what we would assume, I suppose. Thoran may even be better given her age and being a nurse. Steadier hands," Grady said. "How did Branson take it. This was his first scene, wasn't it?"

"Yeah, he has been conveniently absent at the others," LaCrosse responded, looking over his shoulder. Branson was walking around to the side of the house, *checking for evidence left behind*, he had called it. "He'll be alright. He is handling it better than Nettles. But she's a rookie. Branson is a vet—"

LaCrosse was cut off by Branson losing his late lunch in the side bushes. LaCrosse turned his back as if he didn't notice.

"I guess I spoke too soon. He'll be fine. Branson's a veteran. I will say this though, this guy must've been a bleeder. There was an excessive amount spilled. Bioremediation is going to have a field day cleaning this place up. You thought Dale was bad. This guy puts that scene to shame."

"That bad, huh? So, what's his story?"

LaCrosse pulled out his notes. "Quinton Hendrick. 27. He was a mechanic for a company that services private owners here at the airport. He must make decent wages for living in a place like this. Although nothing screams, *Hey, come kill me*."

"Make sure they take photos from every angle. We need the same images as we have here for comparison. Not that it matters.

We know who it is. More just may give us something new to go on. Every clue matters."

"Understood. I'm going to check if Branson found anything on his *perimeter search*. I'll check in if we find anything." LaCrosse smiled and hung up.

Grady laughed as he set down his phone, writing the info on Mr. Hendrick down for Carmen.

Carmen had been looking into locations for Tanner when she received Grady's information. She switched screens and discovered that, much like the other victims, Hendrick led a solitary life. He didn't have many connections other than a couple of beer buddies. He came home to an empty home and not much else other than a tabby cat who now needed a new home.

After a couple of hours, Carmen took off her glasses and tossed them on her keyboard. She leaned back and massaged between her eyes. "Did they find the cat?"

"No one said anything about one," Grady said, entering the room from Masters' office.

"Well, my mom has two. She'd never forgive me if I left the poor thing out in the cold."

"It's in the 80s."

"Figuratively," she said with an arm wave.

"Gotcha," Grady said. He dialed LaCrosse with the BOLO for Hendrick's tabby.

"Mom would be pleased," Carmen smiled. "Thank you."

"Just have her send in some of that world-famous Paella you're always gushing about."

"10-4."

"What else have you found out about Hendrick?"

"Not much." Carmen retrieved her glasses and pulled up a file for Grady. "He's like all the others. Solitary. His job was his life. He kept to himself. No run-ins with the law. Not even a parking ticket. He was popular within his field, though. He knew his stuff. I called around, and his name came up on several lists of mechanics who the airlines wanted. He was fully certified to work most types of aircraft, and he had the years to boot; been in mechanics since high school. Other than his job, he was a hermit."

"Just like the others."

"Just like the others. Not even a lady friend. A drink or two with the buddies, but that was it. Work, home, repeat," Carmen said.

"Confirms our theory that our perp seeks out these loner types. It makes it harder to find Thoran. How can you find someone who seeks those who like to hide in the shadows?" Grady said. "Any word from the other teams in the field?"

"Just false alarms. We're all on edge. But better to report anything than to report nothing and miss something. Clarke had a call in what turned out to be a neighbor snooping around. The idiot almost got himself shot. The plain wrapper had a couple of kids snooping around the abandoned house. They had to shoo them off. Wasn't sure if they were customers or squatters trying to gain access to an abandoned home. Either way, if Thoran was watching, their cover was blown. Do we call them in?"

"No. Let them sit there," Grady said, then touched his temple. "We need to let her think that place is off-limits. If we leave and she has eyes on our eyes, waiting for us to leave…"

"… then she will have those eyes contact her that we left."

"Right."

"All bases covered. Right, boss."

Grady smiled. It was the first time Carmen had called him *boss*. It felt out of place but good. "Anything else?"

"No. Dispatch has nothing to report. Sarge said she would alert us of anything out of the ordinary. Even a hiccup over the airwaves would come up to us."

"Good to know."

"So, what's next?" Carmen asked.

"We keep our eyes open and our ears to the ground." Grady exhaled. The truth was they couldn't do much until evidence found a mistake or Thoran popped up on radar.

"What do you need me to do today?" Nettles asked as the gate buzzed, then shut behind her. She looked a bit lost not having a partner. She and Grady had been working together and she had half an expression of expecting the same this go around.

"Good afternoon, Detective," Carmen said, waving Nettles over to her station. "I've been working on Tanner's past hangouts. They are old; before he supposedly went straight. You and Grady could look into them to see if perhaps Thoran made contact. Thin, but it's something to do." Carmen's fingers danced upon her keyboard, and the glare of the screen hid her eyes. "There. I sent the list to your phone, Nettles. A couple of bars, a gym, and amazingly enough, a church. He volunteered at a soup kitchen."

"Part of his make-over, I suppose?" Grady shrugged.

"Got it. No stone unturned," Nettles said, thumbing through her phone. "Guess I'm your navigator."

"Let's head out," Grady said to Nettles, then to Carmen, "You know where to reach us."

"10-4."

Grady notified Masters and Atwood at the front desk, then he and Nettles pulled out of the motor pool.

The first bar gave them no clues to where Thoran could be. No one knew a Tanner or a Thoran. They had better luck at the second bar, Big Eddie's. Grady approached a hulk of a man who was lining up a shot at the pool table. He dropped a photo of Tanner on the green felt surface. "You ever seen this guy?" Grady asked.

The big man knocked the 7 ball into the corner pocket. "Yep."

"You want to tell us where we can find him?"

"Why? What's he done?"

"He died," Nettles shot back.

"He died, and you can't find him? Pretty crappy detectives."

"Someone might look like him," Grady explained, trying to salvage the situation.

The big man lined up his next shot and gently nudged the 11

ball into the side pocket. "Too bad for them," he said, laughing at his own joke.

Grady tossed a photo of Thoran in the path of the man's next shot. "What about her? You know this woman?"

The man picked up the photo, took a swig of his beer, and grinned ear to ear. "Nope, but I'd like to? She got a name?"

Grady snatched the photo from his large hand. "If you haven't seen her, then it doesn't matter." Grady turned to Nettles. "Let's go. There's nothing here." Grady replaced the photo of Tanner with his card. He held up Thoran's photo again. "If you do see this woman, you would be smart to call me. You don't want to have anything to do with her, trust me, pal."

Once outside Nettles mused, "Makes perfect sense when you think about it. Why would anyone believe we're looking for a dead guy?"

At the gym, they had no better luck. Not because no one knew him, but because it had been shut down for the past six months. The neighbor, a friendly grocer, said it was due to health code violations. From the grease-covered windows to the warped wooden sign, it looked like it had been abandoned for six years.

"So, all we have left is the church," Nettles said.

"Yeah, don't think she would be hanging around a place of worship after such an ungodly act," Grady said. "That would be the last place someone would go."

"Or the first," Nettles offered, "Contrition. Besides, it's the last place on Carmen's list."

"Yeah. And it's getting late. We need to wrap this up," Grady said and headed toward the church.

The Savannah Church of the Sacred Heart was at the south end of the main road leading to the station. Another reason they left it until last on their list. Grady was familiar with the church. It was not the one they attended but was one that Elizabeth had on her shortlist. They went once. The pastor was a gentleman, the church welcoming, but was too far from their home. Grady thought closer to the station would be an advantage, but it was further from her office. The church they did find was a perfect match for their driving needs and where they felt they needed to be.

Grady pulled into the parking lot, and both he and Nettles were surprised that the church windows were lit up.

"Bingo night?" Nettles suggested.

"Mid-week service, or more likely soup kitchen. This is where Tanner frequented before he went dark. Hopefully, this will be the place we get our answers. If anyone remembers who he is, it will be a minister. They're trained to remember faces."

Grady found a parking spot, and he and Nettles walked up to a set of double doors with a plaque that read, *Dwight D. Wall Memorial Hall.* It paid tribute to the man who funded the building they were about to enter. When Nettles pulled open the door, the scent of baked goods and a voice calling out "B-4" greeted them.

Nettles smiled. "Told, ya."

"Score another one for the rookie," Grady said.

"I always know a bingo crowd when I see one. My aunt back home was a sucker for a bingo hall."

"You take the lead then, bingo master," Grady said, feigning a bow.

"10-4, boss."

Grady smiled.

The room was near capacity; all ages and types. The die-hards were easy to spot. They had the most cards and lines of good luck charms—anything from candles to dolls with colorful hair. This hall had its share of them. Nettles tapped Grady's shoulder a couple of times, pointing them out. Grady would chuckle under his breath and nod. He highly doubted Tanner would hang out in this crowd.

An older gentleman in a striped tie and thick-rimmed glasses approached them. He had a stack of bingo cards in his hand. "Good evening, sir and madam. Five dollars for your first card, two dollars per additional card. Cash only. How many will you need this fine evening?" He smiled, revealing a gleaming teeth any dentist would be proud of.

"No cards, sir. I'm Detective Gradiosa from the Savannah PD. This is Detective Nettles. We have a few questions about a gentleman who may have attended or helped out here a couple of months ago. Have you been around that long?"

"No, I'm sorry, Detective. I've only been here a month. But Pastor Armstrong may be able to assist you. He's been here ten years and knows everyone. He's over in the main sanctuary."

"Thank you, sir. How do we get there from here?" Grady asked.

The gentleman pointed across the hall, "Through those doors. Just follow the signs to the main sanctuary."

"Bingo!" called out a silver-haired lady across the hall. Her arrangement of knick-knacks nearly toppled over. The crowd mumbled its dismay—those one number away with the most disdain.

The announcer called back the numbers, verified her win, and announced her prize, a 50-piece Tupperware set, to which she squealed with joy.

Grady and Nettles followed the hallway and found the sanctuary. The rear doors were open as parishioners were exiting a late service. A gentleman, who they assumed was Pastor Armstrong, was at the entrance, smiling and shaking hands and with as many as he could. They waited near the front row of pews until most of the congregation had exited, and only a few stragglers were left behind, and then they approached him.

"Good evening, Detectives. What can I do for you this evening?" Pastor Armstrong said, his hand extended.

Nettles accepted the greeting first.

Grady accepted a firm handshake, "Hello, Pastor Armstrong. I am Detective—"

"James Gradiosa, as I recall. You and your wife Elizabeth attended not too long ago."

"Impressive, Pastor. It's has been quite a while, and it was only a visit or two."

"Photographic memory. It's a blessing and a curse, I suppose.

I can remember all my church members' and visitors' names and birthdates, but I can also remember the heartache of every departure as well."

"A tremendous burden. My uncle had a photographic memory. He couldn't stand it," Nettles said.

"It's most certainly a cross to bear," said the pastor. He turned, closed the doors, and faced the detectives again. "Now, what can I do for you this evening?"

"Given your memory, you can be quite helpful. Did you know Stephen Tanner? Our records show he used to help out around here?" Grady asked.

"Yes, I knew him. He was around here a couple of months ago. Very helpful. He was dedicated to his work and the Lord. He asked a lot of questions regarding spiritual matters. It was sad when he just stopped coming around."

"When was this?"

"Just over a month. That was when I brought in Teddy. I assume you met him next door."

"Yes, we met him," Grady said with a smile.

"Did Mr. Tanner let you know where he was going or leave a forwarding address?" Nettles asked.

"Nothing. He was here one day and gone the next. We even had lunch and a stimulating discussion on spiritual matters. He was a learner, especially deep theology. You would never have thought it by looking at the guy. One of the reasons I've learned to never judge a book by its cover." The pastor said, pacing to the front of the aisle. Grady and Nettles followed.

"What types of questions was he asking?"

"Spiritual questions. The afterlife. Getting things right in his head, I suppose. He wanted to know if spirits were real or fake. That after we die, if our spirits do live on, or if this was it. I explained that we are spiritual beings. We will live on past our deaths; that's how God created us. That our bodies are mere shells, and once we die, our spirit is separated from our bodies and is united with Christ in Heaven."

"And he understood this," Nettles said.

"As far as I know, yes," the pastor said.

"Wow," Nettles said, sitting on the front pew, exhaling loudly.

"Why? What's wrong? Has Stephen done something?"

"Not sure how much you've read in the papers or saw in the news, Pastor, but Stephen Tanner was the man who was found in the condos in Forsythe Park back in February," Grady explained.

"The one who almost killed that man and then took his own life?"

"Yes, I'm afraid so," Grady said.

"No, I had just heard the story. Didn't know the names," Pastor Armstrong said, sitting next to Nettles.

"I'm afraid there's more. Much more," Grady said.

"I'm glad I am sitting then," the pastor said.

"We have a theory that there is more to this than meets the eye. And Tanner talking to you about spiritual matters is adding to it. Have you ever heard of the term, transference?"

Pastor Armstrong's complexion went pale, his eyes darted left, then right, and he licked his lips. He took a deep breath and released it. "I'm familiar with that term. I don't like to be, but I am."

"Did Tanner bring it up with you?" Nettles asked.

The pastor leaned over, elbows on his knees and his hands wrapped around the back of his neck. "Just once. Right before he disappeared." He sat up. "I didn't think anything of it. I thought it was just banter. We always had discussions about things he had learned in prison that were wrong. That was how it worked. He asked questions, I answered according to what the Bible taught."

"And this time?" Nettles asked.

"I asked where his questions were coming from? He said it was something that he had heard, but he was curious if it was possible. I was honest with him. I told him the spiritual realm could be dangerous if you start messing with the wrong powers. I explained that type of thinking was not of God, and he should not be considering those thoughts. I tried to show him that anything of Satan would only hurt the progress we were making."

"Well, pastor, unfortunately, he didn't listen," Nettles said, laying back in the pew and placing her hands over her eyes.

"What's happened?"

"Crazy as it sounds, we have reason to believe the transference worked. Twice so far. Tanner has moved into two different bodies. But that's not the worst part. It seems that there is a ritual that coincides with the 'Transference.' It involves a ritualistic murdering of three people, and the fourth becomes the new host. So far, he has already completed two cycles and one in a new cycle. That murder occurred this morning. We have time before he begins seeking out his next victim."

"I think I'm going to be sick," the pastor said.

"It's not your fault," Grady said.

"I think it may as well be. If I had seen more of a threat in Tanner, I could have said something and stopped this even before it began. I'm supposed to be a reader of people. Some visionary I am," Pastor Armstrong stood and paced the front of the sanctuary.

"Pastor, we all missed it. I'm a police detective. It's my job to see these things too. Perhaps even more than you. I have evidence on my side. And it wasn't until recently that we discovered all the puzzle pieces. We know the who and how; we just don't know the where and when. We have a timeline, however. Right now, we are exploring Tanner's past. Places he could go as a refuge to hide out until he is ready to seek out his, or rather, her next victim. He is currently occupying a female host, if I hadn't mentioned that already."

Pastor Armstrong stopped pacing and gripped the back of his neck. He exhaled. "What's her name?"

"Sophia Thoran. We don't know her connection to anyone. Just a random person who was as disconnected from society as most of the other victims.

"Name doesn't sound familiar to me either," the pastor said, barely audible. He exhaled and continued, "I read up on this transference after Tanner brought it up. It's some serious stuff. It requires three blood sacrifices, followed by the fourth, *the new host*, and then it begins all over again. It all coincides with—"

"Lunar cycles," Grady said. "Yes, we have learned that much. You've confirmed the information our scientist, Dr. Glavine has given us."

"It will continue as long as Tanner continues," the pastor said.

"Can you tell us anything else about Tanner? Places he would visit or hang out? We're hoping to find Thoran in hangouts or maybe shelters Tanner would hide out in."

"Not any place for a woman. Mostly taverns."

"Yes, we have already been to those. No dice," Nettles said, sitting up. "Almost had our heads taken off at one of them."

"What about his brother's place over in Lakeview?"

"He has a brother?" Grady asked.

"*Had* a brother. It's a place he and his brother bought down in Harris Neck."

"The National Refuge?" Nettles asked.

"Yeah. He talked about it all the time. He would go down there to get away and think."

Grady and Nettles exchange glances.

"You think he, *er* she, is down there?"

"That's what we intend to find out," Grady said, extending his hand to the pastor. "Thank you for your time, Pastor Armstrong. You've been a tremendous help."

Nettles shook his hand, and both she and Grady reassured him the situation couldn't have been avoided, and he was not to blame. Then they headed to their vehicle.

"Now we know where Thoran is hiding out," Nettles said, her car door squealing in agreement.

Grady felt they finally had the upper hand on Thoran. He relayed their info to Masters and agreed on a meeting point. He hung up and started the car. "Let's go make an arrest and end this."

Friday, March 6, 09:00

Masters made sense. It didn't take much to convince Grady that if Harris Neck was Thoran's hideaway, it would be doubtful she'd go there, at least straight away. She would be exposed if followed. "She's most likely at a secondary location and laying low until everything blows over," Masters had said. And after talking with the pastor, it seemed that location may have been the hideout when Tanner was on his own spree.

Grady called Pastor Armstrong and asked him to be careful in case Thoran visited him and forwarded a photo of her. He could hear the worry in the pastor's voice as he hung up. It concerned Nettles enough that she made Grady call the front desk. Atwood wasn't happy when she was asked to pull another team to *babysit*, as she called it. But Atwood understood the stakes and agreed to send officers to the church to protect Pastor Armstrong.

The team on the church reported no activity overnight, as was expected. It had been just over 24 hours since Thoran committed her crime. She wasn't going to make an appearance anywhere, Grady surmised. "She's probably sleeping it off in some hotel room down off the highway somewhere. Perhaps awake and planning her next victim, but not galivanting in public," he said.

"The next first quarter moon is on April first. That's when she'll make her next move," Lacrosse said. He exhaled and scratched his head. "Not to state the obvious, but we have three weeks."

"Yeah, I know we have time. I'm just getting tired of waiting. It seems like all we do now is wait. We know who the perp is, but there's nothing we can do about it. Meanwhile, some poor innocent soul out there has their name written on a list," Grady said, pacing the diner.

After another rough night's sleep and another early morning, Grady kissed a sleeping Elizabeth, who barely moved, and headed out to the staging area just south of town. The team had just finished breakfast, and Masters was on the phone with Carmen. That morning she confirmed the existence of Tanner's cabin in Harris Neck and attempted to pull up a satellite image on GPS, but the trees obscured it from view. There were a couple of trails leading to the area and one leading out to the creek.

"I marked where it should be on the map I sent to Grady," Carmen told Masters, "but I can't confirm. Be careful. You never know what's out there. My uncle owns a cabin up north. To keep trespassers out, he sets traps. He also has motion sensors that set off alarms in the house."

"Somehow, I don't think these guys are that sophisticated. But we catch your drift," Masters said. "Thanks, Carmen."

"Gotcha. I'll keep you posted if anything comes across the wire."

"10-4," Masters said and disconnected the line.

"Did you get the map yet?" Masters asked.

"Just now," Grady said, scrolling his screen. "Sheesh, nothing but trees and streams. A couple of paths here and there."

"The dot is where we need to get to."

Grady handed his phone to Nettles. "Any ideas, Rookie?"

Nettles bit the corner of her bottom lip as she scrolled the screen, squinting now and then. "If he's serious about privacy, then there will definitely be countermeasures."

"Yes, Carmen mentioned possible booby traps and a security system. But I doubt it. Tanner doesn't seem the type, but we need to be prepared for anything."

Grady took his phone back and made a few taps. Everyone's phone rang with notification tones. "I sent the map to everyone."

Branson scrolled his device. "What's our approach? We can't come from the creek, too exposed, not to mention we're not equipped to handle the conditions. We can't see the paths from this angle. Who knows what it looks like from there to the cabin? The fewer of us, the better, I'd say."

"Agreed," Grady said. "If we head in as a group, we're made. We have to play the part. Hikers who got turned around."

"Well-armed hikers," Nettles said.

"That's for sure," Branson said.

"Does that creek have any boating activity? Who's to say we can't have one craft just cruising as a pair of eyes?" LaCrosse paused a minute, scrolling his device. "Yeah, I can see docks and a couple of boats through Satellite Maps."

"Let me get Carmen on this," Grady said. He dialed Carmen, and she pulled up the area on her system that was leagues better than a Satellite Maps feed. "Hey Carmen, you're on with everyone."

"Between us on land and the boat, we have two sets of eyes on the place. Be careful, though. You don't want to get caught snooping," LaCrosse warned.

"I won't be snooping. I'll be a bird watcher," Nettles said. "I can easily fake searching in all directions. I'll have an open bird app, jot down in a notebook, ooh and ahh when I see a favorite species. They can easily watch me as I am watching them."

"That could work. Okay, we'll have Branson and LaCrosse on land from the southwest. You and—" Grady began to say himself.

"Ryan will be with me on this one," Nettles interrupted.

"Ryan?" Grady said. He hadn't heard about him moving up to their team.

"Yes, he's on his way down. Since he knows the case and has first-hand knowledge of who and what we are dealing with, Masters called him up."

Grady thought about it and agreed that no other officer would be a better replacement for Mesa. He and Clarke had dealt with Tanner himself. Just as long as he kept personal feelings out of it, he would fit in perfectly.

"Where is he now?"

"Making things official with Atwood. All that legal mumbo jumbo, you know how it is," Nettles said.

"Then it will be you and Ryan on the boat. We'll need to get you two set up with the equipment you need for your bird-watching expedition."

"I have it," Carmen's voice spoke. "I have most of it in my vehicle. I can send it down with Ryan."

Most of the team was silent. Carmen took notice. "You guys think my life is just circuit boards and keystrokes?"

LaCrosse shrugged, sticking out his bottom lip. "Yeah, that's about it."

"Shyaddup and go shave that worm off your face," Carmen said into the speakerphone, tossing her keys to Ryan, who had just entered the floor.

"Good morning to you too," Ryan said, catching, holding up the keys, and jingling them.

"Hold on a sec," she said to the phone, then to Ryan. "It's a silver Jeep. In the back, you'll find a crate with a camera and lenses. There is another with sound equipment as well. Take both cases and head down to Harris Neck. I already sent the location to your phone. Check with Atwood. She will assign you a vehicle from the motor pool. Head down there straight away."

"Yes, ma'am," Ryan said and disappeared down the stairwell.

"Okay, I'm back," Carmen said to the speakerphone. "Ryan's en route."

"10-4," Grady said. "What do your maps tell you that Satellite Maps leave off?"

"Well, for one, the latest SM image is four, no, six months old. My image shows the creek is a bit lower. But you still should have no issue getting a boat down it. There is a rental place two miles upstream from you. Craw-and-Dad's Bait and Tackle. Emily Crawford is the co-owner with her father. The site says they have boat rentals. Not many, but I'll look into it when we get off the line."

"Alright, I'll let you get on that. When you get the info, send it to Ryan and have him head over there. Send it to Nettles as well. She will meet him there."

"10-4."

Grady disconnected and tossed his keys to Nettles, "Not a scratch, Detective. I'll have your badge."

Nettles caught the keys and punched his shoulder, "It's that place with the large crab out front when we turned off the highway, right?"

"You have a good memory. I suppose so," Grady said as Nettles got into his vehicle. "When you get up there, ask about Tanner. When was the last they saw him, if they've seen Thoran, and if so, when was the last time they saw her?"

"10-4, boss."

"Short thang, lil' over five foot?" Emily Crawford said, "Yeah, we seen her. Strange person. Keeps on askin' about cops stoppin' by. Guess I have my answer now."

"Miss Crawford, it's important that she doesn't know we're looking for her," Ryan said.

"Yes," Nettles followed. "It's for her safety. If she knew, it might cause her to do something that could harm her. So, for her safety and honestly your own, don't alert her to our presence. Please."

"Well, awright. If you say it's for my safety and all," Emily said with her face scrunched in confusion.

"Thank you, Miss Crawford," Ryan said.

"When was the last time you spoke to Miss Thoran?" Nettles asked.

"Last night. She came here and picked up some ice, soda pop, couple of them microwave meals, and other stuff."

"So, the cabins have power then?"

"Some do."

"What about the Tanner place?"

"Yeah. They do. But why'd she be goin' there? She's no Tanner. They only have boys, and there are only two of them. Now they're both are dead. Y'all should know that. It was you who did it."

Ryan didn't say a word. Images flashed before his eyes of Tanner's final moments; the gleam in his eyes, the grin on his face, the words he uttered, 'Glatchka mondavka insinivicus.' Ryan shook his head, bringing him back to the shack. "She's a family friend, staying up there. We just have a few questions for her. That's all we can stay, though," he said, ignoring her latter commentary.

"I s'pose," Emily said, calming down, her face still bearing lines of skepticism.

"Thank you," Nettles said with an extended hand. Once accepted and shook, she held out a card. "This is our boss' card. His name is Detective Gradiosa. My number is on the back. I am Detective Emily Nettles. This is Officer Chet Ryan." Ryan tipped his cover. "If you need us, you can call either Detective Gradiosa or me."

"Remember, don't let her know we were here. It's for her safety and yours," Ryan reminded.

Nettles and Ryan stepped out into the humid afternoon. "What do you think?"

"Hard to read. But I think she'll keep quiet," Ryan said, opening the water bottle he had purchased and taking a sip. "If it had been Tanner himself, it may have been a different story."

"Agreed. She would be on the phone with him right now. She has nothing to gain from tipping off Thoran," Nettles said, walking toward their vehicles. She couldn't help but notice how much newer Ryan's looked. His had yet to be on the backroads of Harris Neck.

"Do you want me to sit on her?"

"No need. We're just here to pick you up and get info from Miss Crawford. We needed to find out if she knew if Thoran was on the premises. You're my backup on perimeter surveillance."

"Perimeter surveillance? I thought there were no roads."

Nettles grinned and opened her car door. "Roads? Where

we're going, we don't need roads." She put on her sunglasses, which were on the dash, and got into her vehicle.

Ryan laughed and followed the dust tracks Nettles left ahead of him, ruining the carwash shine he had just paid $20 for to impress his new boss.

After a couple of quick turns, Nettles pulled up to a smaller shack next to a long narrow pier. It was a duplicate of Crawdads, same color and trim, but about four times smaller. Two small fishing boats floated at the end of the pier.

"No roads, eh?" Ryan said, shutting his door.

"We're water support. The cabin is about two miles upstream from here. We're supposed to be bird watchers," Nettles explained.

"Ahh," Ryan said, a light clicking on in his eyes. He walked back to the trunk and opened it. "That's what these two cases are for. Bird watching equipment, I presume? They must be important. I had to give blood and promise my firstborn before Carmen would give them to me."

"Just your firstborn? You got lucky." Nettles took one case, Ryan the other, and closed the trunk. "We assume Thoran is held up in a cabin on the bank upstream. We are to cruise up, assess the area, and report to Grady. Then maintain position as they make their approach, and report any movement should she detect them."

"You a rookie, Nettles?"

"Couple of years out, why?"

"You still talk like one. The tech speak," Ryan said, scribbling in the air, ending with a checkmark.

"Yes, Mesa, my former partner, would get on me all the time," Nettles pointed toward the shack, and they walked toward the entrance. "He would tell me to relax, that the tech speak was not that important in the field."

"Forgive me asking, but how did you bypass being an officer and get straight to Detective?"

"I didn't. I was an officer for a year. But I'm good at what I do. I broke a major case, and Masters heard about it and requested that I be brought over. My CO was not happy about it. They hate to lose good talent. Rumor has it I was used to cover a poker bet between him and Atwood."

Ryan laughed. "Either way, they made a good decision. Masters doesn't bring over just anyone. I've known him for a few years. He's picky about who he works with. And I'm sorry about your partner. I know that must have been difficult."

"Thank you, and yes, it was. But I can't let it get to me. I understand it's part of the job, and I need to move on because the job moves on. If I slow down, people get hurt. In this case, they can die. So, I will focus and catch this one."

The front of the shack-sized building had a sign that read **Craw-and-Dad's Marina**. There was a large window with a raised covering above it. Reggae tunes rang through the opening, and a male voice hummed and yelped along. Nettles couldn't help but giggle. Ryan mimicked what he envisioned the acapellist to be doing. Nettles backhanded his shoulder and motioned with her head to keep going. The tune faded out, and to keep from going unnoticed before the next tune, Nettles cleared her throat.

"Oh, sorry, didn't see ya' there. How can I help you two? Officers, right?"

"I'm Detective Nettles. This is Officer Ryan. Our colleague, Carmen Albanese, called ahead of us?"

"Yup, she did. I have our best Princecraft here for ya. She's a Yukon. Has a Mercury strapped to her. Will get ya to where ya goin' in no time at all." The man's grin swallowed his eyes. Nettles thought if he wore suspenders, his thumbs would be stretching them out.

"Very nice craft, sir," Nettles said.

"Many thanks, dear," the proud owner said. "Where are my manners. The name is Arthur Crawford." Author Crawford extended his hand, both Nettles and Ryan shook it. "You met my youngest up at the store."

"Yes, we did. You have a pleasant daughter," Nettles said, not sure what else to say. "Do we need to sign anything? The department will handle the payment for your services."

"Already taken care of, Miss Albanese already paid for the day."

"Wonderful. Are there keys?"

"Just your arm, dearie," Arthur said with his toothy grin.

A little embarrassed, Nettles said, "Sorry, yes, it has been a while."

"Y'all need anything? Snacks, water, life jackets?"

Ryan looked wide-eyed at Nettles. She grinned.

"No to the snacks and water. We have all we need, thanks to your daughter. Yes, to the life vests. They would be prudent."

"A medium for the lady. An' you Officer? A large, I'd reckon?"

"Yes, sir," Ryan said. He took the bright orange vest and gave it a once-over. "Do you have anything less…"

"Eye-catching?" Nettles said, finishing his sentence.

"I have pink?"

"Orange will do, thank you," Ryan said, taking the vest. Nettles grinned ear to ear.

"Bright is for safety reasons. Can't save what ya can't see," Arthur said with a wink.

"Thanks again, Mr. Crawford. Which craft is it?"

Arthur grinned again and pointed down the dock. "The one on the left is your vessel."

"Thank you, sir."

"Smooth sailing, my dear."

Nettles and Ryan walked down the pier; the unfinished boards creaked below their feet. Ryan looked over his shoulder every other step while he held tight to the vest in his hands. Nettles was more sure of herself and began to outpace Ryan. After a few steps, she stopped. "You okay, Ryan?"

"Yeah. I'm good. What makes you think otherwise?"

"You seem a bit hesitant?"

"You can say water and me don't get along so well."

"You have aquaphobia?"

"No. Not at all, Detective. I wouldn't call it a fear. Just an apprehension. I don't like the thought of drowning."

"Neither do I. But you'll be fine. We'll be fine. Just keep your mind on the job, let everything else go. Think of the target, why you're here. It'll keep you focused."

Ryan dropped his hands to his side and closed his eyes. He took a deep breath, and when he opened his eyes, Nettles saw a different person. She smiled.

"There you go, Officer. That looks better. You ready?"

"Ready as I'll ever be. Let's do this."

Chapter Twenty-Six

Friday, March 6, 15:30

I can't see anything through this brush," Branson said. "This is just as dense as it is overhead."

"We can hear the creek, though. It's on our three. It's faint but getting louder," Lacrosse said, gesturing toward the sound.

"There are a few squirrels, maybe a raccoon over there," Branson nodded and pointed toward the trees ahead of them.

"How can you tell?"

"Their gait. Vocal noises they make mostly. Each is distinct."

"Huh. Learn something new every day," LaCrosse said.

"How far now? We should be close."

LaCrosse consulted his phone. The blue dot told him they were a half-mile from the cabin. "Not far. We should keep our eyes open for sensors and cameras."

"Maybe even look for a side trail, through the trees, and get off the main path."

"Yeah, we're a bit exposed. Even if we have a story, this area looks more like a private road." LaCrosse looked behind them. The road was disappearing under their feet. The once-level path was wearing away. It was more rugged dirt than anything now.

"Do you have us, Carmen?" Branson asked.

"Yeah, I have you," Carmen said in both of their ears and in the ears of Nettles and Ryan, who were on the water not too far upstream from their location.

"What's your 20, Nettles?" Branson asked. "Do you have eyes yet?"

"Coming around the bend now," Nettles said. "I can see a clearing, but not the house. There is a dock but no boat. We just passed a single boat tied to a smaller dock, but there was no structure around it. I do see two boats further downstream about 50 yards. They are up against a dock. No activity surrounding them. All is quiet here. Permission to proceed."

"Do you see anything out of place, Branson?" Grady asked.

"Nothing. All is normal," Branson said.

"Just FYI. Those docks are about 50 yards long. They are separated from the shore by marshland."

"10-4," Branson said with a cringe.

Grady sensed his team's apprehension, "It's okay, guys. If we were to need Nettles and Ryan to enter the picture for support, they would most likely go unnoticed, and we'd still have the element of surprise."

"Unless Thoran has the dock monitored as well," Branson said.

"True, but forgive the pun, but we will cross that bridge when and if we come to it. Hopefully, the situation won't come to that. Right now, let's stay focused on your and LaCrosse's entry point."

"Understood," Branson said.

"We're getting off the main path and heading into the trees to avoid detection," LaCrosse informed Grady. "The trees are thick but not so thick that it would prevent our movement. The ground is also clear of foliage, no twigs under feet to alert anyone of our approach."

"Still, keep your eyes open. Don't get comfortable," Carmen said. "There could be anything out there. Motion sensors can look like anything nowadays. They're not pretty white boxes anymore. They can look like bark or rocks. You'd never know you set one off one until you had bullets whizzing by your head from a trigger-happy landowner."

"We get the picture, Albanese. Now quiet down, or we won't hear Elmer hunting wabbits," LaCrosse jested.

The air went silent for several minutes. Even though the ground was clear of debris, it still crunched under both their feet. Every footfall threw the announcement of their presence toward their target. LaCrosse and Branson reassured each other it was all in their heads, that their noises were not carrying that far. It was all they could do to keep moving on.

"The heat helps," Branson said. "The humidity will absorb most of the noise."

"Look," LaCrosse said, grabbing Branson's arm, bringing them to a halt. The cabin was in the distance through a clearing.

"We have a visual on the cabin," Branson radioed in.

"10-4," Grady said. "Any activity?"

"Too soon to tell. We'll radio back in as we approach."

"Understood."

The two men toed closer to the cabin. After another hundred yards, they stepped into a small clearing. LaCrosse stopped and looked around, hesitant.

Branson looked side to side across the empty area, "You really think this guy is going to layout tripwires?"

"Gal. And I'm not sure, but this clearing is suspicious," LaCrosse said.

"It's a firewall, you moron," Branson laughed. "Small clearings help keep brush fires from reaching structures. It's common in wooded areas. Keep going."

"Just wait a second. We need to be sure it's not monitored," LaCrosse held out his arm, preventing Branson from entering the clearing.

Branson rolled his eyes and resigned to LaCrosse's hesitation. He scanned the tree line up and down the clearing, but he did not find any sign of surveillance. "I don't see anything, Detective. Are you happy?"

"Something doesn't feel right. But I agree, I don't see anything, and we aren't accomplishing anything just sitting here. Let's go. We just need to have each other's backs. Keep your eyes open."

"Don't we always? Let's go. But let's make it fast."

With those words, both men sprinted across the clearing. It was only 30 yards, but it felt like 200. Being that close to the cabin and out in the open, Branson and Lacrosse found security behind two oaks that pulled them into a bear hug of safety. Both men, out of breath, rested backs against their trees. After a moment, they looked at each other and fell into hearty laughter.

"I need to hit the gym more," LaCrosse said. "Lieu says I don't go enough."

"You and me both," Branson said. "If I had to chase a perp now, they'd certainly have the one up on me."

Catching his breath, Branson gave a glance over his shoulder to check their progress. The cabin was now much closer. He could make out the windows and details of what Tanner kept on his porch.

"What do you see?" LaCrosse asked, still winded.

"Windows on this side are covered with storm shutters. I can only make out half the porch. There are crates of some sort."

"That's it?"

"From this angle and through the trees that are there. Yes."

"Damn."

"We need to circle around to get a better view," Branson pointed with his head.

"Wait," LaCrosse readjusted his vest that had come loose during their mad dash.

"Someone needs to cut out the dough—"

A loud ricocheting ping splintered the tree bark above Branson's head. He dove to the ground with a loud, "Ooof!"

"You alright?"

"Yeah. You?"

"I'm fine," LaCrosse said, his mustache covered in dirt and leaf shards.

"Well, I guess we've lost the element of surprise."

"You ran too slow," LaCrosse said.

"Hey, I got over here first."

"So now what?"

"We sit and wait."

LaCrosse reached up to his chest and pressed his COM button. "Hey guys, we have a situation."

"We heard it from here," Nettles said. "What's your sit-rep?"

"We decided to take a nap and wait it out," LaCrosse said out loud to no one in particular.

Branson rolled his eyes and answered the COM. "We're pinned down on the edge of a clearing. One shot fired just above our position. It appears to have come from the cabin. Permission to return fire?"

"Negative. We need to take her into custody," Grady said. "Don't take lethal action unless it is necessary. Remember, you're dealing with Tanner, who is inside Thoran. Thoran is innocent. If we can spare him, then we can save her."

"Are you sure that's what Dr. Glavine said?" Branson asked.

"He concluded that if we can find a way to get Tanner out of Thoran, we can save her," Grady said.

"Has the good doctor found that way yet?" Branson asked.

"He is still conducting his research. He has a theory. But he doesn't like to speculate before he has all the answers available to him."

Branson rolled his eyes again and made an obscene gesture with his hands. LaCrosse shook his head.

"Relax, Branson," LaCrosse said. "He has his hands tied. You know the Doc. He never says anything without knowing all the facts. He will never speculate or give an opinion without evidence. If he isn't saying anything, there is a good reason. It isn't Grady's fault."

Branson took a breath and nodded in agreement. He closed his eyes and glanced over his shoulder at the cabin. "I don't see any movement. If we're going to move, now is as good of a time as any. He could be trying to flank us."

LaCrosse scanned the tree line on either side. "If *she* were, *she'd* be just as exposed as we are. I agree. Relocating now is our best move."

"*She*, yeah, thanks for the reminder, partner," Branson said, raising his gun upright to his chest. "Ready?"

"On your six."

Branson crouched as low as he could and moved through the trees toward the front of the cabin. The closer they approached, the more cover they received. Bushes were more abundant, and an occasional boulder sheltered them. Before long, they were directly in front of the cabin.

After taking in their situation, LaCrosse and Branson agreed that there was only one frontal approach; a stairway leading up the porch and the front door. A second stairway at the right end of the porch, ascending from the gravel driveway. It could hide their approach, but the gravel would be problematic.

To their benefit, on this side of the cabin, the window shutters were in an open position. However, they still couldn't see inside through them; only one had the blinds drawn. That window was on the porch near the crates they had seen before that shot went over their head.

"Can you see anything?" Branson asked.

"Nothing."

"What I wouldn't give for a pair of binoculars," Branson said.

"Can't help you there," LaCrosse said. "But I can get up to that window and take a peek."

"That six-foot frame of yours? Good luck with that."

"I'm light on my feet."

"Could've fooled me the way you were clodhopping back there."

"You want me up there or not?" LaCrosse said.

Branson took another eye sweep of the area. Then, he shook his head. "Wait, a second." He keyed up his walkie. "Sit-rep?"

"You first," Grady said.

"We are now dead center of the cabin, 50 yards from the porch, behind brush and a large boulder. All is quiet—no activity since the single shot that went over us. We have four windows to the cabin. All shutters are open, blinds inside shut in all but one. That window gives us a view of the inside, but not from our vantage point. Requesting permission to get a closer look."

"Can you get closer without being spotted?"

"Not sure. Without knowing where the shot came from, we are unsure of where the shooter's perch was," LaCrosse said.

"Then stand down for now," Grady said.

"Hold on," Masters said.

"Stand by, LaCrosse."

"We may just have to take a risk here," Masters said. "I know it's something you don't want to hear, but it was just one shot. Tanner/Thoran had plenty of opportunities to shoot again, but she hasn't. She may have gone into hiding or is trying to plan an escape."

"So, we let one approach while the other provides cover?"

"Precisely."

"What if we give her something else to worry about?" Grady said.

"First, let's give LaCrosse and Branson the chance to feel out the place. Look for weaknesses," Masters said.

Grady keyed up his radio. "Nettles. Ryan. Sit-Rep."

"Ryan here. Nettles is currently enjoying the scenery. She says that the window shutters on this side are all open wide. The blinds are open as well. She can see into the cabin but has not witnessed any activity. She also says that it's difficult to see with the sun's position giving her a bit of a glare. If we wait too much longer, the sun will be dancing straight off the glass into our eyes, and we'll be worthless."

"Understood," Grady said.

"Wait," Ryan said with a startle. Grady could hear Nettles' voice in the background. It was fast and sharp. Ryan responded, "We see something, or rather someone, in the kitchen area. They appear to be alone. We can't make out gender at this distance or if they have any weapons… Oh, okay. Nettles says the suspect appears to be female, based upon supposed hair length."

"10-4," Grady said. "Keep your eyes on her. If she makes any sudden moves, let us know."

"Got it."

"LaCrosse. Branson. Move in for a closer look, but use caution, just in case she's not alone," Grady said.

"And watch your six for man-made devices," Carmen said.

"10-4," both men reply.

"After you, boss," LaCrosse said with a wave of his hand.

"Yeah, now you readily acknowledge my seniority."

Branson took a few steps toward the cabin; LaCrosse followed, always looking in the opposite direction of Branson, the eyes in the back of his head. They both moved at a quick stroll, careful not to encounter any devices or wires that may have been placed in their path. Having spent time in the service, Branson knew how to spot a plate or charge buried in their path. They made it to the steps without a misstep or hearing a peep from the voices in their ears.

"So far, so good," LaCrosse whispered.

Branson kneeled at the steps, inspecting each one, looking for any pins, wires, or loose boards. LaCrosse, being an ex-carpenter, knelt beside him and examined them to check for problems in how they were installed. Between the two of them, they gave the seven steps the thumbs up and slowly ascended them. "Watch for creaking," LaCrosse said. "These are fairly old."

Branson nodded in affirmation, then stood and toed the first step. LaCrosse remained kneeling, watching Branson carefully. Not a sound from the first. The second peeped at them but nothing more than what they could hear. The third and fourth were silent as the first. The tension let up because Branson took steps five and six in quick succession, and letting his foot off of five gave a low-range croaking that the neighboring county could've heard. Both men cringed, and Branson froze.

LaCrosse remained on his knees but unholstered his weapon and fanned the area, looking for signs of movement. Branson remained still, his gun raised to his shoulder. He opened his eyes and met LaCrosse's stern gaze. Branson shrugged, then whispered, "I'm sorry, but all this—"

An ear-piercing explosion threw Branson off the sixth step and right into LaCrosse's chest. Both men tumbled to the ground, knocking the wind out of both of them. Not wanting the next shot to be through them, Branson rolled to the side of the staircase, and LaCrosse crawled closer to the porch and into the gravel garden beside the porch.

"You Okay, Daryl?" LaCrosse asked.

Branson gasped and coughed, refilling his lungs with air. "Oh man," he said. "That's gonna leave a bruise. Yeah, I'm alright. You?"

"I'm fine. Did you see where that came from?" LaCrosse asked, coughing in between words.

"No, I was too busy saving my ass."

"Yeah, and knocking me on mine. Seriously. Any flash or idea where she's at?"

"I don't think she was firing at us, but it sure felt like it. And that one was definitely not a rifle. She has two weapons in there."

"Agreed. It was close but not aimed at us. Sounded like a shotgun aimed in the air," LaCrosse said.

Branson reached for his radio button. "Hey, Gradiosa. I thought you were supposed to be eyes and ears?"

"Don't know what happened. She was in our sights one moment, then gone the next," Grady responded.

"We heard a gunshot. You two alright?" Nettles said. "Do you need backup?"

"Negative. We're fine. A couple of bumps, but we are tucked away right now. Could use a status report."

"Yes, stand down, Nettles," Grady said. "We can't give away your position. Don't react to the situation. Proceed with your assignment."

"Ryan here. Nettles is scanning the house again." Ryan was silent, getting information from Nettles. "Okay. No sign of activity from the cabin. The sun is starting to glare off the windows. Nettles says it's making it difficult to see. She—Oh, hell."

"Ryan?" Grady asked the silent radio.

No reply.

"Nettles? Do you copy?" Grady clicked on the radio again.

Grady shook his head and shrugged.

Masters took the radio, "Nettles. Ryan, report," he barked.

Neither officer responded.

Grady and Masters exchanged a thought-filled stare. Masters nodded in affirmation and paced to the end of the room.

"LaCrosse. Branson. Do you copy?" Grady said.

"10-4, we're here," Branson said.

"Move in at your discretion," Grady said. "I repeat. Move in. Watch each other's six, but you're a go. Move in, now."

Chapter Twenty-Seven

Friday, March 6, 17:05

The front door splintered behind the force of LaCrosse's kick. "Savannah Police," LaCrosse yelled as he entered the cabin, weapon held high, aiming ahead. Branson crouched low, looking left. Neither officer saw evidence of a shooter.

The cabin was dark. The only light that lit the room came from the one window with the drawn blind. Their outside vision only made the darkness worse.

"Dammit," Branson said.

"Didn't you close your eyes before we entered?" LaCrosse asked.

Branson didn't answer, which gave LaCrosse his. "Just hush and sweep the room."

LaCrosse did as instructed and inched forward. From what he could see, the room was clear of activity. It was empty for the most part. A wooden table and two chairs sat in the center of the room. A tall cabinet was against the far wall. It lined up with the window that had the open blind. Near the door they entered to the right was a table with various items he couldn't make out in the darkness. He pictured keys, change, and other pocket items. Two doors lined the wall ahead of them; both were closed. Finally, there was one entryway that appeared to be a hallway that immediately made a right turn.

"This is a bad idea," Branson said, his eyes adjusting to their surroundings.

LaCrosse keyed his radio. With a whisper, he said, "We're in.

The living space is empty—two doors to our front—one hall leading to the rear. About to sweep the rooms. Stand by."

"10-4," Grady replied.

"We should have a third," Branson said, sweeping his weapon across the door behind him.

"We'll be fine. We've handled worse," LaCrosse said. "Let's do this."

Branson remembered the stand-off to which LaCrosse referred. A couple of years back, they had been dispatched to a robbery in progress where a man was holding two clerks hostage at a convenience store. He was upset that his fiancée had called off their nuptials to run off with his best friend. That stand-off had put many lives in danger. They had to go in blind on that one as well, but when lives are in the line of fire, it was always worse.

Branson took a breath and pointed at the door. "Far side first."

"10-4," LaCrosse confirmed.

Just as they proceeded through the woods, they made their way toward the far door, back-to-back. With each step, the boards beneath their feet continued to creak. Not as loud as the stairs, but enough to give away their position should someone want to know where they were or blast through the door when they stood in front of it. LaCrosse took a deep breath as they paused in front of the first door. Then he reached for the handle.

The door gave under the weight of his hand with a light snap. LaCrosse gently cracked it open, allowing the light from the window to illuminate his face. He could see a bed, its sheets crumpled; recently slept in. The sun's warmth gave the room an aroma of damp wood and body odor, making LaCrosse shudder. He took a step back and nudged the door open using the back of his gun hand, careful to keep his peripheral vision as open as he could. He was relieved to find the room was empty. But that just meant that Tanner/Thoran was elsewhere in the cabin.

LaCrosse nodded sideways at Branson to move to the next room. Branson repeated the process on the second room; this one was empty as well. The same musty odor was there, only the bed in this one hadn't been slept in. This room had a desk in addition to the bed. It was up against the window. Branson walked up to it, but there was nothing on it but a layer of dust. Both men stepped back into the living area.

Branson keyed his radio, whispering, "Both bedrooms to the south cleared. Living area cleared. Proceeding to north, creek-facing interior now. Over." He immediately turned the radio down. He turned to LaCrosse. "Ready?"

LaCrosse nodded. Being on the left, he took point. He stepped back and aimed his weapon toward the hall. Branson, his back against the wall, edged his head around the corner. He took a quick glance down the hallway. He nodded to LaCrosse, who then stepped into the hallway aiming high. Branson remained in a crouch, staying low. Both stepped into the hallway and ended up in a kitchen area with an island in the center; there was no sign of Thoran.

Both men stepped into the kitchen and lowered to the floor. They sat behind the island, weapons at their shoulders. The room was well lit by the setting sun. "Now what?" LaCrosse said. "We're sitting ducks with this much light in the room."

Branson shrugged. He bit his lower lip in thought and took a deep breath. "I have an idea," he said in a low voice. Then, with a shout, "Thoran. We just want to talk. Give yourself up."

No response.

"You can make this much easier if you put down your weapon and surrender yourself," Branson said.

Still no reply.

"Thoran."

Nothing.

"You've killed two officers, shot at two more. You really think this is going to end well for you? If you value your life, you will surrender now," Branson said.

"Yeah, that's giving her incentive to surrender," LaCrosse said, rolling his eyes.

Still, not a sound came from the room. Branson nodded his

head toward his side of the room, then to LaCrosse's. LaCrosse agreed and shifted his weight. Branson mouthed a countdown, "Three… Two… One…"

Branson rounded the island with his gun trained wherever he thought a target could be. LaCrosse followed the same pattern on the left. The room was well furnished. Far better than the front of the house; filled with more probable hiding places: chairs, a couple of couches, two end tables, a dining set, and a gun cabinet. On the far wall was a fireplace, but it seemed improbable she would hide in there. No additional rooms led off of this room. Only two exit doors led to the patio; both were closed.

"Clear?" LaCrosse asked.

"Clear," Branson said. He keyed up his radio, "Grady. Do you read?"

"10-4. Status?"

"We have made our way through the cabin. The subject isn't here. Repeat. Thoran is not in the cabin."

"Understood," Grady said.

"Nettles? Ryan?" LaCrosse asked.

"We're fine," Nettles said, keying in. "She knows we're here. When she shot at us, Ryan's com fell out of his ear and into the creek. He almost fell in after it. I'm sorry I failed to respond. My concern was getting us out of her firing range."

"Understood. Glad you two are alright," LaCrosse replied.

"Yes, we're upstream now, awaiting orders."

"Standby," Grady said. "We're blown and not sure how to proceed."

"Glad everyone is okay," LaCrosse said to Branson.

"Okay," Branson said. "Let's not forget we have a serial on the loose here. Possibly armed. Stay focused, people. Where could she have gone? We need eyes. She's back in the woods somewhere."

"Well, she's not getting out by road. We're guarding the entrance," Grady said.

"And we have a lookout at Craw-and-Dad's, so she can't go there," Nettles said.

"The terrain is too rough or marshy to attempt on foot," Branson added.

"Does she have a boat?" LaCrosse asked.

"No. We didn't see a boat on the dock while we were patrolling," Nettles keyed in.

"But she's not above stealing one," LaCrosse added.

No one spoke.

"Permission to patrol the water, Grady?" Nettles asked.

"Granted," Grady said. "But be careful. She may still have a weapon, and she knows what you look like."

"Understood."

Nettles and Ryan continued downstream, toward the cabin. In their retreat, they had nearly made it back to Craw-and-Dad's dock. Now, heading back to Tanner's cabin, they passed the dock with the lone boat. Only this time, the dock was empty. Nettles and Ryan exchanged glances.

"You thinking what I'm thinking?" Ryan said.

Nettles keyed her radio. "We may have a problem, Grady."

"Go ahead," Grady said.

"This may be speculation, but earlier in our approach to Tanner's cabin, there was a boat docked to a pier not too far upstream," Nettles began.

"And now it isn't there?" Grady asked

"No, sir, it isn't," Nettles said.

"Have you witnessed any activity on the water?"

"No. Nothing at all?"

"Understood," Grady said. "Return to Tanner's dock. But proceed with caution. Then head up to the house and meet up with LaCrosse and Branson. Keep your eyes and ears open, Nettles."

"10-4," Nettles said.

Ryan aimed the boat toward the Tanner house, and they arrived in a few minutes with no interference. They pulled the boat close to the dock, the way Arthur 'Crawdad' Crawford had instructed them. Ryan tied the boat and stepped up to the pier as Nettles kept an eye out. Then Ryan returned the favor.

Once settled, Nettles nodded. "I think we're clear. Just be ready." Nettles again nodded toward the house, and the two of them walked the narrow pier toward the house, Nettles taking the lead.

"It's quiet out here," Ryan almost whispered.

Nettles looked to the right and left. She could hear the same noises as she heard on the creek—birds chirping, the wind brushing the tree branches, and the occasional lap of water on the shore, only now she could hear the boards creaking below their feet. "Not used to silence, officer?

"Not really. I'm used to the bustle of the city. Don't make it down this way much," he said as if he was afraid of disturbing nature.

"Ha. My parents are nature freaks. Always were in the woods, brush, or places like this. It's the city that is too loud for me."

"I suppose," Ryan said. "Sorry. Guess we should hush it. Need to be listening for Thoran."

"10-4," Nettles said, pointing her thumb behind her. "Just be glad the sun is behind the trees now, or this walk would be blinding."

The two creaked along the deck the rest of the fifty meters and came to shore. Nothing was disturbed along the way, Nettles noticed. She pointed to the ground and directed Ryan to go right as she went left. The shoreline was clear both ways. "Check for anything that may be disturbed. Footprints. Anything out of the ordinary."

"Understood," Ryan said, unholstering his weapon and heading off. He scanned the tree line on each side of the shore. On his side of the cabin, his walk led him up a small incline. He was able to see through the tree line in front of him. While he couldn't see a path in the distance, he was able to make out the dock where the boat had been.

Nettles' path was flatter. Ryan could see her the entire way. He nodded as she made a gesture toward the house. The two officers crossed a hill covered with dead grass with their weapons facing the ground. They met up at the center of the path that led from the deck.

"See anything?"

"Nothing other than the deck where the missing boat was," Ryan said.

"That confirms our theory. Thoran must've escaped on that boat," Nettles said.

"Damn," Ryan said.

"You took the words out of Masters' mouth."

Nettles keyed her radio. "We're approaching the house, Grady. We're on top of a knoll and have a pretty good view of the dock where that boat got away. Good chance it was Thoran."

"Damn," Grady said. "Still proceed with caution."

"Understood."

"Do you see LaCrosse and Branson?"

"Not yet. We're approaching the house now," Nettles said, stepping up to the rear entry.

Branson opened the door. "Welcome to the party."

Nettles laughed. "There was a boat tied to a dock about a quarter-mile upstream when we approached earlier. It was still there when we retreated. When we were asked to return, it was gone. We believe it was part of this property and how Thoran slipped out of here."

"Damn," Branson said.

"Seems to be the phase of the day," Nettles snickered.

Ryan stepped onto the deck, catching his breath. He held up one finger and took a deep breath, then exhaled. "There are heavy footprints heading in the direction of the pier leading from the house. He—"

"She," both Branson and Nettles said in unison.

"Yeah," Ryan said. "Well, whoever made those prints was running fast. They begin here and go to the pier. If it was her, Thoran left on that boat."

LaCrosse joined them, and Branson updated him on the situation. LaCrosse radioed it to Grady and Masters. For the next two hours, the four officers went through the cabin collecting evidence. The only two rooms with much of anything were the bedroom they had initially entered and the living space. There was no first aid equipment; it appeared Thoran's wounds were healed. The living space, just as they found in Laguna Way, contained food wrappers and clothing. Only here, there was an element of comfort. Items were folded and stacked, not haphazardly strewn. There was a wastebasket with a liner; Thoran didn't expect to be discovered.

"Have you seen any weapons?" Ryan asked.

"Not one," LaCrosse replied, shaking his head.

"Radio it in," Branson said.

LaCrosse stepped into the living area and informed Grady of what they had learned, then he reentered the room and began stepping on boards with the tips of his boot.

"What are you doing?" Branson asked.

"Carmen asked us to check for hidden compartments. If Tanner had hidden weapons, maybe Thoran put them back before she fled. So spread out. This would be the only room she could have hidden the guns if she didn't take them with her."

LaCrosse went back to toeing his area around the living space, Branson looked to his left near the fireplace, and Nettles and Ryan checked the dining area. The room was filled with an orchestra of creaking boards. When one of them didn't creak but gave a hollow thud, two men and one lady turned toward Ryan.

"What you got?" Branson asked.

Ryan was already on his knees. He pushed the chair that was covering the board aside. The board was about six feet long and four inches wide and had a snug fit. Ryan flourished his pocket blade and pried the panel loose. The smell of fresh powder hit them before the visual evidence of a gun did.

"Well, at least we know she isn't armed with either of them," LaCrosse said.

"Yeah, just glad we weren't hit with them earlier. Either would've done serious damage," Branson said.

"Yeah, ten," LaCrosse concurred.

"Bag 'em and tag 'em," Branson instructed to no one in particular.

"We found two weapons," LaCrosse told his radio. "A rifle and a shotgun, both recently fired. They were hidden under the floorboards. We're sending Nettles and Ryan back on the boat to Craw-and-Dad's, then to you. Send a ride to us. We are *not* footing it back to the road. We'll remain here and continue searching this place until our limo arrives. LaCrosse out."

Chapter Twenty-Eight

Friday, March 20, 09:15

So, what brings you to see me today, Detective?"

"Please, call me James. I'm not on the job here, Pastor," Grady said to Reverend Eldon DeMarcus. "Well, maybe I am, I don't know. While my questions are spiritual, they do relate to the case I'm working on."

"Go ahead, James," Pastor DeMarcus said, crossing his leg over his knee. He leaned back in his chair and folded his hands on top of his chest.

"I'm not sure where to begin. Again, it concerns a case I'm working. It has thrown us for a loop. I'm doing my best to deal with it, but I'm at a loss now."

"Okay. What has you troubled? Have you dealt with difficult cases before?"

"Yes, of course. But nothing like this. That's why I'm here. This has a… spiritual aspect to it that has all of us stumped."

"Spiritual?"

"Yes, sir. I've heard you preach about Heaven and God and angels unaware, but I've yet to hear you speak of, how do I put it." Grady lowered his head and raised his eyebrows. "The other side,"

"You mean the devil and demons," the Pastor said, matching Grady's gaze.

"Yes. Exactly," Grady said, snapping up raising a palm out toward the Pastor.

The Pastor sat up. "Please, explain."

For the next hour and a half, Grady did just that. He told

Pastor DeMarcus every detail about his investigation. From the first meeting with Tanner to the latest murder the night before that brought Thoran's kill count to three, counting the nurse in the hospital. He explained the gruesome method Tanner/Thoran used, which didn't seem to affect the pastor. He also went into the details of the numbers and the significance of the transference. That seemed to pique the pastor's interest.

"You're saying that you believe Mr. Tanner is *possessing* Sophia Thoran?" Pastor DeMarcus said.

"*Believe?* No. It's a fact. We've seen first-hand evidence, Pastor. There's no doubt." Grady sat back in his chair and exhaled.

The pastor did the same. He nodded his head and stroked his peppered goatee. "I'm not sure what to say."

The room remained quiet for several minutes, with nothing but the clock filling the silence. Grady studied the pastor's face as he studied whatever he found interesting on the wall. "I wish I had answers for you, James. I could tell you this isn't real and that it's your imagination. I could tell you that Miss Thoran is faking it. There are many things I could *tell* you. I wish I were as experienced in the dark spiritual as you anticipate me to be.

"The fact is, I am not. I *can* tell you that I will pray for you and give you this advice; always be cautious about the spiritual realm. We don't take it near as seriously as we should. When we fail to, it's then that Satan attacks us. Keep your guard up. I will keep you in prayer. I'll pray about this for answers and study up. Should I discover anything, I'll get back to you."

Grady was a bit disappointed. He had hoped for more than what he was getting. He wanted to go back to the squad room with answers in case he had to face another scene like yesterday. But he understood. He shook the pastor's hand, exchanged pleasantries, and headed for the door.

Before leaving, Grady turned to the pastor. "I just want you to understand that this is a serious matter. Lives are at stake. I wouldn't have turned to you unless I believed you could help, and your expediency in this matter is crucial. Please, get back to me as soon as you know something."

"I will, James," the pastor said.

Grady walked through the foyer of the church and out the front doors.

It was a little past eleven when Grady started his Tahoe and headed to the station. He had already explained to Masters he was following a lead and would be in later than usual. He just wished he had more than, *I'll get back to you*, as filler for his notes. Before he headed upstairs, he walked down to meet with Dr. Glavine. There wasn't anything new with the latest scene; it was the same ritualistic murder. Thoran left nothing new. At least they believed it was Thoran. She was never spotted at this scene.

"I know you want me to say something, Detective," Dr. Glavine began, "but I have nothing substantial. Same ritualistic murder scene. Nothing of worth to report. Same instrument. Same length incision, same depth, nearly same amount of blood loss. If I were writing a textbook, this would be it. I'm sorry."

Grady thanked the doctor and climbed the stairs up to the ground floor. He was in no hurry to get up to the squad room. He felt as if he were a batter down to his last strike. There was no winning today. He was tired and just wished this case was over. He was done finding bodies and not having a say in saving the next victim. It was their job to protect the innocent, and if they couldn't do that, then what was the point?

The gate buzzed, and Grady dropped his keys, holster, and jacket on his desk and sat. His demeanor told the story, and he assumed it was what led others to leave him be. He leaned back in his chair and let out a deep exhale. He looked up at the board, and the victim's names stared at him, mocking him. The photos beneath each were a complete blur now. If you didn't know the cases, you would almost swear they were the same. One was female in her twenties, the other male in his forties, but at this point, what did it matter. At least, that was how it was beginning to seem to Grady.

"You okay, Grady," Carmen asked, peeking out from her array of screens.

"Yes. No," Grady said. He exhaled and stood. "Tell me you got something, Carmen."

"I wish I could," Carmen said. "It's just like the others. Clean scene. No witnesses."

"The victim?"

"Just like the others," Carmen typed on her keyboard and nodded at the screen. Grady stepped behind her. "He has no story. No local family. Lived alone, except for his goldfish. Well, a couple of Platys, but that's not important. That's the only thing that all these victims have in common."

"Well, we can't put an officer on every loner," Grady said, rolling his eyes.

"I would need two," Carmen said, elbowing Grady's arm, drawing a smile.

"Anything else?"

"We have an unmarked staking out the cabin. More like camping out. Literally. They are across the Creek within eyesight of the cabin. If Thoran returns there, we will know."

"I bet that threw Sarge for a loop."

"I didn't submit the requisition. Masters did."

"Oh, to have been a fly on the wall for that one," Grady said, rubbing his hands together.

"It did *not* go over well," a gruff older voice said behind them.

"Sorry, boss," Carmen said, exchanging smiles with Grady, not turning around.

Grady turned, and Masters motioned for him to join him in his office.

"Right away," Grady said, then to Carmen, "Thanks, Carmen."

"You got it."

Grady followed Masters into the office.

"Close the door," Masters said with a firm voice. Grady had heard that voice before; the day he started. He sat behind his desk and motioned for Grady to take a seat himself.

After Grady sat, Masters stared for a long moment. His eyes were sizing him up. He felt like that rookie officer on day one again. Masters sat up and stroked his stubble, and he let out an exasperated exhale. "So, where are we on this case, Detective?"

Detective? This can't be good. Grady took a moment before answering, attempting to choose his words and find out why the sudden formality. "Carmen has confirmed our victims all have a solitary life in common. Our latest included. I met with Dr. Glavine this morning. We still have no new forensic evidence from yesterday's vic. Thoran left nothing behind. I haven't spoken to our team across the creek; I just learned of their position this morning. I'll get with them after our meeting. Ryan and Nettles are checking out Skidaway Island. Branson and LaCrosse are at Laguna Way."

"And you?"

Grady couldn't help but give a deer in the headlights stare.

"You're doubting yourself, Detective," Masters said, still sitting upright in his chair. "What can we do to resolve this predicament?"

"I'm tired of this bastard getting away with it!" Grady snapped.

Masters let the words hang in the air, then he smiled, "Bastardess."

Grady couldn't help but laugh.

"You need to lighten up, Grady. When *you* begin to lose control," Masters pointed at him, then to the door, "your team sees it. If you become disheartened, they will reflect that behavior. Don't forget this is *your* case. *I* put you in the driver's seat. Don't let me down; don't let *them* down."

Grady leaned back, closed his eyes, and rubbed his temples.

"Hell, if anything, remember that Branson is looking for anything to put you back in your place."

Again, his boss gave him a reason to chuckle.

"I want to put this one to bed." Grady began, "We know who's doing it; we just need to catch him, or her, whatever. They have one more random before we know the actual date. I hate to sign another person's death warrant, but my eyes are focused on April first."

"Is that what's bothering you? The sacrifices that may need to be made?"

"I suppose," Grady said. "I don't like to think any life should be sacrificed. That life matters. He or she should have the chance to live. We should make every effort to save them just like we should try and save April first."

"And we will. No one said we're not going to try and stop Thoran. But we shouldn't beat ourselves up if we fail. If we did that over every failed case, then we'd never get our job done. We shake it off and do better on the next case. Yes, we'll do our best to save Thoran's next victim, but we won't lose it if we fail."

"Will we fail?"

"Hell no," Masters said with a wink.

Friday, March 20, 19:15

"How much?"

"Twelve," Elizabeth said, grinning with pride.

Grady sat up in his chair. "On one sale?"

"Yes, sirree," she said, slapping the arms of her own.

"Intense. When does that become official?"

"As soon as the client signs the paperwork. Tomorrow. End of the week at the latest."

"Wow."

"I know, right?"

"Just. Wow."

Grady stared at his wife's glowing face. It shimmered in the light of their dining room chandelier.

"You're beautiful," he said.

"It's just the Georgia humidity."

"Maybe," Grady said. "Either way, you're beaming like an angel, Lizzy."

"I'm glad your home," Elizabeth said.

"Me too. I'm sorry this case has been taking up so much of my time."

"It's not just you." Her gaze turned to the table. "This sale has taken me away too. You're not the only one who hasn't been home. You just don't know it 'cause you're not here. I've spent most of the time at the office trying to get better at this job. I've been driving around the city learning where things are, at the office studying laws, anywhere but here. So, it's not just you, my love."

Elizabeth's eyes met his. The shared burden eased Grady's guilt, but he still felt he should've been around more for her or cared enough to check in more. But her eyes revealed that she felt the same way. The unspoken words shared that further apologies were not needed. They understood each other—that was enough. Love had a way of doing that.

Elizabeth's gaze turned to a smile, signaling that everything was okay. He returned the gesture and poured her another glass of tea. "So, when will this wave of good fortune hit the bank account?"

"Sometime next week."

"Well, there goes a steak dinner tonight," Grady said, grinning.

"Well, Detective. Can't you pull some strings and get us a table somewhere?"

"We haven't been here that long, Lizzy. Plus, with all your touring, you may have more pull than I would," Grady chuckled. "The best I could do is a fancy sandwich shop on the south side."

Elizabeth raised her eyebrows, "How's their au jus?"

"Ha, never got that far," Grady said, laughing and rolling back in his seat. "I had the Reuben."

"Should have known." Elizabeth smiled, stood, and headed for the fridge. "You want something?"

"No, I'm fine."

They spent the rest of the evening without a word about the past few weeks—no discussions of clients or serials. The world could have erupted around them, but in those few hours, all that mattered was the two of them, like newlyweds. It was what they needed. They moved into the living room and shared space on the couch, then to the bedroom and shared each other in the way married couples intimately knew each other. They fell asleep spent of energy and with the assurance that everything was going to be alright.

Sunday, March 22, 10:30

Grady opened his church bulletin and read the morning sermon topic. **Heaven and Hell: Topics We Never Discuss**. He wanted to crawl under a rock. Even though only he and the pastor knew of their discussion, he felt that he would somehow end up in the spotlight. Even Elizabeth didn't know the depth of the case he was on. Grady didn't want to worry her. Now, if the pastor would even glance in his direction or mention his name, what would he do?

He closed the bulletin, took his seat, and smiled the best he could. He shook hands with others and gave his best Baptist *church* display that he could. The choir sang their songs, the Pastor gave announcements of coming ministry opportunities, and the music minister's wife sang a song about Easter in a few weeks. When she sang her final note, she sat, and Pastor DeMarcus stood and straightened his tie, adjusting his lapel mic. He approached the pulpit and swiped the screen of his tablet.

"Thank you, Anne Marie. That was beautiful, as always," Pastor DeMarcus began, looking to Anne Marie, who was sitting on the left side of the church. His eyes looked up the rows to the back of the church, then to the opposite side and back to the front, and locking eyes with Grady and holding them a bit longer than the others. Pastor DeMarcus then cleared his throat, "Our sermon this morning, if you haven't seen your bulletin, is titled, 'Heaven and Hell: Topics We Never Discuss'"

Grady held his breath and thought he wouldn't be able to

let it go again until he was safe at home. Elizabeth must have noticed because he felt an elbow to his side, which did two things; enabled him to breathe again and drew a puzzled look from her and the row in front of them. *Sorry,* he mouthed.

For the next twenty-five minutes, Grady was reminded that people would emphasize the Heaven part of salvation and forget that there is also the Hell portion of it. "We must realize that Hell is real and understand that there are people in this world on the path there," the pastor emphasized. "There may even be people in the sanctuary where we are sitting that were heading there."

The uncomfortable silence that followed made even Grady nervous, and he was confident of his salvation.

Pastor DeMarcus wrapped up his sermon with a reminder that people didn't need to feel lost or be doomed. They could turn to God and toward salvation because God sent his Son, Jesus, to save the world from sin and Hell. If Grady hadn't already been saved, he would've been first up the aisle. Others must've also felt the pull because there was little room this week. The fear he felt earlier had lifted and was replaced with a peace that those at the front were comforted by turning to the One who could save them.

Grady felt a new sense of strength. Masters was right. He needed to get his head on straight. And this morning was just what he needed. Last night with Lizzy gave him purpose for himself, personally; today gave him purpose, spiritually. He was ready to complete the job that needed to be done. Tanner was now no match for him. Grady understood the odds. Grady and his team were going to save the life of the next person on his list.

Pastor DeMarcus prayed for those at the altar, those new souls bound for Heaven rejoiced as they stood, everyone, including Grady, shouted their, "Amen!" with new confidence in what lay before them.

Grady was so excited that he didn't notice his phone buzzing in his pocket. He failed to notice the blinking light of the voicemail that was left behind. It was only when he reached the car that he heard the voice mail that would put his newfound strength to the test and set the finale in motion:

"First message, sent, Sunday, March twenty-second, twelve ten p.m. ... BEEP."

"Well, hello, Detective Grady," said the female voice, "You may not know me. Oh, hell, who are we kidding? You know me all too well. This is Sophia Thoran. You may also know me as Stephen Tanner. You and I have much to discuss...."

Chapter Twenty-Nine

Monday, March 23, 08:30

Well, hello, Detective Grady," said the female voice, "*You may not know me. Oh, hell, who are we kidding? You know me all too well. This is Sophia Thoran. You may also know me as Stephen Tanner. You and I have much to discuss. It's too bad you are busy with your family at church. I was looking forward to speaking with you.*

"*As you can see, this number is blocked, so your Albanese can't trace this to my location. Maybe I'll call you back, maybe I won't. The anticipation is killing me. Who will be next? When will it be? The clock is ticking, Detective, and you can't save them all. Good-bye, Grady,*" the call ended, and Grady hit the red button.

"Wow," Carmen said.

"Yeah, no kidding," Grady said. "I just wish I had seen the call come in."

"You still would've ignored it," Carmen said. "Who answers an unknown number. We all expect it's a spammer and let it go to voicemail."

"Well, I'm for sure answering the next one."

"We have nine days until she makes her final move," Masters said. "Between now and then, we are confident she'll take one more life."

"If Tanner/Thoran sticks to their pattern," Branson said, folding his arms.

"Have they ever strayed?" Ryan asked.

"Not when he was Tanner, not when he was Nelson, we expect nothing less now that he is Sophia Thoran," Masters said.

"The last time Tanner called in to Sarge, he was with his final victim. I don't know if he did that with Nelson or just with Thoran. But we can expect she'll do that this go-around. We need to be prepared," Grady explained.

"I want to go over your recording, Grady," Carmen said. "I'll listen for anything distinguishing in the background. It's worth a shot. Hey, it works in the movies."

"Worth a shot. Thanks," Grady said.

"What else can we do?" LaCrosse asked from the back of the squad room.

Grady hated to ask them to do what they had been doing the last couple of weeks. The very thing that led them to strike out and to rush to the body of their latest victim. She had been a thirty-year-old yoga instructor the neighbors labeled a recluse, and no one knew she had been murdered until the ambulance showed up.

"We keep our eyes and ears open," Grady looked down and took a breath. "I'm sorry. It's the best we can do. I'm not happy about it either. I understand the risks."

"Yeah, another person has to die," Branson said.

"You don't think we understand that, Branson?" Masters said, raising his voice with an extended hand.

Branson lowered his head and took a breath, "There must be something we can do."

"If you have any ideas, we're more than happy to hear them," Masters said, sitting upright, arms folded.

Branson didn't have any ideas. Nor did anyone else. Thoran had them. The team could only wait for her to make her next move on the name on her list. While Grady's mind was waiting for the grand finale on April first, he was still determined to do all he could to save the next person. Even though he feared it would be a lost cause. He said a silent prayer to calm his spirit.

"I don't want whoever is out there to die any more than you do, Branson," Grady explained. "But if we are out there instead of in here, we have a greater chance of saving the next victim.

All we *can* do is wait. Unfortunately, waiting is the game we have to play."

Branson looked to the ground and nodded.

"C'mon, partner," LaCrosse said, tugging at Branson's sleeve. "I know a good coffee shop we can set up. We can drown our sorrows and have a danish or two."

Grady watched Branson and LaCrosse head out of the squad room. He exhaled and sat at his desk, opening up the latest two case folders. Masters came up behind him.

"And stop letting Branson get to you. His little remarks don't need to get under your skin. You're above that. We've gone over that," Masters said.

"He didn't get to me," Grady smiled. "He got to *you*."

Masters was silent for a moment, looked at the gate, then back to Grady. "Okay, you got me there. He's been negative since he started. I've let it slide, but now it matters. Guess I'm just beginning to notice how irritating it is. Thanks," Masters said, rubbing the stubble on his face.

"My pleasure," Grady said, standing and patting Masters on the shoulder. "I want to be out there too. You're my ride, so let's get going, boss."

Thursday, March 26, 02:35

A nudge woke Grady, the one only a wife could give if she's disturbed from her sleep.

"James. Your phone," Elizabeth said, with another punch to his shoulder.

Grady glanced to the nightstand at the glowing screen, and once his vision cleared, he read the words, UNKNOWN NUMBER. Those words sobered him faster than a cattle prod to the tail end. He quickly swiped right. Grady had turned off voicemail so the phone would ring endlessly until the caller gave up. This caller had not given up.

Grady took his phone and went into the hall, gently closing the door behind him. He cleared his throat, more to wake himself than anything, "Hello? Tanner, er, Thoran?"

"Ha. I suppose it doesn't matter what moniker you use. You are correct. Use whatever name pleases you, Detective," the caller said.

"Thoran," Grady chose, "where are you? You need to turn yourself in. This needs to end."

"Nice try. It doesn't work that way. I'm not calling to give myself up."

"Then why are you calling?"

"You intrigue me, Detective."

"And how is that?"

"I see more than you know. I know more than you see."

"So, we're on to riddles now," Grady said.

Thoran gave a bellowing laugh. "Not exactly. I've been following you while you've been following me. You see, Detective, the best place to hide from someone who is searching for you is behind the one who is searching for you."

Grady sat at the dining room table, speechless. Had he been that clueless?

"Are you there, Detective? Cat got your tongue?"

"I'm here. So, what's next? Who's next? Wait. Let me guess? It doesn't work that way."

Grady could feel the smile through the phone, "Now you're getting it. See, we understand each other. And I think you know what comes next, Detective. We've played this game before."

"Can I ask you a question? Out of curiosity?" Grady asked, unsure if he would get a straight answer, but even Dr. Glavine couldn't answer this question.

"I'm in a good mood. What's your question?"

"Where's Thoran? Is she in there somewhere? Or have you completely taken over, Tanner?"

The line went silent. Grady didn't think he was going to get an answer, much less the truth. He heard the sound of a deep breath and an exhale.

"The truth is, Grady, I don't know how this works. All I know is that it does. And I must keep doing it. There is nothing you or your team can do to stop me, much like tonight. It's already over. We both know this has to happen. Jeremy has to die and die he will. Then Sophia Thoran will have no more use for me."

"Wait, who is Jeremy?"

"Does it matter? He's a nobody. He doesn't play into the grand scheme of things. Just a stair-step toward our grand finale. A quarter that makes part of the whole. It's the next one that matters. C'mon, you know this. If you don't, then you are not the Detective I thought you were."

"Please, let me save him. Just leave him there and move on. Where are you?" Grady said, dialing the precinct from his home phone.

"Do you really think that's going to work, James?"

"What?"

"You are trying to call the station from home?"

"How do—"

"I told you, I see more than you know. Shame on you. I thought we had trust here?"

"Trust? You're murdering a man as we speak."

"You still aren't paying attention. His death must happen. That's beyond my control. Even if you sent paramedics now, they wouldn't make it. I'll even prove it." With that, Tanner/Thoran hung up the phone.

"Tanner," Grady said. "Thoran? Dammit," Grady looked at his phone and saw that the line had disconnected.

The phone rang two seconds later, this time with a phone number. Grady answered it even before a second ring.

"Hello?"

"Here is your proof, Detective. Make your call. Trace that phone. I will make it easy; I won't even hang up. But I'm gone. Try and save Jeremy here. But I make these final two incisions, and he's done. Heck, I don't even need to. He is barely breathing as it is; he was a bleeder," Thoran laughed. "Passed out after the first incision."

Grady had already dialed the station and given them the agreed-upon code. The trace on Grady's phone had begun. This also triggered wake-up calls to the entire team, who would then roll out of bed and head to the station or the designated muster area. Grady wished Carmen had a Masters-like bunker in the office. She would already have the address and a helicopter with a SWAT team over the location.

"Are you listening, Detective?"

"Yes, I'm here."

"Tell me I am in control."

"Now, why would I want to do that?"

"Because I am."

"Well, as you say, Jeremy dies anyway. So, why would I want to give you the satisfaction?"

"There are others who could die, you know?"

"Nuh, uh. Not your style. You stick to the plan. You're meticulous. The nurse in the hospital was an accident. It wasn't part of the plan. You wouldn't have done it if it weren't necessary."

The line went silent. Grady felt the bluff had been called. "You do know me then. You *are* the Detective I thought you were. But you do understand. I *am* in control."

"If you say so, Thoran," Grady said. He heard a click, then a female voice mumbling, then chanting.

Grady could hear Jeremy's cries as Thoran made the final incisions, then silence. Thoran/Tanner never came back to the phone. Then came a rustling in the background, maybe her preparing to leave, maybe Jeremy fighting for his life.

"Thoran?" Grady said, knowing he wouldn't get a response. "Tanner?"

Grady dialed Masters. He picked up on the second ring.

"You have anything?"

"Nothing yet. Carmen is doing her magic on limited resources from her home. She said it would be quicker than trying to make the drive in."

"10-4," Grady said. "And the team?"

"All up and on their way to their locations."

"I'm dressing and heading out the door," Grady said. "Let me know the second you have anything."

Chapter Thirty

Thursday, March 26, 03:05

Grady was sitting in his idling car near Santa Josephine's Medical Center. He hadn't pulled up a minute before his phone rang; it was Carmen. "He's on Isle of Hope. Best I can do."

"10-4," Grady said. "I've got you on speaker. Direct me."

Grady traded rubber for asphalt and headed East on the highway. He put his light on his dash and slipped in between sedans, semis, and construction cones.

"That's the Moon River District," Carmen said.

Grady accelerated. Eight minutes later, he exited the highway and onto the empty main street. His red light lit up the street signs ahead of him. He found the road sign directing him into the District.

"Okay, where to next?"

"You're going to come to a T in the road, hang a right," Carmen instructed.

"Then where?"

"Half a mile, then a left. There will be a shopping center on your left."

"How close am I?"

"Less than two minutes."

"Do you have an address?" Grady asked.

Silence.

"Carmen, do you have an address?"

"I have the neighborhood. You're lucky to have that. It's the best I can do. It's a burner phone and has minimal software."

"Sorry. Thank you."

Grady made the left, his tires squealing. A second sedan pulled up behind him, the same red swirling light.

"On your six, Grady." It was Nettles and Ryan.

"Good to have you," Grady said. "Just follow me."

"10-4."

"You're on Normandy," Carmen further instructed, "the street you are looking for is Lentil Road. It's on your left. It'll take you back and end at another T; that's Pierce. Take a right. You're on your own from there. Sorry. It's within a quarter-mile from that turn."

Grady found Lentil Road, then the T. He turned off his emergency light to get a better view of the neighborhood. Even in the darkness, Grady could see the well-manicured lawns of middle-class families, boats and RVs, and shiny new vehicles sitting in the driveways. These were families, not the type Tanner targeted. House after house told the same story.

"There is a side street up here," Grady said to Nettles. "Take the left and look for houses that only have one or no cars. We need evidence of single living."

"Understood," Nettles said.

Grady switched channels. "Dispatch, can you read?" Grady said to his mic.

"Yes, Detective. This is Officer Mason. Sarge won't be in until 0600."

"That's fine. I just need you to send EMS to the Moon River District. We will have an address by the time they get here."

"I'm on it, Detective. Mason out."

Grady turned left onto a side street and saw a house without a car in the driveway. He slammed on his breaks because there were words painted on one of the double garage doors.

NOT HERE DETECTIVE

Was this a joke? Was Jeremy in there? Grady thought back to their conversation and pulled away. Jeremy wasn't there. This *was* a game, but Tanner respected him enough not to pull silly mind tricks like that.

Grady passed another car-less house two doors down...

NOT HERE EITHER

The street curved...

GETTING WARMER

"Everyone get to my location, now," Grady barked into his mic, "New Haven Road. Inform EMS. You'll see my light." Grady hit the gas. He figured speed wouldn't matter. If Tanner/Thoran had been leaving these calling cards, she would be highlighting the grand prize—He wasn't disappointed.

YOU FOUND ME!!

was written on a garage door half a block down. Grady turned his wheel, and tires squealed partway into the drive. His headlights illuminated the red-painted billboard. He reached into the passenger seat and pulled his weapon from its holster.

The creaking car door announced Grady's visit, and as he approached the garage, he realized Thoran's proclamation was written in blood.

Thursday, March 26, 06:45

"There was nothing you could've done, Grady," Masters said with his hand on Grady's shoulder.

Grady held the coroner's sheet from Jeremy's body. The blood was already coagulating on his T-shirt. He was bigger than he had anticipated, probably had fifty pounds on Thoran, and at least five inches taller. "How could she overpower him?"

"What?" Masters asked.

"How could a woman of Thoran's size overpower a man of Jeremy's size?"

"Maybe this transference does something physical as well? Could she have Tanner's strength?"

"That's insane," Ryan said, standing at the door to the room. "Sorry. Didn't mean to snoop. The house is clear. No sign of Thoran anywhere. No evidence she was even here. Forensics still has to dust and process the scene. Dr. Glavine says he has a team on the way."

"Thank you, Officer. Has Nettles returned from the other homes yet?" Masters asked.

"Yes. She said that it was spray paint, not blood, at the other homes. The words here were the only ones written in Mr. Warren's blood."

"Presumably, his blood," Masters said.

"Right. Yes. Forensics," Ryan said.

Grady lowered the sheet and exhaled. "Thank you, Officer. Tell Nettles the same. Drive a perimeter of the area a couple of times, and then you're released for the morning. Grab something to eat and meet us at the station at 12:00."

"10-4," Ryan said and left.

Grady looked over the scene they were all too familiar with—the moved furniture, the centered coffee table, the pooled blood; no other marks or disturbance otherwise.

"What's on your mind, Grady?"

"Guilt," Grady said with a soft tremor.

"There was nothing you could've done. We were too far away to get here in time," Masters said. "Even if—"

"That's not what I mean," Grady cut him off, meeting Masters' eyes.

Grady wasn't experiencing guilt over the loss of Mr. Warren; he was relieved. Now they could focus on April first. True, it was unfortunate that a man had to die, but that was now in the past. Masters was right in saying they did all they could, but Grady felt he should have more grief over Mr. Warren than what he was experiencing. But now that it was a lost cause, his focus could switch to April first. He already knew the when and what. He just needed to make sure they were the ones to be there.

"Don't beat yourself up," Masters said. "Let's get out of here and focus on the next one. We both know there is nothing here. Tanner is too meticulous, and being this close, he's going to be extra cautious. Branson and LaCrosse have already photographed the room. They'll finish processing it after Mr. Warren is removed and forensics shows up."

Grady nodded and took one last glance at Jeremy as the coroner loaded him onto a gurney. He followed Masters to the door. LaCrosse scribbled in his notepad, and Branson watched a cleaning crew remove the now brown stained slur off the garage door. Grady figured blood was more important than the paint several doors down. Masters started to speak with LaCrosse, but Grady placed his hand on Masters' shoulder and took over the conversation.

Grady filled LaCrosse in on the plans he and Masters had discussed. Branson joined them when the brown stain on the garage door was now a brown puddle on the concrete. They gave affirmation of their orders and headed into the house. Grady and Masters headed to his vehicle. Grady couldn't help but notice Masters' pride in him taking charge, as they had discussed the week before. Grady knew it was what he had to do. It was what the team needed.

"Great job, rookie," Masters said with a wink, getting into the passenger side of Grady's car.

Monday, March 30, 10:30

Grady's phone was silent, as was the department floor for several days. As they had assumed, the scene was just as the previous murders had been, routine. Tanner/Thoran had left no clue behind. The phone that Thoran had called Grady from had no fingerprints and no call history. He was waiting on its history from Carmen. Not that a video of Thoran buying the phone would do them any good. She was smart enough not to walk next door to where she was hiding to pick one up.

"Ha," Carmen said, reading her screen. "You'll never guess where Thoran purchased her phone."

"Craw-and-Dad's," Nettles said, looking up from the morning paper.

"Okay. Maybe I was wrong. How did you know that?"

"Because they sold prepaid phones," Ryan said through a mouth full of kolache. He swallowed and continued. "Sorry. They had a big sign about not getting your expensive phone wet." He waved his hand like a banner, "*Use a prepaid phone. Activate in seconds,* it advertised."

"Nice work, officer," Nettles said.

Ryan tossed a balled-up napkin at her. "You don't have to be a detective to detect, Detective."

"That still doesn't help us," Grady said.

"True," Carmen said. "Though we can see if she purchased more than one. If they keep track or remember those things."

"Nettles, make the call. It's worth a shot," Grady said.

"I'm on it."

"Wait," Grady extended his hand. "No stone unturned, right?"

"Has been, always will be, boss," Nettles nodded.

"Then take a drive down there. A call is short-changing it. Maybe seeing the two of you will spark Ms. Crawford's memory better than a phone call."

"You're driving, rookie," Nettles said.

Ryan shrugged, swallowing another bite, taking the keys thrown at him.

"I'd listen to her if I were you," Grady said. "I've ridden with her. No use arguing. And let her choose the radio station. She's got great taste."

The buzzer sounded, and they headed down the stairs, leaving Grady and Carmen at her screen. "Find anything else?" Grady asked.

"Other than the phone, no," Carmen said and let the room fill with silence. "It was good of you to relieve Branson and LaCrosse for the day."

"What good would it do to have them here. We're just waiting for Wednesday. All Branson would do is complain, and all LaCrosse would do is be upset that Branson is complaining. Let them get some rest."

"Still, it was a good gesture. It shows you care about your team." Carmen looked over from her screen and smiled, then turned back to what she was doing.

"Thanks. You could've taken it off too, you know. You're the hardest worker here."

"Ahhh, someone does notice," Carmen's face beamed. "Nuh, uh, though. You know me better than that. No one touches my keyboard but me. Even Masters knows better than that. Plus, I would lose that title if I took a day off."

"You could take a week off and still reign as queen," Grady said with a bow.

"Ha." Carmen raised her hand. "Rise my subject. We need to figure out whatever are we to do next?"

That managed to get Grady to smile, "Agreed. We need a general location to begin our search. We know Tanner/Thoran is going to call, or if she sticks to the pattern, she'll get her next victim to call Dispatch. If it means anything, I'd like to find her before she makes that call. And we have a day and a half to do it."

"Haven't seen her," Emily Crawford said, pushing a shop broom across the wooden porch. "Guess y'all scared her off."

"Do you recall her purchases the last time she was in here?" Nettles asked.

Emily stopped pushing the broom and leaned on its handle. She looked into the distance contemplating her answer, "I already told you that. Snacks and stuff."

"Yes, but what was the *and stuff*," Ryan said, "did she purchase anything electronic? Flashlight, batteries, a phone maybe?"

Emily's face lit up, "Yea, she purchased a couple of cell phones."

"A couple?" Nettles asked.

"Yeah, two of 'em," Emily nodded. "I remember thinkin' *Why would a person need two phones?* We sell 'em cause the fishermen are always tryin' to tell us we need to pay fer their phones when they drop 'em in the creek. So, Pop decided to start sellin' disposable phones."

"So, she purchased two of them?" Ryan asked.

"That's what I said," Emily said with a contorted face.

"Sorry," Nettles said. "Just needed to be clear on the number. It's important."

"Yeah. Just two," Emily said.

"How many of those have you sold since Miss Thoran purchased hers?" Nettles asked.

"I haven't been here the whole time. We do have some help. Comes in a couple times a week. I'd have to ask."

"Don't you have to track the phones?" Ryan asked.

"Yeah. We got a scanner in back that does all that. We scan 'em when we put 'em out here."

"Can you please check if you've sold any?"

"S'pose," Emily said, rolling her eyes. "Watch the front. I have to go to the back fer a minute."

Emily went to the back, and a few minutes later she came back with a piece of paper in her hand. She was reading from it as she was walking. She confirmed that including Sophia Thoran's purchases, one other phone had been purchased. The numbers were not sequential, nor were the serial numbers. To their benefit, the Crawford's had only purchased twelve phones. Two boxes of six and only one box of six had been opened. She handed the paper to Nettles.

"Keep it. It's a copy," Emily said. She pointed to the paper, "I highlighted the three numbers that were bought. Don't know which ones were hers."

A bell rang at the front of the store, and Emily went to the register. "S'cuse me, Detectives."

"Thank you, Miss Crawford," Nettles said as she left. Nettles eyed Ryan, who shrugged.

"Remember, Ryan, you're not on the street anymore. It's not about how firm you are in getting an answer. Kind words can get you further when you have the choice."

"Understood," Ryan said.

Ryan thanked Emily and made a courtesy purchase on their way out.

Chapter Thirty-One

Tuesday, March 31, 09:30

Do you know what today is, Detective?"

"March Thirty-first," Grady said.

"And tomorrow?" Thoran asked.

"April first."

"More detail, please."

"First quarter moon."

"Very good. You *have* figured it all out, then," Thoran said, pride evident in her voice.

"All but the where. But we will."

"Do you know where I am right now?"

"Why don't you enlighten me?" Grady said. He looked over to Carmen, who circled her hand in the air, signaling for more time.

"Don't bother with the trace. I'm not where you think I am and not using that silly phone you think I'm using. I threw that thing away."

"Did you now?" Grady asked.

There was silence on the line.

"Maybe I did, maybe I didn't. This game wouldn't be as fun if you couldn't find my final location now, would it?"

"Where is the final location, Thoran?"

"Detective. Would this be a game if I told you everything? What? You want me to use the restroom for you too?"

"Just thought you would want to raise the stakes. You have done that so far," Grady said.

More silence.

"What makes you think I've raised the stakes?"

"When have you ever called to speak to us? To me? Much less used a cell phone in any of your crimes. You're taking chances, Tanner. You want to be challenged—you have raised the stakes."

Longer silence.

"Thoran, are you there?"

"So maybe I have," Tanner/Thoran said with an edge to her voice. "You and your team have become less of a challenge to me, Detective. I'm bored. This was once fun. Now it has become tedious, something I must do to survive. So, I have to raise the stakes to make it interesting."

"And talking to me is part of this game," Grady said.

"Of course, it is, Grady," Thoran said. Grady could hear her sinister grin through the phone. He looked to Carmen.

Carmen shrugged. "The only thing that can explain this is if he were on the move," she whispered. "She appears to be moving South on 95," Carmen raised her hand at her computer screen, "I think. Toward Harris Neck."

Grady nodded to Masters, who was sitting at Grady's desk. He texted the team and informed them to head toward the cabin. Branson and LaCrosse were nearest and were on I-95 in minutes. Nettles and Ryan were North near Port Wendle. They gave their acknowledgment, threw their light on their dash, and danced through traffic. Masters gave the thumbs up.

"But you lose at the end of the game," Grady said.

"Do I? Only this vessel losses. I move on to bigger and better," Thoran said.

"Is that a clue?"

"Not really. It's not a matter of who, it's a matter of being. I get to start over. I just won't make the same mistakes I made with this weak vessel," she said.

"The escape from the hospital?" Grady asked.

"Yes. That was rather idiotic on my part. It slowed me down. I made my move far too soon. But I saw an opportunity and made my move."

"And murdered an officer in the process," Grady said deeper than he intended.

"Oh, your Detective Mesa," Thoran said as if remembering something. "Nearly forgot about him. Yes, things like that do happen. I'm sorry. So, I suppose the other one survived, or you'd be as bitter about her."

"Yes, she's fine. Walks with a bit of a limp, but she will be just fine," Grady said.

"Neither here nor there," Thoran said. "Her survival doesn't absolve me of anything."

"True," Grady said. "So, where are you?"

"Ah. Ah. Ah. Detective. Mind games won't work on me. You can't distract me that way."

"Fair enough. You said you made mistakes. So did we. You can rest assured we won't make those same mistakes. Even if you do manage to make your transference, you won't get away from the hospital. We will let you rest and heal. But the only place you'll get away to is a prison cell. Then the only moon you will see will be through a prison cell window, if you are even lucky enough to have one of those."

Silence.

"Tell me, what happens if you miss one of your quarter moon deadlines?"

Silence.

"Thoran?"

Silence.

"Tanner!"

"I've never missed one," Thoran/Tanner said, again smiling through the phone line. "And you know, Detective, there are bodies in prison."

"Don't they have to be single, live alone, and have no connections?"

"A dossier you and your department created. I don't need someone coming home or calling when I'm busy. Loners make the best candidates. Nobody cares about them. I do just enough to bring curiosity, then let nosy neighbors do the rest. By the time you guys get there, I'm long gone. Inside a prison, it doesn't matter. I will choose whom I see fit."

"It doesn't matter. You won't have a choice. We're going to find you and stop you even before you get to your next victim," Grady said, his teeth bared as he stood staring out the window.

"You're already too late, Detective. I've already found him. He is already me. I'm already him. Or… is it a she? I will see you on the other side," Thoran said and hung up.

"Thoran," Grady said.

"She hung up," Carmen said. "All I can tell you is that she was heading South on 95. She kept pinging off towers. She was using that second burner number we have."

"She said she had already found him," Grady said.

"Yeah. She was either tailing her victim or giving us a false trail to follow," Masters said, then softened his voice to match Thoran's tone. "What's your impression, Detective?"

"Oh, shut up," Grady said.

"Well, she is obviously taken by you," Masters said. "What *is* your impression?"

Grady looked at his page of notes. He looked to Carmen, who had a silent smile on her face, then back to Masters; his grin had vanished, Grady knew what he was looking for.

"She was on his tail," Grady said. "She wants the challenge of almost getting caught. She said it herself. She's bored. The *getting away with it* isn't fun anymore. I don't believe her final words were a slip-up. She told us she was going after a male."

"I agree," Masters said, nodding his head. "Where was she, Carmen?"

"She last pinged just South of Newpark, where Nelson dropped his vehicle," Carmen said, the computer screen glowing off her lenses.

"How far is that from Harris Neck?"

"Ahhhh, thirty miles to the exit," Carmen said. "Give or take. But she can't go there. We have it staked out. If she does, we got her."

"She won't go there. Thoran is smarter than that. Plus, she has her mark. That's where she's going to stay." Grady said.

"Well, her last ping was off a cell tower five miles South of that Newpark exit."

"Okay, we have a starting point. Better there than sitting up here," Grady said.

"There's a Qwik Stop on I-95 and 84. Just outside of Holloway," Masters said. "We can set up there."

"Call the team and let them know," Grady said, nodding to the phone.

Masters nodded back and called Ryan and Branson, directing them to the service station. "We're all set. The kids are en route."

"We should get going, too," Grady said. "We still carry overnight bags, right?"

"Prepare for every situation. Our team's motto. We planning a sleepover?" Masters asked.

"Yeah. Is there a motel at that Qwicky place?"

"Qwik Stop," Masters said with a chuckle. "Yes, it's a service station with a truck stop."

"We need to stay down there. It's going to be a long night."

Chapter Thirty-Two

Tuesday, March 31, 23:30

The smell of exhaust fumes met Grady as he crossed the Qwik Stop lot to get coffee for the team. Truck drivers from Charlotte, Atlanta, and Jacksonville filled the limited parking spaces to the rear of the facility and spilled out onto the highway. The grinding hum of diesel engines almost silenced the ringing of Grady's phone. With his hands full of coffee and pastries, he had nowhere to set them down. The top of a nearby trash bin around a corner was the best he could find.

It was the same *Unknown Number* displayed as before.

"Hello?" Grady said.

"I was beginning to think you weren't going to answer, Detective," Thoran said.

"Was in the shower," Grady said.

"Or you are trying to trace this call, which you'll have no luck. I've taken certain safety measures to ensure my anonymity."

"Of course, you have."

"Just hours from our big day."

Grady didn't say anything.

"You must be excited. The big stage; you and me. We have a game to finish."

Grady's eyebrows raised, "Do we now?"

"Of course. I won the last one. You couldn't get to Jeremy in time."

"This is a game to you? Life is a game?"

"Why shouldn't it?"

"I believe life is about more than who wins and who loses, Thoran," Grady said.

"Why do you say that?"

"It just is."

"What? God?" Thoran said, her voice raising an octave.

"Yes. God. He has more power than you'll ever have."

Grady could hear Thoran laughing. It wasn't her usual laugh; the pleasant female laugh that would make a man smile inside. This was a sinister, almost growl that sent fear through Grady.

"Let me tell you about God," the new voice said. The female subtleness was there, but it had deeper undertones. Was it Tanner? He couldn't tell. "I have risen from the dead more times than your God has, Detective. Who has the power now?" Grady wasn't sure how to answer Thoran's challenge. Her question had validity. Tanner and Nelson died. And yet that spirit now lived in Thoran. One spirit, three hosts. Tanner had managed to be raised not once but twice. Christ had only risen once. It should be no contest. Once versus twice. It's in the numbers. Two is more than one.

"The numbers don't matter," Grady said, half convinced. "Christ only needed once."

"Keep telling yourself that, Detective. That is why you don't see him anymore. He is weak. Once and he was done. It's what makes us more powerful. We are still here," Thoran said.

"We?"

"You think I'm the only one? Boy, are you naïve. Who do you think I learned this from?"

"The internet," Grady said, half-joking.

"Don't patronize me, Detective," Thoran said, a sharp edge to her voice. "I have been nothing but polite and honest with you."

"Calling my God weak is being polite?"

"No, but it's honest," Thoran said. She took a deep breath, and when Thoran spoke again, her voice had returned to normal. "But we are getting way off topic here, Grady. Our game is the only subject I'm concerned with at the moment.

And our time is running out. We've less than twelve hours until showtime."

"Right. Six o'clock." Grady said, checking his watch. "So, with so much time before the show, what's the purpose of your call?"

"I've already told you," Thoran giggled again. "To give you a sporting chance to win our game."

"Either way, I win." Grady said. "We've already gone over this. I'm just waiting for the call to come and get you."

"Yes, Detective," Thoran sneered. "You've said that already. You're wrong. We both have a chance of winning. That's the point of this challenge—the fun of it. It was fun with Officer Ryan. He looked like he was going to wet himself before I transferred into that kid. Then those two security buffoons messed things up with Thoran. I had to take a different route. This time I want it perfect. You are a worthy adversary—the best. And you will be there, no one else. Mano y mano. That's the purpose of my call."

"You want me there, alone?"

"Alone."

"What purpose would that serve?" Grady asked.

"Ever heard of a quick draw, Detective?"

"Of course."

"Consider this something of the sort. Just ask Ryan. He won. And lost."

"If I am there, you won't get that far, Tanner," Grady said, pointing to the ground for emphasis.

"Now we're talking," Tanner/Thoran said, her smile reaching through the phone. "Tell you what. I will call you later with the details. And don't tell anyone about our conversation. Tell them you were on the phone with your precious Lizzy or something. And no, not even Carmen can see that I am using this phone right now. But you better hurry back to your team, the coffee's getting cold."

Grady almost dropped his phone as his head spun around, but he saw nothing suspicious. The handful of vehicles that were there were empty. He looked around the corner at the rows of semis, and the sounds and smells hit him again. He considered her hiding in the cab of a truck but shook his head in doubt and headed back toward the room. A few vehicles were exiting the highway and even more entering it. It made no sense sounding the alarm. If she had been there, she was gone by now.

Wednesday, April 1, 00:05

Grady entered their room, and Carmen had not called. He halfway wanted to contact her privately to see if she had seen anything, but he didn't want to tip his hand. He handed out coffees and made small talk to ease the nervousness building inside him. After fifteen minutes had passed, and nothing happened, he knew that Thoran was telling the truth. She had a way of making calls under the radar. Her contact with him was the only way of finding the location of the final victim. Thoran was going to use that to her advantage and play her game.

Grady thought about telling the team about his phone call. *What was the point of hiding it?* There was nothing that Thoran could do if they were to come down there in full gear and stop her from doing anything to the man she is bearing down on right now. *Tell them now, get suited up, and fly down there the instance they get a notification.* Forget all the secrecy. Thoran told him to make an excuse. To say he was on the phone with Elizabeth. Wait. Grady sat up in his chair— *'Tell them you were on the phone with your precious Lizzy or something—She said Lizzy, not Elizabeth. How could she know my pet name for her?*

"You okay, Grady?" LaCrosse asked, sipping off his coffee.

Grady shook the look off his face. "Yeah, sorry. I just remembered I was supposed to call Elizabeth earlier." Grady looked at the time. "Guess I'm in the doghouse now. But better at least leave a message." Grady stepped out into the warm air.

Grady found her name and hit the dial icon; four rings later, it went to voice mail. Being so late, he figured he would have to try a couple of times before waking her up enough to answer. Elizabeth never had her phone on vibrate. It was a habit she had that he hated. The only time she would tolerate the buzz was at church. But like clockwork, even before the car was started, she would have her bird chirping ringtone back full blast. His call went to voicemail a second time and a third. This time he left a message.

"Lizzy. Where are you? You need to call me as soon as you get this message. It's important. Wake up or whatever, just call me. I love you."

Grady borrowed one of Masters' trademark phrases. Which he quickly asked forgiveness for.

Grady doubted Thoran could have anything to do with Elizabeth not answering the phone. Thoran was further South than they were, miles away from their home. Plus, it was out of character for her to deliberately harm anyone outside of the pattern. Mesa had been an act of desperation. She didn't seek to harm him. Nor did Grady believe Thoran would hurt Elizabeth, even under their new rules.

Grady took another look around the lot, took a deep breath, and exhaled. He closed his eyes and said a prayer for Elizabeth and his strength. He didn't want to be caught with his guard down. And right now, he was letting Thoran get to him. Her death and resurrection rantings had caused him to forget about God's power. It didn't matter how much power Thoran claimed to have; God's would always be greater. His death was once and for all. He didn't have to die multiple times to prove anything, as Thoran seemed to want to flaunt. He was ashamed he had forgotten and doubted.

The door to the room cracked, and Masters stepped out. He patted his arms and rubbed them up and down. "Chilly out here."

"It's 60 and humid," Grady said, knowing the conversation starter. "Not so much."

"Everything okay?"

"Yeah. I spoke to Elizabeth for a couple of minutes. I felt

bad for waking her up. But better her upset about a little bit of missed sleep than not calling at all," Grady said, faking a laugh not making eye contact.

Masters bit the corner of his lip and nodded. "Well, glad everything is okay. Wouldn't want her to miss your call or anything." Masters held his stare a moment longer then went back inside the room.

Grady looked back at the door and exhaled with a growl. "What am I doing?" he said under his breath.

The wind started to kick up, and he felt the chill Masters spoke of. A front was moving through. He realized how disconnected he had been the last few days. He hadn't even realized that the weather was changing. His whole focus has been on Thoran and solving this case. So much that he had even forgotten to call his wife. He had done so well the last couple of weeks mending things, turning over a new leaf. No wonder she didn't pick up. She was home. She was just upset. Maybe she did turn the phone to vibrate.

Grady went back into the room, ate a danish, and finished his coffee. He checked his phone a couple of times, looking for a message from Tanner/Thoran, feigning looking for something from Elizabeth. Once turned into twice, and twice turned into three times. They talked over scenarios and how they planned to take Thoran/Tanner in. Side entries, frontal, even window entries were on the table. Any way to bring an end to this. They were planning on a single-story home, much like the profile showed the other houses have been.

Grady couldn't help but feel he was being studied from across the room. He understood that stare well. Masters knew how to read every page of Grady's book. The real game, as Thoran put it, would be getting out of the room when she did call. By the way Grady handled the situation before, he couldn't talk his way out of another confrontation. Masters wouldn't allow it. He knew the call was coming, and he needed an excuse to leave the room. He figured his best option would be taking the empty pizza boxes out, but that would be a quick trip and couldn't be timed with an incoming phone call.

"So, what do you think, Grady?"

Grady looked up from the boxes and his wandering thoughts, "I'm sorry?"

"We need to distract her," LaCrosse said. "Then take her from the sides."

"She won't be armed. The knife will already be hidden for her successor to find," Ryan added.

"Then EMS takes over. We already know that she plans for him to survive, so we have the time. What do you think?" Nettles finished.

"It will depend on the room."

"Yes, of course, but we just need her *not* to invoke those… incantation, or whatever you call it," Branson said.

Grady did believe it was a decent plan, anything to keep the transference from cycling. But he wasn't sure what would happen to Thoran if that cycle weren't completed. He never got an answer from her. The truth was, he wasn't sure she knew the answer either. The simplest solution *was* not to shoot Thoran. Let her evoke her incantation and not fulfill her death wish. Her death is what released the spirit that spills into the new host. That stops the transference.

"You would need someone to distract her enough for the others to make their move," Grady said, knowing what was coming next.

"That's where you come in," Masters said, his eyes still boring holes into him. "He, err she, loves gabbing with you. A face-to-face would be a dream come true."

"All we need is a location," Grady said, looking to Masters, meeting his knowing stare.

Masters nodded. "How much time?"

"We will know when we get the dispatch call, like the times before," Branson said.

Grady's eyes never left Masters'. "Yes. Only this time, I think it will play out a bit differently. We should stay on our toes. Be ready for anything."

"What do you expect?" Masters asked.

"Tanner/Thoran likes to play games. But she also likes to change the rules." Grady looked around at the team. "So don't think this last one will be like the others. She, rather he, has already broken many of his own rules by contacting us. It doesn't mean he won't—" Grady heard his own voice. If Tanner has broken his own rules of contacting them, what other rules has he broken? What other patterns has he stayed from?

"What's wrong?" Nettles was first to ask.

"What's the one rule he cannot break?" Grady asked, standing up.

"The timeline," Masters said. "Six-twenty-one in the morning, the next victim he transfers into."

"So, all the other rules, patterns, and similarities are fair game?" LaCrosse asked.

"Thoran did say that there is no connection other than they are easier to prey on," Nettles said.

"What about their names. Dr. Glavine found the odd anagram-like connection there," Branson said.

"What if that's the difference this time? What if that's the break?" Grady said.

"Then he could go after anyone, not a limited list," Masters said.

"But that makes things worse. We never knew who he was going after to begin with. Even with a limited list," Branson said.

"Right, it opens up to the possibilities of who it could be and removes the limits of who it couldn't be," Grady said. His gut tightened, and reality settled. He looked up at Masters and tried not to reveal what he already knew. Elizabeth was the next transference.

Chapter Thirty-Three

Wednesday, April 1 05:00

So, does Tanner have her?"

"What are you talking about?" Grady said.

Masters had followed him out to the trash bin. Grady lowered the lid and found it more difficult than he anticipated from the frontal breeze keeping the lid from closing. He swore again and kicked the edge of the bin.

"Take it easy, Grady. Care to explain what's going on?"

Grady's eyes were red and swollen, and it wasn't from the dust or diesel exhaust. He looked toward the motel and back at Masters. "I don't know."

"But you suspect."

"It makes sense."

"But you don't *know*," Masters stressed.

"I need to leave to find out. I have to go home. My only concern is, what if Elizabeth isn't there. If he *has* thrown out the playbook, he could have abducted her and taken her away from the house. The phone tracking tells us that much."

"Calm down, Grady," Masters said, placing his hand on Grady's shoulder. "We don't know anything yet."

Grady sat on the short parking barrier. "He wants to play a game. He said he would call with instructions, and I'm to follow them. Alone."

"He gave no clues?"

"None. Just that he would call."

"Well, the closer to 06:20, the closer he is to us," Masters said.

"That's another thing. Thoran/Tanner knows where we are."

"I figured as much. Tanner allowed us to track his cell. He wanted us this far, if not as far as his cabin."

"We are 35, 40 minutes from my place. Thirty from Harris Neck." Grady said. "Has our team across the Creek reported anything?"

"Nothing since the last check-in. But if they did see anything, they would call in immediately."

"When he does call, I need to go alo—" Grady's phone began to buzz.

"Carmen can," Masters began, but Grady cut him off.

"Nope. She hasn't the last few calls. Blocked. Now go."

Masters walked away, back to the room.

Grady answered the phone. "I'm here. I had to get out of the room for privacy."

"Do they expect anything?" Tanner/Thoran asked.

"Of course not. I can keep my cool." Grady said, his voice showing quite the opposite. "Now, let's get on with this."

"What's with the attitude, Detective?"

"I think you know very well what the problem is."

"We aren't going to get very far if you feel the need to behave this way, Grady. If you can't deal with the issue at hand, then I have no use for you, good-bye," Thoran said.

"Wait," Grady said.

"I'm listening," Thoran said.

Grady put his thumb over the mouthpiece. He swallowed back every emotion that was surfacing. From hatred to fear, he pushed it down as far as he could. If Thoran did have his wife, Elizabeth deserved every bit of strength he had within him.

"I'm sorry," Grady said. "I apologize for my outburst. It will not happen again?"

"Much better, Detective. Now we are getting somewhere. We were wasting precious time. Time you know we do not have."

"Yes, I'm aware. What's next, Tanner?"

"Please, let's stick with who I am right now. Sophia would be nice, But Thoran will do. It's her final act; we must bid her a fond farewell."

"Okay, Thoran. What's next?"

"We need to get you from there to here. We have just a little over an hour, and you have to drive here still."

"Where is here?"

"C'mon. Do I have to make it that easy on you, Grady? You're the Detective. Detect."

"How am I supposed to meet your deadline if you don't give me anything?"

Thoran didn't respond. Either Grady was getting through, or she was thinking of a clever retort.

"Your team is not looking in the right place. What is your heart telling you, Grade?"

With that, Thoran disconnected their call and confirmed two things. One that he did have his wife, and two that he was not at Harris Neck; he was at their home. Some things had changed, but not everything.

Grady checked his pockets. He had keys and his wallet. He picked the vehicle they belonged to and headed to the highway. His phone buzzed when he hit the interstate. He pressed the button for speaker, "What do you want now, Tanner?"

"Tanner? Oh my, no, this is not Tanner, Detective. This is Dr. Glavine. I have been up all night going over everything. I came across something interesting. I know this is the morning the transference is to take place."

"Go on," Grady said.

"You remember how I said that you could stop the cycle by ending Thoran's life at just the right moment?"

"Yes. In fact, I am just about to take care of that right now."

"I'm glad I caught you then," Dr. Glavine exhaled. "Be careful who is around. This is why Tanner waited until the end to recite his incantation. After the incantation is recited, the spirit is released and searches for a susceptible host, meaning the one that is prepared as in the photos. The moment it finds the prepared sacrifice, it will enter it."

"So, what are you saying?"

"The host terminates its life and transfers its spirit to the new host. If you are thinking of only ending Thoran's life, you still have to deal with the new host. To truly end this, you must ensure there is no new host to enter."

"I have to kill the new host?"

"Precisely, Detective. It sounds brutal, but if your concern is ending this cycle, it is what needs to be done. Only it must occur after Thoran recites her incantation, but before the spirit enters the new host. Timing is everything. Then, when the spirit does not find a new host, it should be forced to cross over."

Grady couldn't find the words to respond. Kill his wife? How could he do that? He shook his head in disbelief.

"Are you sure this is the only way?"

"Without question," Dr. Glavine said.

"Can't I do both? Shoot one, then the other?"

"My belief is that the transference is instantaneous. You only have one choice, Detective."

"What if I shot Thoran before she recited the mantra?"

"To be honest. I don't know. My theory is I don't believe she would die. If they have the rapid regeneration you spoke of, it is highly likely bullets wouldn't affect her the way you think they might. But that is merely conjecture."

"And the cycle? Is she stuck with just the one?"

"That I don't know definitively, either. I would assume she could wait until the next first quarter moon. It may require another round of sacrifices," Dr. Glavine said. "I also couldn't tell you what would happen if she were unable to make those sacrifices."

"That was my next question," Grady said. "So, this is it. We need to end this here. Or we do this all over again with more bloodshed."

"It appears that way, Detective," Glavine agreed.

"Thank you, Doctor. I need to go now. I appreciate the information."

"I'm truly sorry. I know you want to save every life, but sometimes sacrifices need to be made to save future lives."

Grady ended the call and sped up. There was no need to tell the Doctor that the sacrifice he was suggesting was his wife. It wouldn't change the facts. Grady pulled off the interstate and onto the highway that would take him to Wilton Estates. He wiped his face and realized tears were streaming down his cheek. Did he have it in him to take his own wife's life?

Grady's phone buzzed again. This time he checked the Caller ID, and it read as *Unknown Caller* again. He answered.

"And just like that, you are ignoring my calls? Straight to voicemail?"

Grady didn't realize he had been getting a second call with the calls going through the speakerphone. "I was driving, Thoran. Must've been is a bad location."

The phone was silent with contemplation. Thoran finally spoke, "Are you close now?"

"I would hope so if I made the correct choice. You're at my home," Grady said, clenching his teeth.

"Very good, Detective. I like it here—very nice neighborhood. You know, once I am her, we can keep on living here. No one needs to know. We can put away this Transference idea and live happily ever after."

The very thought of it made Grady sick to his stomach. "Not going to happen, Tanner."

"Tsk. Tsk. Tsk. What did we say about the attitude, Grady? I can always slit dear wifey's throat and leave with your petulance. We can just play this game again come May."

"No," Grady yelled. He swallowed hard. "No. Don't do that. We can continue from here, Thoran."

"Much better. We can talk about it when you arrive," Thoran hung up.

"What did you find out."

"Everything you ask me to."

"Great. Send it to me."

"Already did."

"Thank you, Carmen."

"You got it."

Wednesday, April 1, 06:05

Grady pulled into his driveway, almost forgetting to put it into park. He ran through the front door, which was unlocked. "Lizzy?"

"In here, Detective," Thoran called out. The smell of cigar smoke hit Grady's senses. He rounded the corner and saw Elizabeth lying on their glass coffee table in a slip and shorts. They were the matching set he had bought her as an anniversary gift last year. She was unconscious, and there wasn't a mark on her.

"I'm here," Grady said. "Now what?"

"What a beautiful wife you have," Thoran exhaled her cigar smoke. She was sitting in a chair next to the table. Her legs were extended in front of her, crossed, as were her arms. The cigar was smoldering in an astray he didn't remember owning on the couch next to her.

"Yes. Thank you."

Thoran pulled out the short-bladed knife that had eluded them for so long. She held it in front of her face and eyed it, tilting her head side to side. "It is amazing how much damage such a small instrument can do, isn't it, Detective? I mean, it is larger than a bullet, yes, but a bullet has mass. This? This is thin." Thoran turned the blade to show how paper-thin the edge was, "You wouldn't think it could cause this much damage."

Thoran leaned over, studied Elizabeth's leg, and looked up at Grady with a sinister grin.

Grady took a step toward them.

"Stop, Detective. One wrong step and this cut goes deeper than I intend it to. You saw the others. You know what happens if I go too deep. You also know that if all goes well, Elizabeth lives through this. It may be painful to watch, but watch you must."

Grady shut his eyes tight, but he knew Thoran was right. He heard Glavine's voice in his head as well.

Grady looked up at the clock he had bought for Elizabeth after their first big fight. He remembered telling her that time heals all wounds. He shut his eyes in time to hear Elizabeth yell out in pain. She didn't regain consciousness, which made Grady wonder what Tanner had been using as a sedative this entire time. It also comforted him to know Elizabeth wasn't awake, being tortured; A second scream followed.

"We can talk a bit now, Detective. I'm supposed to allow some time between incisions. But not too much time. As you know, we are on a timetable."

Grady didn't know what to say. He watched Thoran as she wiped the blade on Elizabeth's top. "How do you expect to hide your blade this time since I am here?" Grady said.

"There you go with your assumptions again," Thoran said, pointing the blade at Grady. "Who said this has to continue with this blade? You, your team, and the good doctor have all believed that everything must remain identical to the others because I have chosen to keep things the same." Thoran stood and paced the room. She waved the blade for emphasis. "You know, in some languages, Elizabeth is Elisabeth. Elisabeth Ann keeps with my pattern. So, I am good, either way.

"But the blade doesn't matter, Detective. It is a simple surgical blade. Regardless, Elizabeth will inherit it and continue our work. It doesn't need to be hidden because you know her. And in May, she will die just as Sophia will die today."

"If she eventually dies, I can just do nothing and let her die today after you transfer," Grady said.

Thoran picked up her cigar, took a long drag, and blew three perfect rings. She chuckled and answered, "We both know that is a load of crap." Thoran leaned her elbows on her knees and met Grady's eyes. Grady knew it spoke to the truth of what Dr. Glavine told him. The spirit would keep Tanner alive in whatever host it was in. All he had to do was complete the transference. Her heart would hold, in hibernation, until it was saved.

"You have no choice but to play the game, as I told you. Now it's almost time for you to get your phone out and call EMS. I just need to make the final incisions," Thoran looked up at the clock again; 06:10.

Again, Grady closed his eyes and cringed as Thoran made her precision cuts to his wife's body, and again she resounded in agony. He didn't care about how she did it. The craftiness that awed Dr. Glavine and others in the medical field mattered little to him. His head beat to the drumming of his heart. He finally had to sit to keep from passing out.

"You still with me, Detective? C'mon, we are almost there."

Grady took a deep breath and stood. When he opened his eyes, he saw the blood beneath Elizabeth, staining the rug they had purchased at a flea market in Charleston; it began to spill over onto the hardwood. Grady was lost in his wife's condition that he didn't hear Thoran.

"Detective? Detective!"

"Yes?"

"Now would be good. Lizzy hasn't much time," Thoran said, tapping her wrist.

Grady dialed 9-1-1 as an attempted suicide. He figured it would draw the least attention.

"Smart, Detective," Thoran said. "Now we just wait. You know this part."

Thoran took several puffs off her cigar, then stood and walked around the room. She peeked into the hall and kitchen, "Elizabeth really did well here. This is a beautiful home, Grady."

Grady's eyes never left Elizabeth. Her raising and lowering chest were slowing, but she was still alive. He had to trust God that she would live if he did nothing. He knew what he had to do in a matter of minutes, but he didn't want to do it. He looked up at Thoran. What harm would it do to let the transfer happen? Maybe Dr. Glavine was wrong? Maybe there was another way? What if Elizabeth chose not to keep going?

Then it hit Grady. It wouldn't *be* Elizabeth. His Elizabeth would be gone. Either now or in three months. Grady unlocked his holster.

"She has a keen eye. Always has, always will," Grady said. "We're still working on it. God has blessed us."

Thoran stood and walked up to Grady. She drew in her cigar and blew the smoke in his face. "Don't you now realize that I am in control here? How is God going to save you now?"

Grady waved the smoke from the air, "Faith," he said.

Thoran laughed, "Is that all you can say? Faith?!" Thoran fan-waved her hands in the air.

"It's all I need. But I don't expect you to understand it."

"I thought we went over this. I am up two to one. Soon three to one," Thoran said, pointing to Elizabeth's body.

"All Christ needs is one. Once was enough. That's one thing you don't understand. One reason you feel the need to compete with Him. His sacrifice was once and for all. This here, is peanuts, Thoran. Sorry." Grady said.

Thoran's face burned. She again drew on her cigar and blew smoke in his face but said nothing. She crossed the room and sat in her chair.

Grady felt a strength he hadn't felt before. He felt an assurance that everything was going to be okay. The fear was still there, and he didn't want to go through what he was about to do, but he was aware of what needed to be done.

Thoran exhaled and extinguished her cigar, "Well, Grady, it's been fun. This game is at its end. Now it's time to finish what we started."

Chapter Thirty-Four

Wednesday, April 1 06:19

Thoran leaned back, grinning as the whine of an approaching ambulance grew closer.

Wednesday, April 1 06:20

Thoran sat forward in her chair. "It has been nice knowing you in this life, Detective. It will be exciting knowing you in the next. Will you give me the same benefits you gave Elizabeth?" Laughing, she leaned back, almost slipping out of her seat.

Looking at the clock on the wall, both Thoran and Grady stood. He pulled his weapon and aimed it at her.

"Ready?" Thoran said.

Thoran began to chant. The same intelligible words many had heard behind closed doors, but no one had been able to decipher. It grew from a shallow whisper to a low mumble. Grady had his weapon trained center mass on Thoran, not to give away his true intentions—according to Dr. Glavine, the timing was everything.

'Mumble-mumble-mumble, words-words-words, louder and louder. Thoran raised her hands as if praying to her chest. Then above her head. She closed her eyes. *Words-words-words, mumble-mumble-mumble—* "Glatchka mondavka insinivicus!" Thoran's eyes opened wide, and she gritted her teeth as her hands lunged toward Elizabeth's chest.

Grady quickly lowered his weapon and took aim at Elizabeth's side. He closed his eyes and held his breath praying for a miracle. His trained finger did not tremble as it fired a single shot into her side. With her shallow breathing, her life ended instantly.

Grady opened his eyes and looked over at both women, Thoran was hunched over Elizabeth, neither of them moved. He couldn't understand. Thoran should've stood from Tanner's spirit reentering her. *Perhaps it was a delayed reaction?* He stepped toward the bodies with caution, in case she was faking and would attack him over his *impudence*. Right away, he could tell Thoran wasn't breathing. She was just as lifeless as his wife.

Grady nudged Thoran with his weapon. She didn't move. He shook his head, picked up the body, and lowered it to the ground, it was then that he noticed the single shot to the upper chest.

"What the— "

"It's about damn time," the familiar voice said from behind him.

Grady spun around and saw Masters, gun in hand.

"How did you know?"

"Carmen."

"You tapped my phone, didn't you?"

"You left me no choice."

"No, I guess I didn't." Grady stooped to his knees near Elizabeth, running his hand through her hair. "But I had no choice either."

Masters thought about it, looked to Thoran, then back to Grady, "No, you really didn't. But you sure knew how and when to communicate you needed help."

"And thank you for helping," Grady said, just above a whisper. "Now, it's finally over."

"Indeed, it is." Masters said. "But it gets better," Masters added, then whistled. "I hope."

Two EMS teams entered the home.

"You almost forgot we had EMS outside. I took the liberty of upgrading our service and ordering a second bus for the situation."

One team focused on Elizabeth. They used the defibrillator twice and found a weak pulse. Grady was quick to her side. He took her hand while two other techs began bandaging her wounds.

"Where did you shoot her?" the first EMS tech asked.

"The side. Just enough to stop her heart and her breathing," Grady said, through the tears rolling down his cheeks.

"Thank you. As long as it was just superficial, she should be fine."

"No, thank you," Grady said. "You saved her."

"Doing our job, Detective. We need to transport, stat. She's not out of the woods yet." They loaded her on a gurney and rolled her to the waiting ambulance, Grady followed. But with the team they had to keep her stable, he wasn't allowed to ride with them. Grady protested, but Masters offered to take him and reminded him he still had a job to do, and he relented.

Grady went back into the house where the second team was still working on Thoran. They had a more difficult time with her. The bullet entered the chest. They had to slow the bleeding first.

"Are you sure it's safe to bring her back?" Masters asked.

"It's what Dr. Glavine said. If she were deceased, Tanner's spirit would cross over if it didn't have a host," Grady assured.

"Yes. But Dr. Glavine didn't say how long that would be."

"We need to take that chance. Thoran's life may depend on it," Grady said.

After the fourth treatment, Thoran's heart began to beat. It was stronger than Elizabeth's, but she was losing blood faster because Masters' shot did more damage.

"We need to get her to County, now," the EMS tech said. They wheeled her out of Grady's home and into the waiting bus, and off to the hospital.

Grady and Masters watched as Thoran's ambulance drove away from Grady's home. The siren squealed, as nosey neighbors peeked through their blinds.

"You know you have to move now, right?" Masters said.

Grady looked over at him and raised his eyebrows.

"Too soon?

Grady nodded. "Little bit."

"Sorry," Masters patted him on the shoulder, "Look. All the

final victims survived because their injuries were superficial. Elizabeth will be fine."

"Masters. The other victims didn't have a bullet hole in their side. I shot my wife."

Masters stood silent. He had forgotten about that. "But you went for the soft injury. You had to expect somewhere inside that there was some recovery in this?"

"I suppose. God always works it out in the end," Grady said. He smiled and looked back at his house. He motioned with his head, and they walked to the door. "I will admit, I was terrified to do what I did. But once faced with the reality, I knew it was what I had to do. If Elizabeth were here, I'm sure she would've told me to take that shot too. She would have been upset if I hadn't."

"Really?"

"Heck ya. I'd rather deal with Thoran's attitude than with my wife at my disobedience at what God directs me to do." Grady shrugged his shoulders producing a shuddering motion.

"Even if she dies?"

Grady looked at the blood-stained floor and sighed. "First, I don't believe she's going to die. But if she did, I know she would proud of the job we did. Think of all the lives we just saved. The lives that won't fall victim to Tanner. If Elizabeth had to die for them to be saved, I'm sure she would have been willing to give her life for it."

"Interesting." Masters shook his head. "I guess I just don't understand that type of sacrifice."

Grady smiled, "Well, partner, let me tell you about it on our way to the hospital."

Epilogue

Saturday, July 4, 14:00

Are you ready, James?" Elizabeth said from the dining room. "We need to be there soon."

"It's not like the food is going to walk away, Lizzy," Grady said.

"It's your first Fourth of July at this station. We need to make a good impression," Elizabeth reminded him.

"I think your potato salad will do well enough," Grady said, walking into the kitchen and removing the lid, ready to swipe a sample. His wife slapped his hand away.

"Stop it, Grade. I'm not sure I made enough as it is."

"This isn't Atlanta, babe." Grady reopened the lid and took a small spoonful, "it's half the force we had up north."

She gave the face she always did, the frozen corner-lip-bite, waiting for the approval of her greatest critic. Grady gave a sour look like he wanted to spit it out.

"Oh, stop it," she said, punching his shoulder. "Really?"

"It's your best yet, Love," Grady said, winking at her. "How are you feeling?"

Elizabeth rubbed her leg, and she looked toward the living room. They had thrown out the carpet. He had, actually, even before she had returned home. Grady cleaned up and replaced it with a new, nearly identical one. He was trying to make it as if the whole incident never happened or was a bad dream. While her surgical scars would always be there—those he couldn't take away, nor could the bullet scar he gave her—he was doing the best he could to put the past behind them.

"I'm fine," she said. "It's all surreal. I don't remember any of it. I mean, I remember the flashes of pain. I still do, but nothing else."

"And the dreams?"

Elizabeth was silent. She would occasionally wake up in a cold sweat, out of breath. The doctor said it was a side effect of the drug Tanner used. They were fewer now than the first couple weeks she was home. The doctor also said it could also have to do with her being in the home where the incident took place. But Elizabeth said she didn't even remember being attacked. It seemed that Tanner snuck in and drugged her in her sleep. He carried her down the stairs and placed her on the table. She never knew what happened.

"I don't have as many. I think they were part of whatever he gave me."

"I'm glad." Grady looked into the living room and back. He realized he shouldn't have brought it up. "I'm sorry. Today is a day of celebration. I shouldn't be talking about this."

"It's okay. I'm okay," Elizabeth smiled. She took his hand and kissed it. "My hero."

Grady rolled his eyes. "Yeah. How many husbands can say they were able to do the very thing they always talked about doing and got away with it."

Elizabeth laughed. "So, how's Sophia?"

"She's doing well," Grady said, scrolling through his phone. He pulled up a photo and showed it to Elizabeth. It was of a young woman with a greying-haired gentleman with his arm around her, kissing her cheek. "That's her uncle, Joseph. He lives down in Ft. Lauderdale. He flew up a couple of weeks ago. It looks like she's going to relocate down there with him."

"That's nice. And her visitor?"

"Tanner? He's gone," Grady said.

"Are you sure?"

"As sure as I can be. I've visited with her a couple of times to be sure," Grady said. "The first time, I didn't announce myself. She didn't recognize me. No threats, no name-calling; nothing."

"That's good to know," Elizabeth sighed. "We both owe you and Masters our lives."

"Don't forget Dr. Glavine. He's the one who figured it all out."

"Yes, our saviors," Elizabeth clenched her jaw, realizing her faux pas. "Well, you know what I mean."

Grady laughed. "I don't know what it was, Lizzy. Well, I do now, but I felt such a peace going through it. Yes, I was worried and scared as all get out, but I knew. I just knew it was what I had to do."

"And you did it right." Elizabeth grabbed Grady's hand again.

"Masters couldn't understand why I had to do it."

"What, shoot me?"

"Yeah."

"What did you tell him?"

"The same thing I told you. I would rather deal with Tanner alive than not obeying what God was telling me to do."

"Good answer."

"Well, that and your wrath for not obeying what God led me to do," Grady laughed.

"Most definitely, mister."

"Will he be there today?"

"Masters? Yes, he should be."

"Good. I'm glad. It's been good to see him at the last few services," Elizabeth said.

"Yes, it has," Grady said, then laughed. "Plus, free bar-be-cue? He'll be there. The Lieu won't turn down a free meal."

Here we are again at the point where I thank the many individuals who contributed to this work. I always shrink back because I know I'll forget someone, so I first say thank you to the forgotten. You are amazing, and this work couldn't have been completed without your contribution.

Okay. I feel better. I first want to give praise to my Lord and Savior, Jesus Christ. Yes, this is an interesting piece. I questioned it at times. But there's a reason for everything He gives me, and there's a purpose behind *The Transference*. I thank God for the opportunity to bring this to you.

Next is the wind in my sails. The reason I keep going, my biggest fan, Carolyn. She made writing this one fun. I enjoyed giving her a block of chapters as I wrote it. Her excitement encouraged me to write. Thank you, babe, for your encouragement to finally complete this one.

Thank you, Mike, and everyone at WordCrafts Press for believing in me and this work. Especially with edits at the final moments. You guys are amazing. Thank you for everything.

Speaking of encouragement, two groups helped me through this one. You may remember the Weekend Writing Warriors with *Little Reminders*. This novel we add #WritingCommunity. Both writing circles have been crucial to my writing process. Thanks everyone for your words of encouragement. Each of you is awesome, and I couldn't have completed this work without you.

Then there is the novel's subject matter. I had to study quite a bit. Much like I did with *Little Reminders* and the medical field, I studied my antagonist's methods. It was an intriguing road studying Law Enforcement. I tried to stay true to what I learned. I thank those who helped me with those details. You know who you are. Thank you for your service and God speed as you travel your beat, study case files, and defend me and my family from the crazy world around us.

I also want to thank my writing accountability partner, Bonniejean Alford. We may have struggled this past year, but know that as long as we keep writing and our eyes focused on the prize, there is nothing we cannot accomplish.

I cannot forget to thank the doctors at UT Health SA Neurology. They continue to assist me with my Neurofibromatosis and Epilepsy. This last year I struggled with a few strong seizures. It made completing this novel difficult and will most likely be the signature for this piece for me.

Finally, thank you, reader. This novel is quite a departure from my routine. I pray you enjoyed it. Carolyn, my greatest fan, says it is my best yet. I don't know about that, but I sure enjoyed writing it. It was a beast, but I'm excited to see how it will be received. As I opened with, I'm astonished that God would give me such a piece to write, but He did, and now it's in your hands. I thank you for your continued support of my journey. God Bless!

In His Exciting Service,

Jeff S. Bray

Jeff S. Bray lives in a small town in South Central Texas with his wife Carolyn and two of their five children. They are members of the local First Baptist Church, serving in several capacities, including teaching Sunday School, working with Men's Ministry, and managing the church's online presence.

Jeff's passion for writing began in elementary school with a short story about a lost kitten. His circuitous literary career started with his personal blog, *Moments for the Heart*, which led to small paid assignments before expanding into magazine articles in national publications.

In addition to *The Transference*, Jeff is the author of the contemporary thriller, *The Five Barred Gate*, the supernatural romance, *Little Reminders of Who I Am*, and the whimsical children's picture book series, *Elissa the Curious Snail*, which helps parents introduce basic faith concepts like prayer, even in the face of adversity, into their teachings in a fun and entertaining way.

Connect with Jeff online at:

jeffsbrayauthor.com